Wanted: Wife

Wanted: Wife

GWEN JONES

AVONIMPULSE

An imprint of HarperCollins Publishers

Excerpt from *The Cupcake Diaries: Sweet On You* copyright © 2013 by Darlene Panzera.

Excerpt from *The Cupcake Diaries: Recipe for Love* copyright © 2013 by Darlene Panzera.

Excerpt from *The Cupcake Diaries: Taste of Romance* copyright © 2013 by Darlene Panzera.

Excerpt from *One True Love* copyright © 2013 by Laurie Vanzura.

EPub Edition JUNE 2013 ISBN: 9780062268044

Print Edition ISBN: 9780062268051

JV 10 9 8 7 6 5 4 3 2 1

Wanted: Wife

Chapter One

Romance Is Dead, Sister

ANDY DEVINE WAS the last thing I needed in my life next to a punch in the gut, yet that morning I got both.

"Hey Jules!" Denny called from the newsroom. "Take a look at this!"

I grabbed my compact and fixed my lipstick, catching my red-rimmed eyes in the mirror. How could I look at anything when all I could see was scarlet? But I wouldn't cry, I *wouldn't*, sliding *Ruby Ruse* across my lips, the skyline of Philadelphia reflecting back into my hand. See, Evil had just walked out of this conference room on seven-hundred-dollar Fratelli Rossettis, the sales slip from Boyds still cooling in my wallet.

"Sorry, Julie, but it's just a bad time for me," Richard had purred just moments before, his glossy hair swooping dramatically, his baby blues bleeding Sincerity 2.0, his bespoke suit wafting Clive Christian No. 1. His fingers brushed my neck as he leaned in for the chastest of cheek pecks. "But that doesn't mean I don't love you. Really, it doesn't."

I groped the table for balance. "You're telling me this now? With two weeks until our wedding?"

Richard's mouth crooked with such a perfect mix of pity and condescension I almost felt sorry for *him*. "Julie, sometimes it takes nearly falling into the brink before you know what's best for you."

"Now I'm a *brink*?"

"No!" His eyes widened. "Of course not. You're wonderful and beautiful and talented—the top reporter at the station!" He palmed his chest. "But *I'm* just a struggling agent. You don't need me dragging you down. And I will, if this deal doesn't pan out."

I slanted him a glance; self-flagellation fit him as well as polyester. "Seriously, Richard? Then why keep telling me your agency has the biggest talent out of Hollywood? That these gamers you just signed are the hottest around?"

"Julie. Sweetheart." He clasped my shoulders, his eyes hooded. "Being on top only means you hit the bottom harder."

Wait a minute. I slinked away. "Why is being on top great for me but terrible for you?"

"You just don't get it, do you?" He shook his head, leaving for the window.

I looked to my hand, his diamond winking at me with absurd perkiness. Two years we'd been together, sharing the same Rittenhouse Square penthouse, the same bank account. We were each other's insurance beneficiaries, our lives so imperceptibly tangled it'd take a blowtorch to break them apart.

"Just what is it I'm supposed to get, Richard? That you don't want to make that final commitment? That you don't love me anymore? Or maybe you never did? Maybe we were just mutually handy, equally able to pick up each other's dry cleaning?" My eyes burned. "But you never thought of me that way, did you? I mean, who could be that shallow? You . . ." I looked up. "Richard?"

His shoulders were twitching. I went to the window, spinning him around. "Jesus! Are you *tweeting*?"

He stared at me, aghast. "I have over 5,000 followers, you know!"

"With number one standing right here!"

He had the cheek to finish the tweet before he slipped his phone in his pocket, crossing his arms as he dropped his gaze to look at me. "This is why you're still traipsing around town chasing midgets instead of murderers. You're so blinded by minutiae you have no grasp of what's fundamentally important."

"But didn't you just say what a wonderful reporter I am?"

He slipped his hand to my shoulder. "In your own little world, you are, but the truth is . . ." He inclined his head. "I'm just too intense for you."

There comes a point where the absurdity of the situation overrides any anger. I shrugged him off. "Let me get this straight. You make your living off of man-children blowing imaginary body parts off of imaginary bodies.

You can't start your day unless you purge, hang by your ankles, and rub some $150-an-ounce buttermilk concoction into your Botox-inflicted face. Most of the time you can't walk five feet without feeding that electronic extension of your over-inflated ego. My goodness, Richard. I guess you must be right. Because if all that doesn't scream alpha dog, I don't know what."

His eyes narrowed. "Now you're just being petty."

I wanted to slap him. "And you're dumping me!"

"Shh." Richard pulled me aside, tucking in a bit of hair that slipped from my combs. "Julie, what's the rush to get married anyway? You're thirty-five, I'm thirty-seven, we have plenty of time. And plenty of time to continue this conversation later. I'm leaving to meet with the MacKenzies in just a little while."

The gamers? "You were just out in Seattle!"

"I know, but there's still some rough patches to work out."

"So send Jarrod."

"Jarrod isn't *me*. This is the biggest deal I've ever repped, and I'm not sending an amateur to blow it." He checked his Breguet. "Damn—I gotta go. The MacKenzies are Mariners freaks so we're meeting at the stadium. As it is I'm running late, and the show—" He shook his head tightly. "I mean the *game* starts at seven-thirty.

My eyes widened. And so did my understanding. "You mean the *opera*."

He blinked. "No, I'm going to a baseball game."

"No, you're going to her." Funny he should've mentioned baseball. Because I sure could've used a Louisville

Slugger right then. His ring would have to suffice. "You *bastard*. You're still seeing that diva." I threw it at him. "Why don't you give this to her?"

"Don't be nuts," he said, snatching it, mid-air. "Annika Eden's just a client."

"Who's always coincidently around whenever you're going to the coast." Apparently this was my comeuppance for stealing him away from the opera singer two years earlier. Fact was, that tarty Carmen nearly shoved him at me, and now she wanted him back? At that moment I was feeling very *Don José*—though, lacking a dagger, I used whatever I had. "I want your crap out of the apartment before I get home," I said. "I never want to see a highlighted hair of yours again."

He laughed. "You want me out of my own place?"

"It's mine as much as yours. Your father said it was our wedding present."

"But there doesn't look like there's going to be a wedding now, is there?"

He finally got me to gasp. Ten minutes ago I was two weeks away from hooking up with him for life, and now I seemed lost on some distant planet. I stared at him, hardly believing what I was about to say. "Then you're really breaking up with me?"

He came closer, eyes leaking market-tested sincerity. "Julie, truly, don't do this. By tomorrow you'll see it's better this way. Now, Curtis showed me a row in Society Hill last week that'd be perfect for you. Five minute walk from the station."

"Last week? You already had me dumped *last week*?"

My God, the city gossips were going to have a field day. "How many people already know?"

"Stop it. Why are you making this so hard?"

"Then why don't you make it real easy?" I shoved past him. "Drop dead."

He grabbed my arm. "Am I going to have to call my lawyers?"

I shrugged him off. "Are you threatening me?"

"Will it be necessary?"

I snapped my compact closed—then threw it across the room. *Ooh!* I thought, burying my face in my hands. How did I not see that that soprano succubus still commanded a performance out of him? I took out my Black-Berry and Googled *Seattle Opera*, and sure enough, there was Annika Eden as Adina in *L'elisir d'amore*, opening over the weekend.

I was such an idiot.

"Jules? You okay?"

I turned to Denny, my cameraman, standing in the doorway. "This ought to please you immensely. The wedding's off." My God, it hurt even to say it.

He closed the door and pulled me into his sinewy embrace. "The bastard. All those preparations. And that dress! You want I should pound him?"

I buried my face into his neck, his halo of blond curls muffling my rather colorful cursing. Every girl should have a gay man like Denny in their life. Who else would malign the waste of an $8,500 gown as well as offer to do damage to the offender? "No, thanks, sweetie. I do appreciate the thought, though."

"Hm." He gave me a squeeze then held me out, his runner's musculature such a contrast to Richard's yoga-and-colonic-toned sleekness. "So, are you done with him this time? Tell me the truth."

I swiped at my eyes—why *couldn't I cry?*—checking my face in the compact Denny had so thoughtfully retrieved. "I'm done with men *period*." I kneaded my temple, feeling a headache coming on. "Oh, Denny, why is it every man I hook up with is a lying, self-indulgent infant? Where have all the real men gone?"

"Allowing for your interpretation?" He shrugged. "Unless it's the kind that burps and farts and mixes stripes and plaids, I don't know either."

"They're a lost race." *Christ, my head hurt.* "I need some coffee."

"What you really need is a diversion. Come and see what Terri's got for us."

WPHA Channel 8 News was the highest-rated local news show in the Delaware Valley, which included my hometown of Philadelphia and its suburbs, the state of Delaware, and all of Southern New Jersey, which roughly meant anything south and east of Trenton. Most of the reporters had a beat, a geographical locale they covered, but not me. My specialty was the offbeat stories featured either at the end of the newscast, or tucked between the 5:30 and 6:00 PM slots, the quirky stuff that kept my finger on the pulse of the local nut base. There wasn't a free drink or a meal I couldn't get in this town, though it could be a real pain in the arse just to take a run down Kelly Drive. *Julie Knott's Random Access* made sure my email inbox was a veritable cornucopia of all that was one electron short of a refrigerator magnet.

"Julie! Denny! Over here!" Terri, the fifty-ish assignments editor and everyone's favorite mom-figure, waved to us from the other side of the newsroom. We snaked through the desks to find her hunched over a bright yellow, slightly smudged flyer.

"Take a gander at this," she said, smoothing it. "I had to take a detour on the way to work this morning. Saw this on a utility pole."

"Don't you live in the Pine Barrens?" Denny said, referring to the scrubby woods that covered a big chunk of South Jersey. "Out in the sticks?"

"Right on the edge," she said. "But this detour took me into it. Look."

ANDY DEVINE SEEKS A WIFE

LANDED, FINANCIALLY-SECURE 40 YR OLD MALE
LOOKING FOR HEALTHY, ATHLETIC FEMALE
FOR MARRIAGE AND FAMILY.
MUST SUBMIT TO FULL DISCLOSURE AND BE
WILLING
TO WORK HARD.
GENEROUS MONETARY COMPENSATION
IF TERMS OF CONTRACT ARE NOT MET.
INTERVIEWS WILL BE HELD AT THE IRON BOG
FIREHOUSE
MAIN STREET, IRON BOG
FRIDAY 27 AUGUST 1:00- 4:00 PM
PLEASE BRING ID

"Can you believe it?" Denny said. "It's positively medieval."

"I searched all the local sources, Googled him, even checked Twitter and Facebook," said Terri. "Nothing's out there on this guy. I have no idea how long the flyer's been hanging on that pole"—she fingered it—"but it doesn't look too weathered."

"Weird," Denny said. "You'd think someone would've picked up on it fast."

Terri sniffed. "If you were a single gal with ten bucks in your pocket, would *you* tell anyone?"

"Yeah," I said, dropping to a chair, "to run in the opposite direction."

She winced. "Oh no, what'd that bastard do now?"

"Richard bailed," Denny said. "The wedding's off."

Terri sniffed, ever pragmatic. "Why am I not surprised?" She tapped the flyer. "The hell with that jerk, work's what you need. This has to be the most bizarre yet, so jump back on that horse."

"Especially since he's looking for a broodmare," said Denny. "Hey, why does his name sound familiar?"

"Because it's the same as the character actor," Terri said. "Ever see that old John Wayne movie, *Stagecoach*? Well, Andy Devine was the guy driving it."

"Oh, *that* Andy Devine. Tall, chubby, real squeaky voice." Denny glanced at Terri. "Think they're related?"

I was feeling nothing but unkind. "Or maybe he looks like him?"

"Well, if he looked like John Wayne," Terri said, "would he be shilling himself at the firehouse?"

"Maybe he's so hot he'll need to hose 'em back," Denny said.

Terri snickered. "The divine Devine."

"He'd have to be," I said. "What sane woman would actually marry someone like this?" I sniffed. "Not that *sane* and *marry* should occupy the same sentence."

Denny leaned in. "*So* happy you're not bitter. You must have missed the line about 'generous monetary compensation.'"

"Like citronella to skeeters," Terri said. "In this economy he's *gonna* need a fire hose."

"I'm getting my gear," Denny said. "If we hurry we can just make it."

Suddenly I felt trapped in one of my own stories. But, as crazy as the whole thing seemed, this Andy Devine was still a man wanting to get married, and how cruel was that? Yet, after so many fits and starts, after so much self-delusion, I should've been surprised if Richard actually went through with it. Though he always seemed one for grand romantic gestures—flower-filled carriage rides, schooner cruises on the Delaware, even proposing to me via the Jumbotron at Citizen's Bank Park—they were always when someone was watching. It was the smaller moments, the early mornings, the hard days nights, that always left him stymied.

I felt Terri's hand on my shoulder. "Forget about Richard, Julie. He never did deserve you. Trust me, there's somebody still out there that will, and until he finds you, there's the work. That's exactly what you need right now."

"The work ..." I said absently. "The *work*," like a mantra.

"It's your one constant." She came around to face me. "Tell me I'm wrong."

"No, you're right." Dammit, she was. "Like Tara to Scarlett."

Soon we were crossing the Walt Whitman Bridge out of Philly and into New Jersey. Though apparently, I had fed the GPS an address a little too low tech for high tech.

I slid the GPS back into the holder. "It keeps saying 'incomplete.'"

"I never liked those things anyway," said Denny, coming up on Route 73. He pointed toward the glove box. "Get the map. What was the name of that town again?"

"Iron Bog," I said, smoothing it across my lap. "Terri said to take 70 into Medford, then to the Red Lion Circle and from there we look for Route 582."

We passed from city to suburban sprawl to farm-land and, quite suddenly, into what is euphemistically known in these parts as the Pines. Covering a quarter of the state to the south, it could be tough to explain to someone from outside the region. Most people think of New Jersey as this cheek-to-jowl succession of refiner-ies, housing and garbage dumps, bordered with crum-bling cities on one side and casinos on the other. But that's a New York City view. From Philadelphia, we see the lower half of the state much differently. If the Jersey Shore is the great cleansing breath we take to clear our citified lungs, the Pine Barrens, the wide, mysterious woods we cross to get to it, is the balm that clears our mind first.

Soon we were in the thick of it: deciduous maples and locusts gave way to scrub oak and pitch pine, the shorter, lankier trees which opened up the forest and cooled the hot August air. A bend in the road led us past a cedar marsh, the scent reminding me of my grandmother's winter coat. I rolled down the window as we lost all sight of houses and habitation, breezes off a big lake chilling us before the woods swallowed us again.

I thought of when my parents would take my brother and me to the Shore as kids, and they'd tell us scary stories about the Jersey Devil, the part-man, part-goat, horse-headed horror that terrorized the Pines. But I couldn't imagine such a monster right then, with my arm out the window, riding in the current. As I fixed on the trees flicking past, the sandy forest floor littered with needles and laurel and fern, I knew all my demons were right there beside me.

"Iron Bog, two miles," Denny said, glancing at a sign. A few minutes later we rolled into downtown.

Iron Bog didn't appear much more than a crossroads, with a general store, a gas station, a post office, Town Hall, and a shiny little place called The Cranberry Café. With geraniums here and there along white picket fences, it seemed the crusty-old Pine Barrens village had taken on a bit of a polish, like the cursory perking-up a house gets when company's coming. And five hundred or so feet later I'd know why. That's where the Iron Bog Volunteer Firehouse was, and from the looks of it, the company had arrived.

"Damn, look at that," Denny said. "There must be a hundred women in line."

I leaned into the windshield, squinting. "And the door's not even open yet."

He parked the van on the opposite side of the street. "Hurry," he said, grabbing his equipment. I grabbed mine and scrambled after him.

We passed women of all shapes, sizes and ages, all glammed to the hilt, some with one or two kids. Seeing Denny with his camera and me with my mic, they tossed us a few scowls, knowing their secret would now get out. When we finally reached the head of the line, we met a fireman in full uniform.

"Hi, Channel 8 News," I said. "We'd like to chat with Mr. Devine before you open the door."

He eyed me skeptically before his mouth widened in a grin. "Hey . . . You're Julie Knott! I love your stories. You know, if it were anyone else, I wouldn't—Oh, go on in."

I gifted him with a smile, on autopilot now. "Many thanks."

As we entered Denny already had the minicam hoisted atop his shoulder, but I kept my mic holstered for the moment. If this Devine was as loony as I figured him to be, I thought it best to ask his permission first. My childhood had been peppered with tales about Pineys, crazy backwoods Jethros who shotgunned first and asked questions later. Through the window I could see the back of a man standing behind a table, and all at once resentment boiled inside me. I took a deep breath, my shirt sticking to me in the un-air-conditioned hall. I opened the door.

"Hello? Mr. Devine? I'm Julie Knott from Channel 8 News. Might I have a quick word with you?"

When he turned, my heart leaped right out my throat.

Chapter Two

The Flipside of Serious

"HOLY MOTHER OF—God . . ." Denny said.

My sentiments exactly. Andy Devine had to be the most stunning man I'd ever laid eyes on.

He was tall, six foot two at least, his black hair swept back to just nick his collar, his skin tanned, his cheekbones high, his shoulders as wide as his waist was lean. He wore dark trousers, a white shirt, a tie, and a vest, but I could tell immediately he was used to more freedom. His body looked sculpted by hard and frequent use, his biceps nearly bursting from their cotton casing, and even in that un-air-conditioned room, he looked as cool and collected as if encased in ice. Putting it all together, he was quite the package, but that wasn't what took my breath away. As I came toward the table, as he moved around it to meet me, it was his eyes that nearly nailed me to the floor: two sharp, liquid arrows so regally blue they looked cut from some empirical standard, and infused with an intelligence so far above any preconceived notions, I genuinely felt embarrassed.

To put it simply: he was *not* what I expected.

"What can I do for you?" he said, the overhead fans ruffling his thick hair.

Not that I would allow him to ruffle me. "As I said, I'm Julie Knott from Channel 8 News, and this is my cameraman, Denny O'Brien.

Denny cleared his throat—loudly—lowering the camera to his side. "Pleased to meet you," he said with surprising steadiness, in spite of his blanch a minute before.

Andy Devine nodded, but didn't reach for either of our hands, which we were too off-kilter to offer anyway. Instead he eyed us with a curiosity I'd last seen at the zoo.

Inwardly, I was a little miffed that any human—insanely gorgeous or otherwise—could invoke such ridiculous reactions, doubly so as I groped for the right thing to say. *My God! When's the last time that happened?* Still, years of experience let me slip into my screen-perfected smile and simpatico interviewer's mode, my voice precisely modulated as I leaned in and said conspiratorially, "Maybe you've heard of me? I do segments on Channel 8 called 'Julie Knott's Random Access.'"

"Can't say I watch much TV," he said. Then his eyes narrowed. "*Random*, as in meaning . . .?"

"You know, out of the ordinary, off the beaten track. Unusual."

"Ah." He considered that for a moment. "You think I'm unusual?"

Only the fact that you're actually saying that with a straight face. "Well, your interview process certainly is. We'd love to do a story on it."

He looked honestly perplexed. "Why?"

I almost laughed. Either this man was yanking my chain, or there were still people out there who could surprise me. "You don't think advertising on a utility pole for a wife is a bit out of the ordinary?"

He leaned back against the table, folding his arms across his massive chest. "No more than when a woman tricks herself out and goes into a bar, advertising herself as available. I'm just giving her a more respectable venue."

His voice was deep and melodious, yet he had the oddest accent, as unmistakably American as it was faintly exotic. The sound of it sent a distinct wave of heat through me. *Good God.* I scrubbed my hand across the back of my neck; I refused to let him throw me. "So, you don't see having them parade before you like horses at an auction as a tad different?"

That seemed to amuse him. "Miss Knott, it's me who's really for sale, and don't think for a moment each one of those women out there isn't aware of it."

I had an image of Mr. Gorgeous being yanked from one frantic female to the other, *One Day Sale!* signs hung around his neck. "That would be true if they were doing the choosing."

"Even the woman I pick still has to agree to it. I'll be making all the promises."

"As in a contract."

"Actually, it's very simple. I'm offering a three-month trial marriage, in which I'll promise to house, feed and provide my wife with anything she needs. All I'm asking of her is to be healthy, work hard and try for a baby. If for any reason she's not completely satisfied—and pregnant within three months—she'll walk away with a generous compensation. So obviously, the risk is more at my end. Their risk is relatively effortless."

"Effortless!" The ways in which this preposterous proposition *so* did not resemble *effortless* nearly made me laugh out loud. "Mr. Devine, I'd hardly call bearing your issue *effortless!*"

He bristled. "I'm not saying it would be. I only thought of children as a logical progression."

Amazing, truly. He wasn't medieval; he was positively Neanderthal. "A logical progression of *what*?"

"Why, marriage, of course."

"So couples that don't have children . . ." I flung my hands in a futile gesture. "Who don't want or can't have them—their marriages are a sham?"

"No . . ." he said, a bit condescendingly. "That would be the logic of their own particular marriages. But in ours, the terms will already have been spelled out. I have a farm. She'll help me run it. And if it's run well, we'll share equally in the benefits and rewards. You couldn't get a better deal than that."

"You talk as if this marriage'll be nothing more than a business relationship."

He looked incredulous. "Isn't that what all marriages really are?"

"Of course not," I said. "What a crazy idea."

"Well, if they aren't, they should be. Because that's what it comes down to at the divorce settlement anyway. A dissolution of a partnership, a consolidation of debts, a distribution of the assets. Are you married, Ms. Knott?"

I caught his glance to my left hand. I shoved my bare fingers into my pocket. "No. Presently unattached." Denny cleared his throat. I tossed him a filthy glare. And when Andy Devine lifted a brow, I knew I'd better offer a quick clarification before my cameraman spilled it. "I just broke it off with my fiancé this morning."

"Does this upset you?" he said.

I could feel the blood rising to my face. "What do you think? We were to be married in two weeks. The man practically left me at the altar."

"Did you love him?"

He was beyond belief. "Of course I did! Why else would I have married him?"

"Probably not for any of my reasons. Because from what I can assume . . ."—he assessed me quickly—"you're probably a good risk. Which just proves how ancillary love actually is."

If the morning hadn't already unhinged me, this Andy Devine threw the door right off the hinges. "You're wrong," I said, my hands clenching so tightly I nearly crushed the mic. "Even after what my fiancé did to me, I still believe the only *logical progression* is people meet, fall in love, get married. *That's* the way it's supposed to be. Because without love, Mr. Devine, your marriage will never be a real one."

He sprung from the table toward me. "Oh believe me, Ms. Knott, with or without love, this marriage will be a real one. In *every* sense of the word."

It wasn't fair, it really wasn't, that this strange man got to set parameters for what he believed a marriage should be, and then have a hundred women lining up ready to agree with him. And then there was me, who always played by the rules, who couldn't even manage to keep one man happy.

Suddenly everything descended on me: the impatience of the crowd outside, the hot room, and then there was the scent of him, a rustic mix of pine and cedar, all wrapped up in a package so enthusiastically male I went a little weak in the joints. I took a step back, teetering against a chair.

Andy Devine's hand shot out. "Steady," he said, ready to assist me.

I straightened instantly. "I'm fine. It's just these chairs, I didn't see—"

"You're a woman of strong passions, Ms. Knott, and I upset you." His gaze skimmed over me. "Truly, I didn't mean it. Please forgive me."

"You didn't upset me. You just kind of threw . . ." The words stuck in my throat because really, talking to him was starting to prove pointless. I wanted to shove him, curse him out for being so presumptuous, but there was something so damn chivalrous about him. *My God*, I thought, *how the hell did his eyes get so blue?* Their swirly, little vortexes made my head go a little . . . I backed away, clearing my throat.

"You're a most unusual man, Mr. Devine," I finally said.

When he smiled, his whole face seemed to glow. "I'll take that on authority, Ms. Knott. You get paid to know."

Devastatingly handsome wasn't enough. He had to go ahead and be witty. "So you do see my point then?"

He shrugged. "Let's just say I see it and leave it at that."

It would be easy to spend the afternoon sparring with this disconcerting man. Why? The outward reasons were fairly obvious. As for the inner, my battered ego relished the attention, as much as I did the idea of digging further into his archaic ambitions. But Denny was making impatient little noises, hardly audible above the restlessness rising from the line outside. But I never did get an answer, did I?

"So what about the story, Mr. Devine? I promise I'll be tasteful."

He shrugged. "Sure. Why not. What do I have to do?"

I explained we'd like to ask him a few questions about himself before he started, then we'd record him as he did the interviews. Each woman would have to sign a release so we could use the resulting footage and their names. We would then ask him a few more questions afterwards, and that would be it.

"Sounds simple enough." he said, turning to sit behind the table. "And as far as whatever else you need to know about me . . ." He slid over a photocopied set of papers. "This should answer your questions."

As he readied himself for the interviews, I perused Mr. Devine's so-called Fact Sheet. He was forty years old, in perfect health (a copy of the results of his recent physical was conveniently attached), no social diseases (bonus), six foot two, two hundred twenty pounds (yikes!), black hair, blue (definitive) eyes, left-handed (?). He was a college graduate (though he didn't say where), had traveled extensively, and was a native of Iron Bog, though he hadn't lived there in "quite some time." He was the outright owner (no pesky mortgages or liens) of a large tract of land in a wooded area outside of town, which included two acres of highbush blueberries, peach and apple trees, mushrooms, a kitchen garden, holly bushes, chickens, and a few "various items of special cultivation," whatever that meant. He also added he was "financially secure," details of which would be further disclosed during "final negotiations." He also had a house on that large tract of land which, he conceded, "needed some work."

Needed some work. Right. A falling down house out in the woods with chickens. I looked to The Catch in question as he straightened his vest. Six-pack abs or not, I had the feeling his dazzley-eyed wife-to-be was going to be in for one big eye-opener.

"All set?" I asked Denny.

He hoisted the camera to his shoulder. "Open the floodgates."

I looked to Andy Devine. "Ready if you are."

He smiled. "I always am." He nodded to the firefighter

at the door. The man opened the door, letting in the first batch of prospective brides.

I must admit the variety of the applicants who came through the door over the next three hours surprised me. Granted, there was a liberal sprinkling of gold diggers, but there were also quite a few professional women: two accountants, a national sales rep for a *Fortune* 500 company, a bank executive, a nurse practitioner, a freelance journalist and even a veterinarian.

"Oh, mushrooms!" the vet said as she read the fact sheet. She was blonde and petite with a curvy figure. "That must be where the chickens come in."

"What do you mean?" I asked her.

She looked at me as if obvious. "Everyone knows you need them to cultivate mushrooms."

"*Chickens* cultivate mushrooms?"

"No," she said dryly, "but their manure does. Industrious little things, aren't they?" She poofed her hair, straightening her pencil skirt. "Just like me."

"So you wouldn't give up your practice, then," I asked, noting it was about twenty miles away in tony Moorestown.

She looked at me as if I were daft. "In a snap, sweetie. I've had it with birthing overbred puppies." She tossed Andy Devine a lascivious glance. "From now on I'll be squeezing out my own. Ta!"

I quickly learned I'd better get used to my jaw dropping. Because it was more of the same with each woman I spoke.

From one of the accountants, a slim, designer-suited

Latina: "From my calculations, we should be able to subdivide some of the land and sell it as farmettes. Plus blueberry demand is way up, and with last year's disappointing yield in Maine and Wisconsin, the Jersey crop is worth a record amount. So after we invest in some more acreage, we can take . . ."

It seemed as if she and Mr. Devine shared the same pragmatic bent. "Sounds like you want to expand the business, make it more profitable."

"The only thing I really want to expand is *this*," she said, pointing to her flat belly. "But if talking profit-and-loss gets that big hunk of *machismo* off?" She leaned in, "*Chica*, I have nothing against spreading myself like Excel."

From the bank executive, dark-skinned and drop-dead gorgeous: "Says here his house needs some work. Well, I'm not afraid to invest in capital improvements. And as far as him being financially secure?" She winked at me, sliding her hand down the trim hip of her tailored pantsuit. "So am I, and I'd love to merge our assets."

Then there was the *Fortune* 500 executive, a willowy brunette teetering atop Louboutins and jittering from too many sips of her venti Starbucks coffee. "This farm he's talking about," she said, her eyes darting from side-to-side, "It's out in the boondocks, right? I mean I gotta know this."

"So he's saying," I said. "Is it important?"

She pointed a Frenched fingertip at my heart, glancing over her shoulder. "Don't quote me on this, and you're a dead woman if you do, but if you hear about someone from some company getting arrested for misplacing ten million, give-or-take a mil, you didn't hear it from—*shh!*" She whirled around. "What was that!"

I scanned the busy room. "I don't know. What do you mean?"

Her eyes narrowed. "Oh, don't play dumb with me." She bolted out the door.

Denny just looked at me and shrugged.

And then there was the nurse practitioner, full-figured, with piercing, blue eyes and an easy smile: "I'm nearly as good as a doctor, so think of the medical expenses we'll save. Plus I was raised on a farm, so I'm no stranger to hard work. In fact, after being cooped up in a hospital all these years"—she tossed her auburn hair—"I think I'd love working out in the fresh air. I also know a bit of carpentry, having renovated my own Victorian, so I could help with the house. And I already have a large nest egg, so he really wouldn't have to worry about supporting me. Plus I love children. I can't wait to start a big family."

She sounded perfect. A distinct air of reason surrounded her, off-setting the room's palpable vibe of lust. So I had to ask: "You seem quite accomplished in your own right. So, what's your reason for coming here?"

At once, she turned somber. "Above all, I'm a practical person. All I have to offer is how wonderful I look on paper. Because when you meet me . . ." She thumbed the waistband of her plus-sized skirt. "This is the only thing they see." Then she brightened. "Which is why I like that he's calling it a partnership, rather than a marriage. Tells me he's willing to look below the surface."

She was perfect, but I couldn't get beyond how short she was selling herself. "Listen, he'd be lucky to have you."

"Thanks." She stood for her turn. "Let's hope so." And she left to sit before Andy Devine. Not a minute later, he was smiling wide.

A *hidden jewel*, I thought. I just hoped he was smart enough to delve deeper. And then the next candidate, the freelance photojournalist, blew that hope all to hell.

I had never seen a more beautiful woman, and that's the truth. She was olive-skinned and brilliantly green-eyed, her hair long and wavy and flowing in lush waves around her shoulders, definitively voluptuous in a simple tank top and khakis. Her gaze was sharp and intelligent, and when she told me about herself, her voice as clear as it was smokily seductive, her reason for being there was as logical as any I'd heard so far.

"I only came out of curiosity, not with any real intention, just having seen the flyer on the pole and thinking I could take a few shots. And probably just like you, I muscled past everyone to take a peek inside. Then I saw him."

I thought of my own first impression. "And when you did . . .?"

Her eyes fluttered and she shivered. "I turned around and got in line." She looked to Andy Devine as he shook the hand of the now-supplanted nurse practitioner as she left. "Oh man . . . you can't get much better than that."

When she went to him—when his jaw dropped at the sight of her, the same as mine had when I first caught sight of him—I knew he had met his match. In fact, he was so transfixed the insanity of it all took my breath away.

Because insanity was what it had to be.

I turned to Denny. "Did you see that?"

"Yeah," he said, still shooting. "I believe we have a winner here."

I tried to look away, but watching those two freakishly beautiful people was as compulsive as gawking at a car wreck. "This is so wrong. I just can't understand how otherwise-sane women could prostitute themselves like this."

"It's as old as the hills, Jules. The classic impetus of love and money."

"It can't be that simple," I said. The woman laughed heartily as Andy Devine's animated hands moved about. "There has to be more to it. Especially with this one."

"Well, she is a writer. Imagine her story now. If you want to be jealous over anything, there's that."

"Jealous? Of that walking Viagra ad?" I could feel the blood rising to my face. "I'm hardly a crone. How could you think I'd be jealous of *her*?"

He lowered the camera, glaring at me. "Calm down, princess, I'm not attacking your feminine pulchritude. I'm only referring to her inside scoop. Jesus."

"I knew that." But, of course, I hadn't. Because this whole thing was beginning to feel a little too personal, and even more weird. I plopped to a chair, my head in my hands. "Maybe this wasn't such a good idea. Not after this morning. Maybe it cuts a little too close to the bone."

Denny squeezed my shoulder. "I don't doubt it. But at least we're almost done. Did you see that?"

"What," I said wearily, not looking up.

"Andy Devine just signaled to the door guy. He's not taking any more."

"What?" I looked up to see the photojournalist making her exit, smiling and waving to me as she breezed past, an apparent triumph. I needed to wrap this up. The whole day had been a bad dream. Then my BlackBerry vibrated against my hip. I pulled it from my pocket. My heart leaped—*Richard*.

He was texting an apology—he had to be! It had been the stress of the wedding. We had fought before, and—as in all normal relationships (the antithesis of which had been percolating in this very room)—we'd live to fight again. Were we any different than any couple anywhere? *Of course not*, I told myself, smug in my normalcy. Suddenly I felt better and I got up, mic at the ready. If the day had been a bad dream, I was awakened now. And more than ready to *carpe diem*.

Denny caught my arm, chin thrust toward my phone. "Don't tell me that was Richard."

"And what if it was?" I said, shoving it into my pocket. "Would it matter?"

His grip got tighter. "Things happen for a reason. Don't do it."

"Do what?" I said blithely.

"The man's a shit, Jules. Consider the morning a lucky break and keep running."

"I've never run away from anyone or anything, Denny," I said, shrugging him off. "You know that."

"I also know maybe this time, you should."

I ignored him and fell back into the swing, whipping

out my mirror to reapply my lipstick. Suddenly, I felt revived. I tucked back a few tendrils falling from my combs and turned to Andy Devine, just rising from the table.

"Let's wrap this thing up," I said, switching on the wattage as I went to him.

The man seemed taller three hours later, seemed broader in the shoulders and leaner in the waist, his eyes now nearly azure, his face more determined. Odder still, in the time it took to travel the twelve-or-so feet to get to him, I became curiously tenuous, as if I were teetering on some unknown brink—no thanks to Denny, I'm sure. Suddenly my heart began to race, an excitement boiling inside me. "Well, Mr. Devine, that last one sure seemed like a winner. Was she the one?"

He watched through the window as she climbed into her Jeep. "She wanted to write a story on me."

"Ooh—competition. Lucky I got here first."

"Yes." His eyes shifted firmly to mine. "Wasn't it, though?"

"So," I said as I raised the mic, "have you found your wife?"

"Yes," he said. "You."

Chapter Three

One Day I'll Look Back on This and It'll All Seem Funny

"YOU," ANDY DEVINE said. "I want you for my wife."

As that statement traveled the neuron pathway to the part of my brain which would absorb, interpret and decide how to answer, I couldn't help but think of all the bizarre I'd seen. From the dog on a high wire balancing an egg on his nose; a three-legged goose; a woman who ate nails; a man surgically altered to look like Chewbacca; a woman living in a refrigerator; an old man who hoisted a truck when it rolled atop his grandson's leg; to a couple whose house had two rooms filled to the ceiling with pennies, I'd seen heroism and lunacy, oddity and insanity. But up until that moment, none of it had made my jaw drop. Because up until then, none of it had involved me.

So, *"What?"* was all I managed to reply.

To which, he reiterated, "I want *you* for my wife."

I smiled, clearing my throat; he had to be playing with me. "I'm flattered, Mr. Devine, truly I am, but what's your real answer?"

He leaned in, his proximity sending numbing signals to my brain. "The same."

I laughed. "You're joking."

"When I'm joking," he said, moving even closer, "you'll know it."

Denny lowered his camera. "Excuse me," he said to Andy Devine, "but are you for real?"

"Pardon?" he answered, unblinking.

"Okay, never mind," Denny said, realigning the camera. "Go on."

I slapped my hand over the lens. "Shut that thing off. Are you insane?"

Denny lowered it. "I ought to be asking you the same thing. It's the best offer you've had in years."

I scowled at him, returning to the subject at hand. "Mr. Devine—a word." Then I promptly crossed to the other side of the room. When I turned, Denny had sunk into a folding chair, and my would-be suitor was standing before me.

"Yes?" he said, calmly attentive.

A part of me was so flabbergasted I hardly knew where to begin, but I retained enough professionalism to override anything. "I'm a TV reporter, Mr. Devine, not a candidate for your fiancée. I'm here to cover a story, not to become one. So, as tempting as your offer may be, I have to decline."

He lifted a brow. "Why, Ms. Knott, are you patronizing me?"

That threw me. "What? No!"

"Because I detect a hint of condescension."

"Then you're imagining things." My hands were sweating; I swiped them on my skirt. "I'm just stating a fact."

His gaze dipped seductively. "So, you don't think I'm worth considering?"

"Mr. Devine, don't take—" Suddenly I was struck by the line of his jaw, so angular and forthright. I swear, he could be a judge or a juror or anyone who's supposed to be capable of impartiality, and yet . . . There was something about it, in his emerging beard and how it sloped toward his mouth, that was so indefinably sexy it knocked all sense out of me. I was fighting a losing battle and I knew it.

I cleared my throat and began again. "Look, I don't want you to take this personally, but—"

"I won't," he said. "In fact, I've gone out of my way to make sure personalities have nothing to do with it. I need a wife to help run the farm and have our children. And if she does, she'll share equally in all the rewards and benefits. All I ask is that she's healthy, able to have children, and be willing to work hard. You, Ms. Knott . . ." He looked me over. ". . . appear to meet all the criteria."

The man was astounding. "But you know nothing about me!"

"What do I need to know beyond what I can see?"

"How about what's inside me, what my interests are, if I'm honest, how I take my coffee—Christ!" I stabbed my fingers into my hair. A comb tumbled out. "Why, if I even *like* you, for Pete's sake!"

He plucked the comb from the floor. "Do you like me, Ms. Knott?" he said with the barest of smiles, the bit of tortoise-shell plastic pinched between his fingers.

I snatched it from him, shoving it into my hair. "That's not the point, and it never was."

He leaned in. "My point exactly."

Good God! He was infuriating. "Look." I took a breath, forcing myself to calm. "I don't even know why we're having this conversation. I came here to cover a story—"

"Like the woman who just left," he interjected, and not without apparent distaste.

I blinked, though I didn't let it throw me. "She was practically your clone. Pick her. She's perfect."

"You're perfect," he said, closing in so tightly my back smacked against the wall. His eyes were like two blue burning coals. "I'm sure your fiancé knew how you liked your coffee, what magazines you read, how you looked first thing in the morning. Yet he left you anyway. Maybe because he couldn't see what I do, even without looking. You're what I want. Sometimes you just know."

He reached into his vest and pulled out a business card. "Take three days to think about it." He slipped the card into the pocket of my blouse. "Then call this number." And with one more rake of those eyes, he walked out of the hall.

He left me a shivering mass of disorientation, wondering how the hell I'd let the man flip the tables on me. I looked to Denny as he watched Andy Devine go. He set his camera on a chair and joined me.

"Jesus—you're white as a sheet." His face darkened. "What'd he say to you?"

I took a moment for my heart to slow, and reaching into my blouse pocket, idly handed him the business card. "He asked me to marry him."

"I already know that." He glanced at the card. "Jinks' Gas? What the hell?"

"He said to call that number when I've made up my mind. Gave me three days."

"From the way you look, you must be considering the possibility."

That snapped me back to reality. "Do you have any idea what kind of day I've had?" I grabbed my gear and headed for the door. "I'm out of here."

"But what's the story!"

"There is no story!"

"Oh, there's a story," Denny said, following me out. "We're just not filing it yet."

Then file this: they were all crazy. This Andy Devine, Denny, all those insane women who thought the answer to their dreams waited inside that firehouse. As if it were that easy to hop into a new life as simply as changing your shoes! Well, I wasn't blinded by Mr. Devine's divineness, and the only thing I'd fall for right now was a stiff drink and my feet propped atop something soft and cushy. I squeezed my eyelids, near running to the van. When would this hell-day be over?

I'D BEEN SO jangled by Andy Devine, I didn't even remember Richard's text until we were at our building. As Denny pulled the news van to the no-parking curb, our press credentials giving us access to virtually anywhere, I dug my phone from my purse.

"I'm coming up with you," he said, already climbing out of the van.

"Oh no you're not," I said, slipping the phone into my pocket. "He's probably left for the airport anyway, and if he hasn't, he knows how you feel about him. I don't want any drama."

"You're getting it anyway," Denny said, cupping my elbow as we entered the lobby. Geraldo, the doorman, looked up from his desk, seeming genuinely surprised to see me.

"Ms. Knott!" the doorman said. "You're here! But I'd been told—"

"We're really not interested," Denny said, sailing past him and into the elevator. He leaned into me as I inserted my key for the penthouse floor, and whispered, "Jesus. Their jaws are flapping already."

"That's weird," I said, the slip for my keycard blinking back red. "It won't . . ."

"But Ms. Knott!" called Geraldo, loping toward us, "Ms. Knott!"

Denny's hand stopped the door. "You saying it won't work?"

I tried the card again. "I think the code's been changed."

"Son of a bitch." Denny looked from me to Geraldo. "Why can't she get up to her house?"

The doorman wrung his hands. "Mr. Sayles had the locks changed. Just after Ms. Knott left." He looked to me, pleadingly. "I'm so sorry. I don't want you to think I—"

"Are you joking!" Denny roared.

Somewhere near the edge of my consciousness I could hear Geraldo apologizing as Denny vented his spleen, but at that moment all my attention was clamped on the digital 'Dear Jane' Richard had left on my phone. *The locks have been changed. Ask Geraldo for access to your things. Call 215-555-8935 for that apt I told you about. I'm so sorry, but it's cleaner this way.* I stumbled out to the lobby, dropping onto a sofa.

Cleaner. "Oh Richard . . ." I said, ready to hit *reply*, "how could—"

"Give me that," Denny said, snatching the phone. He dropped it into his pocket and grasped me under the arm. "All right. Let's go."

I gaped at him, unable to mouth the word, *Where?*

"You're coming home with me," he said, dragging me toward the door. "I have plenty of extra tooth-brushes."

"I'm sorry," Geraldo said again.

"Yeah, yeah, we're all sorry," Denny muttered, "until we do it again."

THE ONE THING I'd always loved about Denny's partner, Brent, besides his eclectic Walnut Street gallery, was his uncanny ability to match the perfect food to every crisis.

"Here you go, love," he said, his English accent like raw silk. I curled my fingers around a mug of hot Dutch chocolate. You wouldn't think something producing such a head of steam would work on a sultry August evening, but right then, as it slinked down my raspy throat, it was comfort incarnate. And it was about all I could stomach at the moment.

"Bastard. Piece of metro-ass shit," Denny spat out, pacing. "I'd like to slam those veneers down his gullet."

"You need to take it down a tad," Brent said, his arm around me. "Why don't you return the news van before they clamp a boot on it? It'll give you a chance to calm down while Julie has a good cry on the sofa."

"I'm not going to cry," I said. "I'm too angry."

"That's what I'm talking about," Denny said. "Better to get even."

"Dennis!" Brent cried, "Will you go already?"

Denny snatched the keys and stomped out.

Brent sighed. "I love the man, but he gives *machismo* a meaning I'm sure no dictionary has ever heard of." He turned to me. "So, my darling, what shall we do now?"

"I haven't the faintest," I said, as various scenarios of

Richard's demise formed in my head. "Besides Denny's most excellent suggestion."

"Oh, come now," Brent said, "you're a clever girl. You didn't see this coming?"

I left the sofa, dropping to a window seat across. "Damn!" I slammed my fist into the cushion. "You have to admit he was perfect on paper. He was so smart and ambitious, and didn't he always know exactly the right thing to say?" I laughed, the irony hitting me. "He must have told me he loved me ten times a day."

"Proving how fake he really is." Brent sunk to the opposite end of the seat. He ruffled his salt-and-peppered hair and pushed the window full-open, the evening breeze sweeping past the brick townhouses of Old City, promising rain. He took the hot chocolate from me and set it on the floor, leveling his gaze to mine.

"I've been with Denny almost two years," he said, "and in all that time, I can count on two hands the times he's told me he loved me. And because of that whenever he does, I'm dead certain he means it. With repetition comes dilution, don't you think?"

I squeezed his hand and leaned back into the molding. "I don't know what I think anymore. All I can see is red. It's not every day your future gets tossed out the window. I can't wait until the 'I told you so's start rolling in."

Brent's mouth crooked. "I promise I won't say it."

I waved him off. "You'd just be another voice in the chorus."

He took a sip of my chocolate, then handed it to me. "Julie . . . this might sound callous, but did you love him?"

It was the same question Andy Devine had asked me earlier. The difference was, my answer then had been knee-jerk, whereas Brent knew me so much better. I stared into the mug. "I thought I did."

"Even though he was still seeing Annika Eden?"

I looked up. "How did you know?"

He shrugged. "Everyone knows, darling."

"*Everyone?*" In many ways, Philadelphia was a small town; I could only imagine how they were laughing at me. "Yet he was still going to marry me?"

Brent cocked a brow, as if obvious. "Was he?"

"Oh, come on! Why would we make all these arrangements together if he never intended to go through with it?"

"Perhaps to keep you around for a while? You're successful, a cash cow. Very good for his portfolio."

I could feel my throat closing up. "And now he doesn't need me anymore?"

"I'm sorry, Julie," he said quietly. "Truly I am."

How much more obvious did I need it to be? *It really was true.* I burst into tears.

"That's it, my dear, get it over with ..." Brent murmured, rubbing my back. "It'll wash him out of you like a good dose of ipecac."

I cried and cried for I don't know how long, first in a gasping torrent, then with a moan or two coloring a few choice epithets, until I finally succumbed to a pathetic whimpering that eventually gave way to the immediacy of the moment.

"Brent—I have no place to live! And two hundred

invitations floating around out there! What'll I tell my family? My job? My *caterer*!"

He shoved a wad of tissues at me. "That you've come to your senses. What else could you say?"

"But he's made an absolute idiot out of me. How will I ever show my face to the camera again?" I honked my nose. "I'm ruined."

"Julie, enough already." He grasped me by the shoulders. "I've every confidence you'll find a way to work it out. Why, I'll bet the next best thing for you is just around the corner. Now, go upstairs and revive that gorgeous face of yours. As soon as Denny comes back we're taking you out for dinner. And cocktails. I suspect we'll need many."

I didn't have the heart to tell him I couldn't eat a bite. But the cocktails were an inspiration, as well as an apt apology. Part of the blame for this fiasco lay with Brent.

Two years earlier I had walked into his gallery, Curieux, to tape a spot on an exhibition of oils created with poisonous plants and venoms. Immediately, Brent took over my story, my cameraman, and—after a couple martinis—my private life, which he began to scrutinize. But I hardly minded. At the time I was still building my brand name, and Brent seemed so well-acquainted with the local oddballs, he became an excellent repository to draw from. So, after a few such tip-offs and their subsequent ratings-breaking stories, I was grateful to call him a friend. Even if he had introduced me to Richard.

"He's a shark," Brent had said. "But if anyone can get you that contract, it's Richard Sayles. He actually talked me into upping Dagor Ruski's commission, and I still made a killing on his show. He's new, but he's hungry. You can't miss."

At the time I had been mainly a general assignments reporter on another station, but my oddball stories were getting more and more popular, and Channel 8 was floating rumors they might be interested in turning my occasional quirky spots into a permanent fixture. I had print media, radio, and a degree from the U of Penn's Annenberg School in my book, but if I ever wanted to become Jeanne Moos' heir-apparent, I absolutely needed to cultivate my signature.

"So you think I should hook up with him?" I asked Brent.

"Hook up?" He cocked a brow. "If you're speaking in the popular parlance—God *no*. The man will disappoint you as sure as clockwork. But as your talent agent? Run and get your pen, darling. He could sell water to whales."

So we hooked up, in more ways than one. Richard got me exactly what I wanted from Channel 8, and I got Richard. Or so I thought. I left for the bathroom and gave my face a good washing, the cold water dousing me with logic: If I were the boost that had launched his rocket, then once he was in orbit, like all boosters, Richard had to cut me loose.

My God, why hadn't I listened to Brent in the first place?

I pulled the combs from my head and, dropping them in the sink, brushed my hair until my scalp burned. It's amazing the delusions I accepted as truths. That our similarities made us soul mates. That whatever he did for me he did *for me*. That he meant it when he said he loved me. That he would marry me.

I reapplied my lipstick, mascara, a bit of powder to hide the shine. I wondered if he ever even *liked* me. I thought of all the things we did together, the restaurants, the group trips to Turks and Caicos, the shows, the bars, the parties too innumerable to tally. I tried to think of the times we sat on the floor in front of the fireplace and just read the Sunday *Inquirer* together; I couldn't picture it past our third month. Did we always have to have an audience?

I gathered up my hair and twisted it into a chignon, fastening it with the combs. The last one slipped from my fingertips to the sink.

Do you like me, Miss Knott?

I started, snatching up the fallen comb. *Do you?* Andy Devine's voice rumbled through my head. *Do you, Miss Knott? Do you?*

I shoved the comb into my hair. He was totally missing the point.

My point exactly.

This was nuts. I grabbed my purse and fled.

HOURS LATER, I was floating out of Amada and up Chestnut Street on four Dark Habits, a brilliant concoction of lime, strawberry and gin. True, we had a few tapas chasers, but they hardly diluted the elation I felt from my complete denial. I spun around to a bemused Brent and Denny, squeezing between them.

"You guys are terrific," I said, flinging my arms up around their shoulders. "Now lemme buy you a drink."

"And what'll that be, sweet piece," Denny said, squeezing me. "A Dr. Pepper? An Ovaltine? How about a Shamrock Shake?"

"How about a sock in the kisser?" I said, tweaking him under the arm. His answer was a nip on the ear.

"Don't tempt me, Jules," he said. "You're in need of a good one."

"Oh, do play nice, children," Brent said. "Let's not waste all that good gin."

I shot Denny a smirk, pulling away. "You just blew your free drink, buster." I caught sight of a bank at the corner. "I need some cash. Hold tight, I'll be right back."

I trotted up to the ATM, the debit card already in my hand. I pressed the arrow for one hundred dollars, the machine whirred, and a receipt sputtered out. I held it into the light. All it said was SEE TELLER FOR MORE INFORMATION.

"Problem?" Denny said from behind me.

"Oh no . . ." I murmured, instantly sobering. "He wouldn't."

Brent plucked the receipt from me, eyeing it. "This is a joint account, isn't it?"

My gaze shot to Denny. "Where's my phone?"

He looked nearly as panicked as I felt. "At the house. Come on."

Five minutes later I dialed Richard; the call went directly to voice mail. "You son of a bitch!" I spat into my BlackBerry. "Don't you even have the guts to talk to me?

Call me! Now!" I delivered the same message every ten minutes for the next two hours, calling and texting. Then I finally gave up all my scruples and sent him a Tweet:

I thought you loved me. Even worse I thought you LIKED me.

I was sinking fast.

The next morning, exhausted and nursing a 'tini head, I stopped at the bank first thing, asking to see customer service. Instead, I was taken directly to the branch manager's office. My account information was already on her screen when I entered.

"Have a seat, Ms. Knott," she said, bursting with politeness.

Without preamble, I said, "Why can't I get at my money?"

She folded her hands atop her desk and looked me square in the eyes. "Whenever there's a dissolution of a joint account, as your fiancé has requested, it's always frozen until the depositors can settle how the funds are to be distributed. For that, we'll need both parties present, and if one of them can't be, then the absent party has to sign this form and get it notarized." She slid it to me. "After that, we can close up the account."

I stared at her, aghast. "But all my money's in that account! You must already have Richard's permission if he's asked you to close it."

She tapped at her keyboard. "It says here Richard Sayles had to go out of town on a family emergency, and he would settle the account when he returns."

"Family emergency?" I thumbed my chest. "*Here's*

your family emergency." I leaned in, *sotto voce*. "He's left me high and dry!"

She smiled sympathetically. "If you like, I can set up a separate account for your direct deposit, and arrange so you can withdraw the equivalent of one pay period. Outside of that . . ." she shrugged. "I'm really sorry. Can't you contact him?"

I swiped my hands on my skirt. "He's in Seattle, and we really didn't part on the best terms."

Her eyes sparkled. "Really?"

What did I just say? I could see my name in Dan Gross' gossip blog before the sun set. "Nothing we won't work out. In the meantime, about that new account . . ."

I filled out what I had to, withdrew $500, and by the time I hit the sidewalk my head was spinning. It was the day after one of the worst disasters of my life, and there were a million things I should be doing, but all I could think of was retreating to the haven of Channel 8. Since I was a kid, the printed or spoken word had always been my sanctuary: from the library, to the school newspaper and the city desk, to the radio and TV stations that had become my second home. On a Saturday morning, Channel 8 was manned by the second string, and most were surprised to see me. All except Gil, the odious station manager. He seemed downright delighted.

"Julie! Look at you, here on a Saturday morning!" He pushed a bit of paunch back under his belt and waved me over to his office. "Come on in and chat a sec."

"Can't it wait, Gil?" I was wearing the same skirt and blouse I'd worn the day before, a bit wrinkled and slightly gin-soaked, but until I could get into my apartment, I'd have to settle for the extra clothes I kept in my desk. '"I'm in a bit of a hurry and—"

"Only take a sec," he said. "Come on."

It was more of an order than a request. I took a seat in front of his desk.

He leaned back in his chair, the statue of Billy Penn rising from the skyline behind him. "Glad you stopped in, Julie. Saturdays are quiet, so it's better."

"Better for what?"

"For this chat." His chair squeaked. "About your contract renewal."

A prickle crawled up the back of my neck. "I thought we had that all settled. Richard said the only thing you had to do was sign."

"Richard. Ah." He pursed his lips, his fingertips steepling. "I saw his tweet about your breaking up. That's tough."

"You saw his—" I couldn't believe my ears. "Jesus— you *follow* him?"

He waved his hand dismissively. "He didn't he tell you, did he? I sent the changes yesterday. Julie. Your spots have been cut."

My jaw dropped. "What?"

"You're fluff, what can I say? Nielson numbers don't lie. Station's in the toilet. Either we cut the chaff or we'll lose the wheat."

I sprung from my chair, leaning over his desk. "Spare me the philosophical analogy, Gil, I make you money. How can you cut me? You must be joking!"

"Hey hey hey—slow down sweetheart! Don't kill the messenger! This comes from on high. Least you're not being fired. We're giving you weekend anchor at eleven."

"Weekend anchor!" It hit me like a blow to the chest. "I'm no talking head! I'm a reporter for Christ sake! You're burying me!"

His eyes turned steely. "Let's hear a little thanks, Julie-girl. You could be one of the twelve people I'm showing the door to on Monday. At least you'll still be drawing a paycheck. Unlike your compatriot, Mr. Denny."

I stared at him. "Denny . . .? No, you can't."

"It's done. Such are the times." Then his face uncharacteristically softened. "Hey, you're a smart girl. Maybe this'll give you time to write a book or something. Isn't that what all you guys do eventually? Now, other people? Well, they aren't so lucky. Maybe you are."

He stood. "Look, I gotta go watch my son lose at soccer, so get those changes initialed by Monday, okay?" Then he left.

I might as well have been hit by a bus. Could Richard have aimed any lower? My God, he couldn't just break up with me; he had to go for complete annihilation. Then my phone *dinged!*—a text from Richard.

He won't say it, so I will. Leave us alone.

Annika? In what alternate reality was I spinning? How did things get so bizarre so fast? I wanted to kill, maim, take them down hard, but how could I when that cowardly bastard wouldn't even talk to me? Is this what futility felt like? I doubled over, hugging myself, when something slid from my shirt pocket to the floor. I looked down at the business card. *Jinks' Gas.*

Maybe this'll give you time to write a book or something.

Suddenly, everything became inordinately clear. I had one chip left to call in and, crazy or not, maybe there was a chance to get my own back.

Oh, I was so taking that bastard *down*.

Chapter Four

Rules of Engagement

"ALL RIGHT, I'LL marry you."

Andy looked as incredulous hearing it as I felt saying it. "Are you sure?" he said.

It was the first time I'd seen him look tentative. "Pretty sure, but don't push it. You haven't passed my tests yet, and let me assure you, they're pretty rigorous."

He smiled. "Give me all you've got."

My God, I went all squishy in the stomach. A decidedly pleasant feeling, yet I couldn't help burying my face in my menu. The man did things to me I'd never imagined.

We met the next morning at the Sage Diner in Mt. Laurel, New Jersey, a little bit more than halfway between our two milieus. I needed neutral ground in the worst way, absolutely demanded of me by my surly, ersatz big brother.

"Yeah, but I never thought you'd actually *do* it," Denny had said the night before.

"That's because you always underestimate me." We had returned to his spare bedroom with all the two of us could carry, having successfully gotten into what was now Richard's penthouse. The swiftness by which my former fiancé had effected my departure was both impressive and astoundingly insulting. In a single day, he had jilted me, packed up everything I owned, and tossed me out on the sidewalk. Then, just as quickly, I'd been replaced, Annika Eden's photo as Violetta from *La Traviata* was prominently splashed atop his Facebook page.

"She's a cow," Denny said, clicking off. "A heifer, a Holstein, a goddamn Guernsey. A freakin' Texas Longhorn. Did you see those ears?"

"Denny, your loyalty is touching," I said, digging into my suitcase. "Especially since working with me probably got you fired. But I can't blame everything on her. You're forgetting what a scumbucket Richard's been."

"So, because of him you have to go ahead and marry that—" He stopped, blinking. "Okay, I'll admit he's easy on the eyes, but I was only joking when I suggested it. How can you marry someone you met two days ago? What is he? Where'd he come from? The man has no Google hits, no Facebook, no *nothing*! Are you out of your mind?"

"If I am, believe me, there's a method to my madness— ah, here it is." I scrolled to an email I'd just received that morning.

"What's that for?" Denny said, eyeing it.

"This," I waggled my BlackBerry, "will be Richard's downfall and my rise. And this"—I held up a leather-bound journal—"will be the bus driving him off the cliff."

"You cramming it down his throat?" he said, sitting back to put his feet on the bed. "I know that'll make *me* feel a whole lot better."

I ignored him. "You know how we were going to Bhutan on our honeymoon, taking this journey into Shangri-La? I planned on recording our mystical transformation, how we dined on exotic food, meditated with lamas, made love atop the Himalayas . . ."

Denny winced, holding up his hand. "Ease up on the metaphors. *Please.*"

"As silly as you think it sounds, I thought it might make an interesting book."

"So now you're all, *Eat, Pray, Love*? Sweetheart, it's so been done."

I waved him off. "The point is, I've been wanting to write something serious for a while now, but my weird little stories were hardly life-altering enough."

"So, you thought a trip into Dali-wood with that fop would be?"

"I'd hoped it would, until my life exploded a couple days ago. But you know what they say—when life tosses you lemons, make lemonade."

He scowled. "What the hell are you talking about?"

"Look, remember that writer we did a story on over the winter?"

After a moment, he said, "The one who typed with her feet?"

"Right. And remember how her editor said if I ever wanted to write a book about my stories to give her a call?" He gave me a blank stare. "Oh come on—Mina Riley! From Haughton House. She was thinking a book of essays. Ring a bell?"

"Vaguely," he said testily.

"I had figured I'd send her the Bhutan book, so I called her this afternoon and pitched this utility pole wife thing instead. Denny . . ." I poked his leg. "She went *nuts.*"

Actually, it had been more like, "Are *you* nuts?" The editor had paused for a moment, laughing out loud. "Jesus, Julie, when I said I thought I could sell a book of your crazies I didn't mean you had to turn into one! Are you kidding me?"

"No, really I'm not." And I had truly affected dead-certainty, even though deep-down the whole thing still felt like a beyond-the-pale prank. "Tell me a better way I could get the real story without becoming it?"

"But even immersion writing has its limits. My God . . ." Mina sighed deeply. "Does this Andy know what you want to do?"

"Not yet, but he will. I intend to be completely transparent about it." Well, not in *everything*, but she didn't need to know that.

"Because if he doesn't, you're skirting fraud, especially if . . ." She cleared her throat. "If I may ask, you *are* going to be his wife in every sense of the word, right?"

"Absolutely." Though it was the one aspect that gave

me pause; he was just so overwhelmingly *male*. "Even if I have to risk pregnancy."

"What?" I heard a bang, as if she'd dropped her phone. "Are you serious?"

"I assure you I am."

She laughed. "Oh my dear girl, do you have any idea what you'd be setting yourself up for? If I were you, I'd take some time and think about this very carefully."

"Actually, Mina, time is the last thing I have. Andy's only given me 'til tomorrow to decide." When she sighed I went in for the kill. "I've already prepared a proposal. Do you think if I sent it right over you can get me an answer today? And . . ." *Oh what the hell, this whole thing was insane so why not?* "A bit of an advance for mad money?"

It took a bit of convincing, but in the end she decided that anyone who had the nerve to go through with such a scheme deserved a shot. "But you better let me know how you're doing now and then," she had said. "I'm *not* financing Bluebeard."

"So," I said to Denny, cramming another skirt into the suitcase, "she just sent me the approval. I have five grand coming right away and another thirty when I finish." I held up the contract. "I'm mailing it in the morning."

"Good Lord . . ." he breathed, "she's as crazy as you."

"Denny, listen. What makes a man who looks like him, who's financially secure and obviously intelligent, pick a wife like he's buying a car? It just doesn't make sense. There's *got* to be more to him than the fancy packaging. I'm figuring it's something big."

"So if it's a Pulitzer you're after, I'm sure you don't have to sign your life away."

"Who says I am? You remember what he said: ninety day guarantee. If it doesn't work out, I'd walk away with a nice severance."

Denny stared at me like I'd truly lost it. "You're doing it for the *money*?"

"I never intend to take a penny from him. I'm doing it for the *story*. But if I'm not part of it, no one, including this editor, will buy it. And if I happen to tarnish a certain scumbucket agent's reputation in the process?" I tossed my hands. "Oh, well. Because I'm sure not going to let him ruin mine. As far as anyone will ever know, I dumped him *because of* our divine Mr. Devine."

He seemed to accept that but only for a moment. "Just make sure your little plan doesn't blow up in your face."

"It'll never get that far," I said, tossing the journal into the suitcase. "Three months is plenty of time to get the skinny, and to make it seem like I gave the marriage a go. So save me a seat at your Thanksgiving table."

"And what if he falls in love with you? Or worse, you fall in love with him?"

I shot him my iciest glare. "The contract says our marriage is a business agreement and that's fine with me. After Richard, I'm never falling in love again."

He laughed. "As if you ever have a choice."

I sat on the suitcase, clicking it shut. "I always have before."

"Then you've never been in love. Because when you are, there *is* no choice."

I wasn't about to argue; love was beside the point anyway. Especially the next day at the diner, when Andy leaned back in the booth and all the muscles in his chest strained beneath his polo. With the bright morning sun streaming through the windows, accentuating the strong bones of his face, I thought: *Who could think of love when all your lust impulses are on fire?*

"I suppose I do owe you a story," Andy said.

"That you do," I said, smoothing the folds of my halter dress, resisting the urge to add *and I intend to make it my best one ever.* "Who knows? It might even be pretty lucrative. We might make some money on this."

He shook his head. "If we do, you keep it. I have all the money I need." He pushed aside a manila envelope. "May I ask you a personal question?"

I laughed. "Like 'Will you marry me?' wasn't personal enough?"

His mouth crooked. "You're right. I suppose it's all downhill from there."

I tilted my head, feeling coquettish. His faint accent, wherever it came from, was doing a number on me. "I'm being facetious." I took a sip of water. "Go ahead."

He paused a moment. "You recently became—how shall we say—*disengaged*, and story aside, I was wondering how much bearing that had on your decision."

Canny, wasn't he? "A fair question, but the answer is, none at all."

"Hm." He considered that a moment. "It's just that I know I can be . . ." he smiled subtly, "rather *insistent* at times."

"That you were." I said, recalling how he loomed over me. "But I can make up my own mind, thank you."

"I'm sure. But I don't want you marrying me because you feel you don't have any recourse."

Something Denny said about this being the best offer I'd had in a while crossed my mind, and if he were there I would've smacked him. "I assure you, it's not."

"Was it your decision to break the engagement?"

Annika's fat little face wormed its way into my head. "No. But if I knew then what I know now, I'd be breaking more than our engagement."

"So you're still angry."

Now here I could be completely honest. "Damn right I am. The man locked me out of our apartment, froze our joint account, and got my TV contract cancelled." I slid my water toward me, surprised I had already drained it. "Plus he left me for a woman he's probably been seeing all along. So if you ask me if I'm angry, I think I have a right to be. But if you're insinuating I'm still in love with him, you're dead wrong."

A little muscle on the side of his cheek twitched. "I would never insinuate, but that last bit is good to know. I loathe competition."

I wanted to add something witty, but when those beautiful eyes crinkled and his mouth edged into a smile, all I could do was laugh. I relaxed almost immediately. "Oh, Andy, I doubt if anyone could remotely compete with you."

He laughed softly, inclining his head. "Thank you."

"For the compliment or for agreeing to marry you?" *He had a tiny mole just below his right ear.*

"For agreeing to marry me, for having breakfast with me ..." His gaze washed over my face, and my stomach fluttered. "For being so clever and so adventurous. But also, for finally calling me Andy."

There went that flutter again. My God, the man was charming. "Well ... it's the least I can do. We *are* engaged." *There. I said it.*

"That we are." He signaled for the server. "Shall we have something to eat?"

Food was the furthest thing from me at the moment, but ... "I suppose I should. Maybe something light?"

"I know just the thing." And a few minutes later, we were breakfasting on coffee, croissants and fresh Jersey cantaloupe. "Enough?" he asked.

"Plenty," I said, spooning into my half-melon. "Now, may I take a turn at the personal questions?"

"Certainly," he said, tearing off a bit of croissant and smearing it with jam before popping it into his mouth. "Ask me anything."

If he really meant that, then I hardly knew where to begin. Charmingly anachronistic or not, I had already caught on to how cagey he could be. "Even though I've agreed to marry you, I do need to know a bit more about you before I do. Your little fact sheet was rather spare, wasn't it?"

He shrugged. "Why give away company secrets before you hire for the job? But since you *are* hired ..." He finished the last bit of his croissant, and then tore into another. "I'm forty years old, this past May. I was born in Iron Bog and lived there until I was thirteen. Then my parents divorced and I moved to Le Havre with my mother."

Why I hadn't caught on sooner was beyond me. "You're French?"

"So, you've finally figured me out," he said with a wry smile. "By ancestry, on both sides, but I've been on the sea so long, it's hard to call any country home."

"And a sailor, too."

He laughed. "I come from a long line of merchant seamen: my father, my grandfather, his father, too. Sooner or later, though, we all end up in dry dock. Like when my father died this past spring, leaving me the farm."

"Which is why, like them, you figured it's time to come home and settle down?"

Something unreadable flashed behind those eyes. "The farm's been in my father's family for a hundred and fifty years. It was only logical that when I married, I'd come here."

Logical. "So your mother left . . ."

"Yes." Andy stiffened almost imperceptibly, his spoon digging into his cantaloupe. "My mother missed her family and the bustle of the ports." Then his gaze shot to mine. "Sometimes the silence of the woods can be deafening."

It was a warning, and I knew it. But I also knew I wouldn't be living there the rest of my life. "I'm from the city. Silence will be a welcome diversion."

"It's good you feel that way. You'll be getting a lot of it." He waved his hand dismissively, lightening the mood. "Anyway, I, too, went to sea after university, and—"

"Where did you go? College, I mean."

"*Université Paul Cézanne Aix-Marseille,*" he said in such perfectly accented Gallic, my head spun.

"Marseille's also a port city, right?"

"On the Mediterranean. Just couldn't get away from the sea." His mouth crooked. "But that's the marvelous thing about New Jersey, isn't it? You're never too far from it."

"A fact appreciated in Philadelphia as well. But come on, Andy, let's be honest." I leaned into him, affecting my most seductive interviewing mien. "You're a handsome guy. Why would you think you needed to pick a wife the way you did?"

He blinked; for a moment I thought I'd caught him. At what I wasn't sure, but there had to be more than he was letting on. "Why fool around with pretense? I want to get married and have children. So I went looking for someone who felt the same way. I knew if I were up-front about my expectations, the right woman would come to me. Was I right?"

"Well, yeah . . ." My second warning. He was certainly setting the ground rules, wasn't he? Yet big story or not, I had my own as well. "But what *are* your expectations? Besides the obvious, I mean. I hope they won't always be more important than mine."

"Since our marriage will be based on *similar* expectations, I would never make you do anything we didn't absolutely agree on. But you should also know this:"—his eyes darkened— "I'm a practical man, Ms. Knott. And a realistic one, too. I'm harboring no romantic illusions about this. We're both in it for the same thing—our own self-interests, so if you have any reservations, please let me know now."

A bit jarring to have it brought down to that level, but there wasn't much I could argue with. "No," I said, just as gravely. "How about you?"

"I know what I want when I see it. But I've also seen how devastating a bad marriage can be. That's why I'm not only documenting these expectations up front, but I'm also giving us a way out if we find we're not up to them. Still, I want you to know that even if our marriage doesn't work out, I'll take care of you. If anyone ever tries to harm you again . . ." His hand tightened around the mug. "They'll have to answer to me."

He left no doubt who he was referring to. "I appreciate that, but last I looked, no one's chasing me with a hatchet. I think I can take care of myself."

"I wouldn't doubt it for a moment. Which makes me wonder . . . why give up everything to retreat to the woods and marry me?"

Should I tell him I had no intention of staying married? That even though we were starting out on a trial marriage, the idea of it ever being permanent didn't enter in the equation? That it was all for the story, that it was *only* for the story, and I could justify it by knowing I'd never take a penny of his money? It wasn't lying. Omission was hardly the same thing. So naturally, I tossed the question back to him.

"I will remind you, Mr. Devine, you rather twisted my arm."

"And I will remind *you*, Miss Knott, we are here only because you phoned me. If you're marrying me just to get a story, then I think you should reconsider."

Damn, if he couldn't see through me. But how could he fault me for taking his offer of a trial marriage at face value? But I wouldn't let that throw me off my game. So I countered with logic—as well as a bit of stroking to his rampant machismo. "Mr. Devine, as juicy as this story may be, I don't know you from a hole in the ground. As a woman, I'm taking an incredible risk. But I'm choosing to believe I'm marrying an honest man who's offering me a fresh start at one of the worst times of my life. At least that's what I'm hoping."

His whole demeanor changed; he almost seemed offended. "I meant every word I said. I will take care of you."

And somehow I knew he meant it, so much more than any assurances Richard had ever given me. "Then I guess that's all I need to know."

He looked visibly relieved, raising his coffee. "Then congratulations to us, Julie. We're engaged."

Julie. When he said it, it sang like poetry. *Zhu-leé*. I clinked my cup to his, suddenly feeling giddy. "I suppose we are, Andy. Shall it be a very long engagement?"

"Only as long as it takes to get the license."

"Really? Shouldn't we get to know each other better?" *No euphemism intended.*

Within a breath he returned to business. "You'll have marriage agreement protection and ninety days with compensation if it doesn't work out. After that, I would like to think we'll be playing it by ear. Of course, I've put this all down in writing." He slid the manila envelope to me. "Does that sound fair?"

It sounded perfect. "Sure."

"And not to seem indelicate, but during that time, we will be trying for a baby. I do want you to know up front that's an intractable clause in the contract."

Had anyone in the world ever said that less romantically? "I get you," I said, feeling my neck heating. I slid the envelope into my purse. "I'll look it over tonight."

"If there's anything you'd like to add or detract, let me know and I'll review it. If you don't mind, I'd like it if we could go get the marriage license."

"Now?" My God, he was in a hurry. "Where?"

"In Iron Bog. I figure we can get married there. Unless you have something grander in mind."

Funny he should mention *grand*; I thought of what I had cancelled just that morning: the calla lilies for me, the gardenias for our bridal party, the $1800 three-layer *dobos torte* wedding cake, the ceremony at the art museum, the 250-guest Four Seasons reception with full orchestra and open bar, the 1934 Studebaker convertible which would have squired us around. I had told all concerned Richard had been killed in a subway accident in the Bronx. Most said they would give me a full refund. The honeymoon to Bhutan, which Richard had been paying for, I left intact for Annika and him to default on. For the guests, I had asked Denny to send out all my pre-stamped and pre-addressed thank you cards with a *Just kidding; stay home*. When I told my parents, I think my mother's tears flowed from a wellspring of joy. I hadn't the heart to let her know what was coming up next. By that time, I was truly exhausted.

"No," I said, "the justice of the peace will be fine."

"Good." He tossed off the last of his coffee. "Shall we go then?"

Since the car Richard and I had shared was most likely stashed in the long-term lot at the airport, I had borrowed Brent's Saab to meet Andy. And although Andy offered to drive us both out to Iron Bog for the license and drop me back, I wasn't ready to relinquish my freedom to my new fiancé just yet. So I followed his old Ford F-150 pick-up past the strip malls and office complexes until they thinned out to housing developments and finally into the Pines, where the trees eventually gave way to the crossroads of Iron Bog and Jinks' Gas Station.

"This is my Uncle Jinks," said Andy. "He'll be our witness for the license."

"How you doing," said a grizzled older man, taking my hand. "I'm really just an old friend of his dad's, but still, I get final approval." He pushed back his cap and smiled with perfect teeth. "So you're the lovely Julie Knott. Pleased to finally meet you in the flesh. You're even prettier in person." He winked. "Which means I approve."

I liked him immediately. "Why, thank you, Uncle Jinks," I said, squeezing his hand. "You say the sweetest things."

"You couldn't be getting a better husband, and that's the truth," he said earnestly. "Though my boy seems to be caught in a bit of a time warp."

"I've noticed," I said, slanting Andy a glance. "He's positively medieval."

Uncle Jinks laughed. "Boy, if that don't fit. Because just like his dad, he's—"

"Jinks," Andy interjected, "isn't that your phone ringing?"

"Bobby!" his ersatz uncle yelled to a young man stacking oil filters. "Get the phone! Bobby! Hey!" He scowled. "Oh, he's had it." He looked to Andy. "Hold on, I'll be right back."

I watched Jinks trot off to the garage. "What's he talking about?"

"That kid," Andy said. "If it isn't his phone, it's his iPod."

"No, I meant about—"

"The municipal building is right across the street," he said, turning toward it. "They're only open until noon today. We better go. Jinks will catch up."

I looked over my shoulder; he was already starting back. Whatever Andy's uncle had implied, I'd have to ask him later.

Applying for a marriage license in New Jersey was a rather simple affair. All we needed was ID, our social security numbers, Uncle Jinks as witness and twenty-eight dollars. Andy signed, I signed, Jinks signed, Andy paid, and the next thing I knew I was one step closer to strapping myself to this stranger for life. At least in theory. I was cross-my-heart sure it was the craziest thing I had ever done, and I'd more than a few times come close to the asylum. I thought of the journalists who had gone deep, like John Howard Griffin in *Black Like Me*, Gloria Steinem in "I was a Playboy Bunny" or Barbara Ehrenreich in *Nickel and Dimed*. Was my story of a utility pole bride just as worthy as those first-person narratives? I glanced at Andy as he walked me to my car.

I certainly hoped so.

"Well," he said, squinting from the sun, "that was easy."

Why did he look so much bigger in broad daylight? "I should be going. I have lots to do." I tapped my purse. "And read. I'll call you if I have any questions."

"Just leave a message with Uncle Jinks."

"Because you don't have a phone? Why is that?"

He shrugged. "You'd be surprised what you can live without. And with."

And with whom. When we got to my car he opened the door; I rolled down the window after he shut it. "Well, I guess I'll see you—"

"Tuesday, right here. Shall we say, three o'clock?"

Not before then? I pulled the manila envelope from my purse. "How about this?"

"Bring it with you when you come. It's pretty cut-and-dried, as long as you agree with it." Then he leaned in, his fingers wrapped around the door. "Thank you, Julie. See you Tuesday." And with a tap on the roof, he left.

As long as you agree with it. To living in the woods. To marrying a stranger. To having his baby. *My God!*

Then it hit me like a head-on collision: this tall, dark, and handsome French throwback-to-the-nineteenth century was my *fiancé*. With one breakfast as courtship, with no engagement ring, with his only endorsement from another stranger, I was actually going to marry him? I fell back in my seat, watching him walk away. He hadn't even touched me, not once. I closed my eyes, remembering to breathe.

It really was a business arrangement, wasn't it?

Chapter Five

Here Comes the Bride

I DON'T KNOW what I had expected, but it probably wasn't being stood up again. Truly, who would think lightning would strike the same woman twice? But there I was, standing in front of Town Hall, teetering on my Ferragamos while the sweat collected beneath my cream silk sheath, the baby's breath no doubt drooping in my salon-perfected hair. Maybe I should have taken up Brent and Denny's offer to drive me, but I just couldn't face another scene. Even though the cab had cost a fortune, I felt much more comfortable with a stranger dropping my baggage to the curb. Since I was marrying one, the stranger theme fit all around.

The point was driven home by the contract I had signed the night before. Brent had asked his attorney, Alvie Ross, to take a look Monday morning, and by that evening, he'd come back with a verdict.

"Purely from a contractual point of view," Alvie had said, "it's a match made in heaven. You'd certainly come out with the sweet end of the lollipop."

I took another sip of sherry, hoping it'd negate the sleepless night I was anticipating. "You really think so?"

"This guy's clean—I can't find *anything* on him." He tapped his pipe against the page. "If you stay married, he assumes all your debts, and gives you half-ownership in his property, bonds and liquid assets. His father's will just got out of probate, and your fiancé was left quite a substantial legacy—over $750,000, some very solid municipal bonds, and acres and acres of property he owns free and clear. He even has a little bungalow down Long Beach Island right on the beach, and with the way things have been selling down there, you can only imagine what it's worth. He has all kinds of insurance in which you'd be the beneficiary, not that he isn't as healthy as a horse, plus there's that three-month out with $50,000 to cry all the way home with." Then he frowned. "But everything's contingent on the one thing that concerns me: within those three months you have to get pregnant, or that gives *him* grounds for annulment. Are you all right with that?"

"A big question to ask yourself, darling," Brent said, squeezing my hand.

"I wouldn't be marrying him if I wasn't," I said, especially since I was counting on it.

"Then I suppose, if you're so inclined . . ." Alvie said, handing me the pen, "you're good to go."

Go where? I thought as I stood on the courthouse

steps. I didn't know where he lived. And the taxi driver had grabbed my $125 and taken off in a cloud of dust. I looked toward Uncle Jinks' garage. I suppose he might know where to find my elusive fiancé, but in the twenty minutes I'd been waiting I hadn't seen him either. As conspicuous as I'm sure I looked, I'm positive he would've come out had he been around.

As I idled, I recalled a childhood notion. Before time and reality jaded me, I used to be quite the romantic, lying back on my twin bed, my adolescent mind pondering: *I wonder what my future husband is doing right now?* Was he hanging with friends, doing his homework, watching television, perhaps even imagining me? I used to wonder if he was dark-haired or blond, tall or muscular, liked horses and Geraldo Rivera and Talking Heads as much as I did. I wondered if one day he'd be working for the network, as I assumed I'd be, or a star reporter for the *New York Times*, or writing a political expose for *Newsweek*. Even from my most tender age, I knew I was a voice to be heard, and as narcissistic as that sounds, it truly wasn't. It was more like there were truths to be unearthed and only I could bring them out, just as there was that one man who had to be working his way toward me.

How moronic.

I checked my watch: three-twenty. According to the sign on the building, the offices closed at four. Which set the timer at forty minutes and counting. I thought of the elaborate wedding I had planned with Richard, and how forty minutes hardly would've gotten us down the aisle. I pushed a drooping curl behind my ear, a baby's breath fluttering to my shoe, and unstuck from my sweaty chest the wilting bodice of my sheath. *What an idiot.* How in hell had I been so stupid to let it happen again? I felt like I'd been had, but for what reason? It hurt, especially considering I was skating very close to scamming him. But at that moment, at the prospect of Andy leaving me hanging, the only thing that concerned me was how the hell to extricate myself from this situation. Then suddenly his old Ford truck screeched around the corner to the curb. He jumped out, trotting to me.

"I'm—I'm so sorry," he said breathlessly, his chest heaving. "Really I . . ."

All at once he stopped and stared, and I had to admit, I did likewise. With his hair wind-tousled, his eyes a frantic blue, he looked so downright gorgeous in his black suit and tie, I think I could've forgiven him anything short of murder. Especially when I caught sight of the bouquet of yellow wildflowers clutched in his hand.

"For—you," he said, handing them to me.

I wrapped my fingers around the stems and buried my nose in the blossoms, even though black-eyed Susans don't carry a scent. "I thought you'd forgotten all about me."

He came closer, his gaze fixed on mine. "I could never forget about you."

Amazing how this man could make my insides go to mush with nothing more than a few everyday words. Yet when Andy looked at me, smelling of fresh air and sounding like music, my angst eased a bit. "Then maybe all we need to do is synchronize our watches?"

"Maybe," he said, so close to me I could see a tiny muscle pulsing on his cheek, "but I'm pretty sure Betsy wouldn't care."

I felt dreamy, ready to—"Who's Betsy?"

"My heifer. She's just about ready to calve." He picked up my stuffed suitcases like he was lifting balloons and pulled back on the door. "So, we'd better hurry," he said, holding it out with his foot. "Uncle Jinks is with her, but we haven't much time."

Heifer? Calve? I hurried up the hallway beside Andy, rethinking the logic of this for maybe the last time. We stopped at a door that said, PAUL S. HINKLE, MAYOR. HUNTING & FISHING LICENSES MONDAY THRU THURSDAY 10-1. Andy set one bag on the floor and opened the door.

"After you," he said and, spreading the door wide, kicked the suitcase in.

We stepped into a tiny, windowless anteroom, chairs lined against one wall, a counter directly across. Five feet or so behind it another door opened, and out walked who I presumed was hizzoner.

"Andy!" boomed a ruddy, barrel-chested man. He thrust a beefy paw at Andy. "So," he said, giving me a languid once-over, "*this* is your intended!"

I tried to ignore the objectification and gifted him with my most gratuitous smile. "Good afternoon, Paul," Andy said. "This is Julie, my fiancée."

He squinted at me. "Hey. Haven't I seen you somewhere before?"

"I don't know," I said. "On a utility pole, maybe?"

"Haw!" he laughed, snapping his suspenders. He pointed to Andy. "I like her! Last chance before I snatch her up myself!"

Andy set down the other suitcase and shook the mayor's hand. "Thanks, but I think I'll keep her. And if you don't mind, we have to hurry. Betsy's about to calve."

His eyes widened and he erupted again, nudging Andy." So it's the *cow*, then? Haw! Guess we won't need the shotgun after all! Come on!"

It's for the story, it's for the story, I kept telling myself, feeling a little ill.

The mayor led us into an office with long windows that looked out on an expanse of tall trees. Between the cab ride and the front steps I had sweated away the afternoon, but thankfully an old Kelvinator window air conditioner chugged away, chilling the room considerably. The mayor shrugged into a jacket and picked up a small leather-bound book.

"Got a witness?" he asked.

"Jinks was supposed to be here," Andy said, "but he's with Betsy."

The mayor thought a moment. "Hold on, I think I got it covered." He hustled into the next room for the phone. "Lila?" I heard him say, "You want to make ten bucks?"

Andy turned to me. "Do you have something for me?"

I looked at him, mystified. "Like . . .?"

"The agreement," he crisply replied. "I need it signed before we start."

It was like a bucket of cold water to the face. The only bigger squish to my romantic notions would be if he'd inspected my teeth. I plucked the contract from my purse and handed it over. "And so do I," I pointed out. "Right by the 'X.'"

He gave it a quick perusal. "No changes?"

"Not at the moment, but I'm starting to think of some."

He arched a brow, suppressing a smile. "Too late." He signed then handed over my copy, slipping his own into his inner pocket. "Thank you."

I dropped mine into my purse. Any further commentary was aborted by an elderly woman being shuttled into the room. "Lila is our town archivist," said the mayor. "She just happened to be in today scanning documents."

"Pleased to meet you," she said, shaking each of our hands, her eyes eagle-sharp. She looked to Andy. "Welcome back, young man. Been a few years, eh?"

"Yes, it has, Mrs. DeForest. I hope you've been well."

Her silver brow lifted. "So you remember me, then?"

Andy smiled. "The school librarian? I used to think you knew everything."

She looked to me and winked, saying *sotto voce*, "And I do, too."

My spirits lifted immediately. *Now here was a woman who might come in handy.*

The mayor opened the Bible. "Ready?"

My heart raced: *it isn't too late, you know.* Yet it was, as I had never bailed on a story in my life. Didn't matter if my hands were shaking or my mouth was dry, or if all the doubts in the world had suddenly been rolled into a boulder and dropped atop my head: I couldn't quit just as the camera started rolling. So I took a deep breath, plucked a flower from my bouquet, and nipping the stem three-quarters up, I tucked it into Andy's buttonhole.

He glanced from it to me, and smiled. "We are now."

"Dearly beloved," the mayor began.

I'm sure the ceremony was no more original or eventful than the thousands of others performed that day. But having just canceled a Wedding of Epic Proportions, I knew immediately it wasn't the Vera Wang gown or Armani tux, an art museum ceremony or a fancy car to an even fancier reception, or even the transcendent honeymoon in Bhutan that made that ceremony any more significant than this one. In fact, the wedding itself hardly had anything to do with it at all. It was the bald fact that *I'd be married.* I looked into Andy's clear, blue eyes. *Married!* To a man I hardly knew!

My heart stuck in my throat. *Holy shamoly.*

". . . as long as you both shall live?" the mayor asked me.

I was long past rational thought. So I simply answered, "I will."

Just as Andy answered, "I will," not a half-minute later.

"The rings?" the mayor asked.

I looked to my about-to-be husband. "I don't think we—"

"Here," Andy said, his hand suddenly lifting mine.

It was the strangest thing, and I thought I knew strange pretty well. But when Andy touched me for the very first time, laying my palm flat upon his and sliding on a carved platinum band, tiny diamonds here and there among the filigree, I felt a connection to something so complex I knew it would take everything in me to even scratch the surface.

The sensation was only compounded when he said, "It was my grandmother's."

I was beyond surprised, by the ring, and by the man before me. "And . . . yours?"

His mouth crooked. "Unfortunately, my grandfather never wore one."

The mayor closed his Bible, beaming. "With the powers invested in me by the state of New Jersey, I now pronounce you husband and wife. Andy—kiss your bride!"

"With pleasure," he said, leaning in.

With his lips slightly parted, he brushed my own in a silky pass, ending with the tiniest of nips to the corner of my mouth. It was quick and chaste yet undeniably possessive. "Mrs. Devine," he said softly, lifting my hand to kiss it.

I felt a little swoony, not even realizing I had closed my eyes. *Mrs. Devine . . .* I thought . . . *Mrs. Devine.* Then all at once my breath caught. Holy crap—*Mrs. Devine!*

A second later I saw myself signing the license, shaking Mrs. DeForest's and the mayor's hands, and then being shuttled out the door. "Thanks, Paul, Mrs. De-Forest," Andy said, leaving a hundred dollar bill on the counter. He hefted my suitcases. "Have dinner on me."

"Wait!" Mrs. DeForest cried. She reached into her purse, pulling out a camera. "You have to remember the day!"

Andy leaned into me and she snapped a picture, then

he grabbed the suitcases and me, and we ran toward the door.

"Goodbye!" Andy said.

"Thanks!" the mayor called after us. "And congratulations you two!"

"To the bride it's always 'good luck,'" Mrs. DeForest corrected him. "'Congratulations are for the groom. After all, it's he who's won her."

That simple statement was so pregnant with implications that my head fairly spun, but now wasn't the time for analysis—especially with Andy tossing my suitcases in the back of his truck and stuffing me into the passenger seat. "Maybe you should call Jinks and see how he's doing," I said.

"Can't," said Andy, climbing in. He started the truck; it exploded to life with a rattle and a chug. "No phone."

"Oh." I reached into my purse, producing my Black-Berry. "You can use mine."

"Wouldn't matter." He looked over his shoulder then pulled out in a cloud of dust. "There's no service out there."

"No service?" I looked at my BlackBerry, checking my texts. Two from Denny, one saying, YOU CHAINED YET? "My phone's working."

Andy looked to me, smiling a bit insularly. "If you're going to use it, use it quickly. It's about to be useless." Then he turned off Main to Forge Road.

Almost instantly, clearings and houses gave way to piney woods and, within five hundred feet, macadam bumped into gravel. Not far after that, the road seemed to lose all sense of civilization as it turned into firmly-tamped sugar sand. Overhead the foliage grew denser from a clumping of tall trees, and I took in their clean scent, their soaring trunks rising out of a shallow stream of water.

"Smells like my grandmother's cedar chest," I said, as we thumped over a short wooden bridge.

"That's because they're cedar trees. And if her chest was made in Philadelphia, the wood probably came out of a bog like this."

As the cedar stand thickened, the afternoon dimmed. The bog was alive with gnats and dragonflies and a thousand whirling, zipping, clicking things. The air was cooler yet fragrantly lush. Soon the road narrowed and the woods opened up, pitch pines and scrub oaks replacing the tall cedars. The sparse undergrowth became a mix of bushes and ferns, laurel clumping near the edges. Even though the Pine Barrens had always loomed on Philadelphia's periphery, I had never taken them for much more than a green filter on the way to the Jersey Shore. Although, once I had done a story on naturalist Howard P. Boyd, author of the definitive *A Field Guide to the Pine Barrens of New Jersey* (tucked into my suitcase, of course), and de facto dean of Pine Barrens ecology. The night before I had crammed like I hadn't done since my college finals. But it was one thing seeing the forest from the pages of a book or as one zips down Route 72 at 65 mph. It was quite another bouncing inside it at no more than twenty per.

I stuck my hand out the window and let it ride the

current, near enough to the trees to flutter a pine swag, when we passed four crumbling chimney stacks rising out of a clearing.

"That used to be a tavern," he said, pointing toward it. "My family ran it when this trail was a post road to Camden."

"Back when people actually wanted to get to Camden," I said.

"Some still do, but not from there." He made a right onto an even narrower trail. "A friend of mine said some folks from Trenton were sniffing around last month—more than likely from the State Museum, looking for relics."

"This friend of yours," I ventured, "does he live in the woods, too?" "Of course. He works for the fire service—*merde!*" The truck jangled as it hit a rut. "Sorry about that. Anyway, he works the tower over at Snakes Ridge. He told me we had a big one near there two years ago. Burned for a week and nearly four thousand acres. Ray's the one who spotted it. Lightning." He shrugged. "What're you going to do?"

"Put it out, I'd imagine."

Again, that insular smile. "That's the general consensus."

Suddenly the air changed. It felt denser, even amid all the humidity, yet it took on a spicy freshness. A slight breeze kicked up. "How far out of town will we be?"

He looked at me, his hair catching the breeze. "Little over five miles, although I prefer to think of it as five miles *in*."

I took a deep breath, settling my hands in my lap.

He reached over, taking one. "Hell of a wedding, I know. But I'll make it up to you, I promise. How are you doing otherwise?"

His hand was warm, his thumb stroking the inside of my palm. "I'm okay."

"Glad to hear it." He gave my hand a squeeze then abruptly let go, twisting the wheel into a sharp right. The over-reaching bushes scraped the side of the truck, the dense foliage overhead closing around us like a tunnel. I glanced to my hand, still warm from Andy's touch and my heart raced, my throat harboring the occasional gulp. Overcome by exploding nature, my senses worked overtime.

A couple hundred more feet and the trail opened up into a large, weedy clearing and a small one story wooden house sorely in need of paint, a long barn with more than a few broken windows, several vehicles of questionable operation, an overgrown garden, and to the left, a dock leading to a wide expanse of lake, tall pines rimming it. A moment later, Jinks barreled out of the shed.

"Jesus, Andy—get in here! I think something's wrong with Betsy!"

Andy yanked off his jacket. "Just what I wanted to hear."

"Ever done this before?" I asked.

"No, but I've been reading a book." He grabbed my hand. "Come on."

We tore from the truck as a lamentable *moooo* emanated from inside. Andy threw back the door and there was Betsy, on her belly on a bed of hay, her soft-brown head thrashing side to side. The stalled barn was rife with the scents of manure and alfalfa, tempered somewhat by the opened windows and the fecund odor of bovine birth. Andy whipped his tie off and tossed it to me, rolling his sleeves as he hurried toward the stall.

"She can't push it out!" Jinks said, frantic, a book in his hand. "She's been like this since you left, yelling and mooing."

"Damn," he said, squatting to get a better look. The heifer's distended belly rippled in a mohair wave, her swollen vulva dripping and contracting. I clamped my hands around the rim of the stall, alternately appalled and fascinated.

"I guess the water's broken," Andy said to Uncle Jinks. "Did you see a hoof?"

"Yeah," he answered, but it was pointing up. And according to this book . . ." He tapped a page, "it's supposed to be facing down."

"Like in a diving position," Andy said. He looked to Jinks, his brow furrowed. "Damn."

"What?" I said. "What's that mean?"

Jinks closed the book. "Means someone's gotta reach inside Betsy here and turn her calf around."

"What!" I cried. "Call a vet or something!"

Again, Andy's insular smile. "She might be dead by then. Or her calf." He pushed a sleeve up over his bicep and loosed a couple buttons of his shirt, his chin jutting toward the shelf across. "Julie, get me that bottle of baby oil over there, please?"

I darted to it, a heel squishing into something I hoped wasn't what I figured.

He held out his arm. "If you don't mind, squirt some on me." When I did, he slathered it up and down his forearm, flexing his hand as the heifer let go with a *moooo*, just pitiful enough to make us all shiver.

"Holy cats . . ." Jinks groaned, "you're really gonna stick your arm up there?"

"You have a better idea?" Andy said briskly. He swiveled around and dropped to his knees, his muscled arm slick and gleaming in the late afternoon sun. "Here goes," he said, and taking a deep breath, he slowly slid his hand into the cow's vulva. She screamed.

Both Jinks and I jumped back, the heifer's head thrashing. Andy lay half on his side, his leg arching up to gain traction as he fell in further, the cow's belly rippling as he attempted to turn the calf around. The beast moaned and mooed, a sheen of sweat breaking out on Andy's brow, the moisture from the cow's broken water bag soaking his trousers. A moment later an undulation tore through her belly and Andy yanked the calf out, its body shimmering with mucus and as slick as a greased piglet.

"You did it! Look at him!" Jinks yelped, tossing Andy a towel. "He's a beauty!"

He tilted his head. "*She* is. We have another heifer." He swiped the mucus from her white muzzle and slid her next to her mother, who immediately began to clean her. "But you're right," he said happily, beaming with relief. "She *is* a little beauty!"

"Yes she is," I said, coming around to stroke a delicate ear. "Maybe you've a future in midwifery after all."

He looked at me, his eyes softening. "Maybe I do."

All at once I felt a rush of anxiety, or trepidation, or maybe something I'd yet to discern. Whatever it was hung there between us for a moment, before Andy stood and offered me his unsullied hand. I took it, rising to meet him.

"Scared yet?" he said.

If it was a challenge, I was up to it. "Of course not."

He smiled. "Jinks, let's go wash up. Mrs. Devine, I'll meet you outside in a minute." He squeezed my fingers. "Don't go away."

What was I feeling just a moment before: anticipation? It had to be. I was a bride about to have a wedding night, albeit with a groom presently up to his elbow with the effluvia of cow-birthing. I glanced over my shoulder; he tossed me a wink from the sink. *A wink from the sink.* I laughed to myself, feeling woozy

I opened the barn door, and all at once I was greeted by a flock of scattering, squawking—*chickens!* "What the hell!" I screeched, momentarily disoriented. I twisted around, only to catch sight of a black and white hell-hound tearing toward me, barking to take my head off, his teeth bared. I bolted toward the dock, the chickens hopping and fluttering past me as I leapt onto it. My heel caught between the planks.

"Andy!" I screamed, and fell promptly into the lake.

Chapter Six

How You Gonna Keep Her Down on the Farm?

Did I mention I was deathly afraid of dogs? I didn't? *I was deathly afraid of dogs!* When I surfaced, Andy and the hellhound were looking down on me from the dock.

"I see you can swim," he said.

I kicked away from them. "Get that beast out of here!"

Andy just ruffled the animal's fur. The black and white dog hunkered down next to him. "You mean Bucky?"

"If that's the hellhound's name!" I threw out my arms, treading the warm water, my bare feet (who knew where my $400 shoes went) skimming the lake bottom's muck. "Damn thing's out to kill me."

"He's not out to kill you. He was herding chickens. Now, come here." He reached out, guiding me back to the ladder.

"Herding chickens?" I said, water raining off me as I grabbed a rung. Andy's hand clenched around mine. "I never heard of such a thing."

"That's what Border Collies do. They herd things. Wait a little while and he'll probably be herding you. Not that . . ."

Perhaps it was my stunning appearance that stopped Andy as I climbed from the lake. Or maybe the mask of utter horror that was no doubt on my face. Because when I assessed myself—soaked to the skin, shoes gone, hair collapsed and hanging around my face and shoulders—I'm sure whatever vision of loveliness I previously affected had melted away with my make-up. Then an engine turned over.

"I see she's met Bucky!" Jinks called from his truck, idling toward the road out.

"Thanks again!" Andy called back, never taking his eyes from me.

I slid my hair back, pins pinging to the dock as the dog suddenly loped off. "So much for your beautiful bride," I said, smoothing my ruined silk sheath.

His arm slipped around my waist, and he lifted me into his arms. "Let's go into the house."

"Why?" I said, looping my arm around his neck, my sopping dress turning his shirt translucent. "Do you think I need to change or something?"

"Or something," he said so smoothly my heart did a little flip.

I could see a tiny muscle in his cheek thumping. I caught his clean, spicy scent—though mixed up with a bit of cow—and felt the hardness of his chest against me. Being this close, I felt a little unnerved, so I looked past his shoulder to the lay of the land. We passed old tires and bottles and crushed Salem packs, barrels of who-knew-what lying against a post-and-rail fence, rusty tools hanging on equally rusty nails on the side of the house. Further out, a picnic table and an ancient barbecue sat near the tree line, a pockmarked and faded bulls-eye nailed to a tree. If this is what he meant about the place needing work, I was starting to get the picture. Even so, I didn't want him to think I wasn't up to it, especially after freaking out over a dog.

"Sorry for acting like an idiot," I said. "But he scared the crap out of me."

He smiled, shaking his head tightly. "My introduction to Bucky was worse. He likes to sleep on the roof of the barn and he jumped me, knocking me into a pile of manure."

"*Eww.* I'd say my intro was at least cleaner."

"And certainly less smelly." He leaned in and sniffed my neck. "Much less."

A shiver shot up my spine. "You don't smell so bad yourself."

"*Eau de* heifer." He set me down on a slate path at the foot of the house's screened-in front porch. "Wait right here while I get your bags. Won't be a minute."

This gave me a chance to assess my new home. From what I could see it looked sturdy enough, one and a half wooden stories of weathered cedar-shakes, most definitely a handyman's special. I leaned over and gave my dress a good squeeze, a puddle collecting at my feet, then climbed the three creaky steps and yanked the door to the screened porch.

I stepped inside to a rusty-springed porch slider, buckets of bottles, a third-hand wrought-iron patio set, and an old refrigerator, desiccated leaves and pine needles strewn across the scuffed, planked floor. Poison ivy grew through a crack amid crushed cigarette butts, and a mop handle was tilted in the corner beside a holey pair of Topsiders. I looked up to see crab traps, fishing nets, and dozens of dried bunches of herbs hanging from the rafters. I pushed aside what looked like basil and pulled open another perforated screen door, revealing the unlocked door to the inside.

The curtains, or what served as such, were closed, and I paused, letting my eyes adjust to the musty interior. After a minute I could make out a stone fireplace about twelve feet away, slats of flattened wood stacked into its hearth. I turned to my left, my feet sticking to the greasy carpet as I went to the window and slid back the ancient curtains. Almost instantly I coughed to split a lung, a miasma of dust and filth shooting straight up my nose, a billion motes poofing into the stream of sunlight. Instinctively I flailed my arms, gagging and coughing, doubling over with a sneeze. When I straightened up, the bright light treated me to floor-to-ceiling boxes, old furniture topped with papers and magazines, buckets of bottles and cans, and so much of what could only be called crap. *Jesus*, I thought, stepping back, *is this what I signed up for?*

All at once something went *snap*! under my foot, my heel sinking through the floorboard. I yanked it out and I spun around, heading toward the door and running face-to-face into something furry and most definitely—

"DEAD!" I screeched, punching aside the hanging carcass of a groundhog or raccoon or whatever the hell it was, which I had no interest in clarifying. I kicked open the door, hobbling off the porch and right into Andy.

"Julie!" he yelped, dropping my bags. "Don't tell me you went inside!"

I scrambled past him and down the steps. "If you think I'm spending even one night in that filthy freakhouse—" I slapped a spiderweb from my arm. "Dammit, Andy, I'd rather sleep in the barn with Betsy!"

"Hey." He jumped off the porch, holding me by the shoulders. "I know the place is a mess, but I've only been here a couple of weeks."

"Is that's why you got married? You need a housekeeper?"

He eyed me wryly. "Because a housekeeper who'll get half of everything I own will be so much cheaper."

I shook myself, feeling skeevy, wanting to jump in the lake again. I shrugged him off. "Look, I'm not trying to be a diva, but there's a dead possum in there!"

"Raccoon," he corrected me. "Rocky, to be exact."

"It's got a *name*?"

"It's a long story. You'd have to know my father."

"Not interested." Though in fact, I was. "Andy, be reasonable! Do you really expect me to sleep in—"

His look was such a grasp of the obvious I blushed right down to my toenails.

Right then we reached the part in our tender marriage where *obvious* morphed very quickly into *awkward*. He grabbed my bags from the porch and beckoned me to follow. "Come on. And stay on the slate path. I want to show you something."

I followed him around the house to the side, past a bramble of flowering vines and the overarching branches of a few deciduous trees, to another screened-in porch which looked out to the woods a dozen yards away. However, this one was newly planked, with nary a hole in the screening, and it sported a freshly-painted wooden table and two chairs and a couple of hanging pots of very pretty, and pretty-smelling, flowers.

"Well, well," I said, truly charmed. "It's certainly an improvement."

Andy looked down, his brow furrowed. "Don't move." He nudged open the screen door, hauling my bags to whatever was on the other side of the door opposite. A moment later he was at my side, lifting me up.

Of course I'd read about this, dreamed of what it would be like when it happened to me, if it actually did. Richard would have thought it terribly anachronistic, something an uber-urban hipster would hardly entertain. But when neo-Victorian Andy carried me over the threshold, I knew it had to mean something more than when he hefted me across a weedy and tetanus-inducing yard. Because it was all so terribly romantic, setting me down in a wooden chair in a gorgeously sunny—and apparently *clean*—little bedroom, replete with quilted brass bed, fireplace, upholstered settee, crocheted curtains, and a dozen other accouterments specifically designed to make me *ooh* and *aah* and swoon with anticipation—which I just about did when he kneeled before me.

"Do you know your foot is bleeding?" he said.

"What?" I said, twisting it.

"I noticed it when you stepped on the porch." He turned it to the side for a look. "Hardly anything at all, just a scrape, but it's seeping." He pointed past me. "Bathroom's right there. You'll find all kinds of stuff in the medicine chest." He stood. "I'll let you get cleaned up, and I ought to do the same." Then he left, closing the door.

I stared at the door, too numb to move. Or maybe just a bit affronted.

My Neanderthal of a husband hadn't swept me off my feet—he'd been protecting his newly-fixed floors. I hopped to the bathroom on one foot, as God forbid I should track bloody footprints across his precious planking or his idiotically quaint throw rugs. I hauled my foot up on his impossibly cute pedestal sink and rinsed the crap out of it, figuring I must have scraped it when my heel busted through the floorboard on the other side of this schizophrenic hovel. I rubbed some Neosporin into it, as who knew what else lurked behind these walls, maybe even an Amazonian monkey virus. Next to me was an equally quaint 1930s-style toilet, and opposite, the *de rigueur* clawfoot tub, with its accompanying wide-mouth shower and curtain ring. I shrugged out of my trash-worthy wedding dress and used them all.

Forty-five leisurely minutes later I was fumbling through my suitcase, my hair turbaned in a ridiculously plush towel. I hit upon a *peignoir* I had picked up just the day before on a whim, its champagne silk slipping through my fingers. It was out-and-out the sexiest thing I had ever contemplated wearing, as Richard was never one for a tease, always preferring to cut to the chase. But with Andy . . . *with Andy* . . . I sighed, flipping past it, and pulled out a more appropriate cotton sundress.

Apparently this marriage would really be no more than a business arrangement. Aside from that making for a less interesting story, I shouldn't have been surprised. He made it clear from the onset. Obviously, I'd read more than he intended (and I should have expected) into his matrimonial kiss, those fleeting hand squeezes and his carrying me over the threshold. Not to mention the alpha maleness the man poured forth like a fire hose. Practically speaking, this whole adventure was a rebound relationship anyway, and everyone knew they never lasted. Still, as I pulled the dress over my lacy bra and panties, I couldn't help feeling a little disappointed I'd never get to flaunt them.

Not that any of this should have mattered. Because the whole point of being there was to get a story anyway. And to accomplish it, there was one thing I could never let him see or I was sunk: a small plastic pouch which I really needed to find a place to stash. I scanned not only for a hidey-hole, but for a spot where I could privately access it on a regular basis. The logical choice was the bathroom; but where?

I went back to assess: a window, sink, toilet, tub, medicine cabinet, a short chest of drawers for linens. No closet. White wainscoted walls and ceiling, planked floor and molding. I jiggled them all; nothing was loose. I sat on the toilet to think, pulling open the chest of two drawers. Towels and facecloths on top, sheets on the bottom. I figured the towel drawer would be opened mostly every day, but the sheets, no more than once a week. I pulled out the bottom drawer; it slid easily and noiselessly. I knelt in front of it and pulled it completely out. Between the drawer and the bottom of the chest there was about two inches of space. I dropped the plastic pouch to the flat bottom, sliding the drawer in and out a couple of times. It slid smoothly. Until I found a better place, my little hiding spot at the bottom of the chest would have to do.

I pulled the towel from my head and, shaking my wet hair, grabbed my lipstick. *No*, I thought dropping it back into my cosmetics case, ignoring my mascara and perfume as well. Andy Devine's new wife was strictly utilitarian, no adornments necessary. So, as I left for the porch, sans make-up and expectations, I prepared myself for the passionless. But as soon as I stepped outside, something more feral took over.

Hunger. My stomach growled. Audibly.

The little wooden table was now covered with white linen, and on it lay a couple kinds of cheeses, a baguette, sliced tomatoes, cucumbers, peaches, plums and two wine glasses. Everything looked beyond fresh and completely gorgeous. I tried to think of the last time I ate, which was likely around ten AM, when I had grabbed a latte and a banana before getting my hair done. Between my anxiety and the hours since, as it was now going on seven, I was beyond ravenous, so hungry I would've eaten the tablecloth if there hadn't been food on it. I reached for a piece of cheese.

"Thought that'd get you out here."

I jumped, dropping my hands to my sides. "What do you mean?"

Andy opened the screen door, letting it slap closed behind him. "Means I thought you'd fallen down the drain." He held a red wine. "Cabernet?"

I loathed presumption. "No."

"Something to eat?"

"No," I repeated, piqued enough to be petulant.

"Hm," he said, peering at me with curiosity. And I did the same. In fact, I had to try my damnedest to keep my eyes off of him. He was freshly showered, in jeans and a white shirt, his hair still damp. Where he had accomplished it all, I hadn't a clue, but he looked delectable enough for a smorgasbord. I stepped away from the table, moving to look at the trees beyond.

"You're not eating because you're angry," he said.

"No I'm not."

"Yes. You are." I could hear him sipping wine. "You're angry at the rushed ceremony, the cow, Bucky chasing you into the lake, scraping your foot on the floorboard, getting the crap scared out of you, and the whole general state of this sorry excuse for a farm. But most of all . . ." I could hear him dropping things to a plate, and a moment later, he was behind me. "You're angry with me."

I inched away. "Really, I'm not."

"Then you should be. A hell of a wedding day I've given you so far."

The art museum, it wasn't. But what had I expected? "You don't owe me anything."

He exhaled. Hard. "I owe you an apology. Will you forgive me?"

I turned, leaning back against the wall. *Good Lord, he was big.* And he was starting to unnerve me. "Andy, there's nothing to forgive."

"Then indulge me." He lifted a peach slice. "Have something to eat."

I could smell it: fragrant, luscious. *Like him.* Yet . . . "I told you—I'm not hungry."

"Liar." His eyes drooped to half-mast, and he leaned in, his breath on my cheek, scented cabernet. "They come from my own orchard. *Our* orchard. Taste one."

The slice glistened in the shafted light, deep yellow and ruby-rimmed. He pinched it between his fingers, a tiny drip of juice hanging on. Suddenly my presumptions began to wither, not to mention my feigned disinterest. But I couldn't let him unhinge me. "Believe me, I'm not hungry." *But I was.*

"Just a taste." He held it to my lips. "One taste . . ." My traitorous mouth cracked open, and that infinitesimal drop found its way inside. I swallowed.

"*Tu sens si bon . . .*" he said softly, tracing the cool peach across my lips.

"O-Ohh . . ." I groaned, startled, as if caught on a live wire. I sucked it back.

"*Ça y est, ma petite* . . ." he growled, grinning, feeding me another, and another. "*C'est bon, n'est-ce pas?*" He pinched another slice, a plum, leaning in to pin me against the wall. My heart thumped wildly, especially when he brushed his nose against my hair and whispered, "*Goûtes,*" before slipping the fruit between my trembling lips.

"*Goûtes,*" he breathed against my mouth, his thumb tracing my jaw line, my bones going to liquid. "*Goûtes-moi.*"

The dish crashed to the floor. My heart skipped a beat. It was all I could do to think, breathe. "*Très belle . . . très belle . . .*" he murmured, his mouth falling over mine.

I don't know if it was the French or the raw feel of his kiss, soft and cabernet-warmed, but when his tongue laced hungrily into mine it was like some crazy bomb went off in my head. For all of Andy's previously standoffish ways, he was suddenly all over me, covering me with kisses and enveloping me like a huge, hungry lion. The icon from afar evaporated before my eyes, and all at once he became real—a living, breathing testament of his desire for me.

I sank into him, no more capable of saving myself than if I were in the middle of the ocean without a ship. Not that I wasn't willing—thrilled, in fact. I arched my neck and let him devour me, Andy kissing my eyes, my cheeks, his mouth sweet and searching and so wonderfully delicious I pressed into him, my hands riding up his chest.

"Tu es magnifique ..." he murmured, stroking my back as he trailed kisses down my neck, the slope of my shoulders, the growl of his lilting French an aphrodisiac like none other I'd ever imagined. *"Ma belle. Je veux être avec toi ..."* he whispered, his breath hot against my skin as he kissed the swell of my breast.

"Andy ... Andy ..." I could barely choke his name out, his big hands encircling my waist as he trailed even lower, his tongue teasing my cotton-covered nipples into hardness.

"Je t'adore ..." He kissed each breast, sucking and nipping through the fabric as I writhed against him, clutching his hair. *"Je t'adore."* He sank to his knees.

Andy lifted my dress, my panties coming down in one swift motion, pulling them over my bare feet before his hands cupped my bottom. My breath caught, my legs shaking as he trailed kisses from my belly to the soft inside of my thigh, where his first furtive tease nearly drove me into the wall. But he held on, pulling me closer, licking, sucking—I screamed, bucking violently, almost blind with pleasure.

He shot to his feet. "Julie ... Julie ... *ma femme*," he murmured, his mouth covering mine, and I threw my arms around his neck, pressing hungrily to him. When he lifted me up, like instinct, I wrapped my legs around him. With his mouth still on mine he loosened himself, and drove himself inside me.

We both gasped: there were no words left, *en français* or otherwise.

Chapter Seven

Coming Up for Air

WHEN WE FINISHED we slumped to the floor, our bodies tangled together. He stared at me, breathless, perhaps equally amazed. "Jesus, Julie, I never thought I'd—"

I pressed a finger to his lips, understanding completely. "And I never thought I'd marry a man without sleeping with him first. What a nice surprise."

He nipped my finger. "You're saying you weren't a virgin?"

"Ha!" I slid a bare leg across his exposed hip, reveling in the feel of him. "Does that shock or disappoint you?"

"Now, let me think ..." He kissed the inside of my knee. "Disappoint, maybe." He ran his hand up my thigh until I flinched, his eyes smoldering with wicked merriment. "There's so many things I would have liked to teach you."

"But I have a terrible memory," I said, stretching back against the floor. "Perhaps you'll need to refresh it?"

Andy smiled, arching over me. "Exactly the kind of refreshment I had in mind."

When he bent to me, my reflection in his crystalline blue eyes, nothing could prepare me for his kiss—a sultry, portentous pass of his lips before he nudged mine open and claimed me. As gothic and beyond anachronistic as that sounded, how else could I explain it? When his muscular arms wrapped around me, I felt a raw, masculine prevalence I'd never felt in another man, refined yet distinctly feral. He was over me, around me, enveloping me, and suddenly out of reach of my own body. *Ma femme* took on an ominous new meaning. As his kisses plunged even deeper, his hands roaming the curves of my traitorously-aroused body, my mind spun to how vulnerable I really was. Even though we had just been intimate, I became acutely aware of the falling darkness, of how alone and deeply in the woods I was with this virtual stranger. For a moment, I even thought of Richard. Panic shot through me and I stiffened, moaning against his mouth as I palmed his chest, pushing him back.

He reacted immediately, breaking our kiss. "Julie . . ." he said, his eyes widened. "Did I . . .?" A look of horror spread over his face, his hands flying from me.

I pushed myself up, my heart pounding, twisting my dress back over me. "Andy—sorry, it's just that you . . . you were kind of intense and I got a bit—" I pulled in my legs, waving him off. "Oh God. Nevermind."

Even in the thin light I could see him pale. "Jesus. You're scared to death." He scrambled back and stood up. After a moment he offered his hand. I took it.

"Julie," he said gravely, holding me out, "I came on too strong, too fast, and for that I'm deeply, deeply sorry. You're very beautiful and I wanted you very badly, but on my life, I'd never do anything to hurt you. Do you believe me?"

Suddenly the idea of him having to ask sounded so ridiculous I was instantly ashamed. Practically speaking, if Andy were a latent Bluebeard he could've picked a more prosperous victim. And then there was the fact he'd called me *beautiful* . . .

I went to him, laying my head against his chest. "Oh, Andy, I'm just being stupid. I wanted you pretty badly myself. Matter of fact, I was more than a bit confused why it hadn't happened sooner. Maybe that's what weirded me out."

He sighed, wrapping his arms around me. "I'll make it up to you, I promise. That is if you allow me to."

What my mind had misconstrued my body remembered all too easily, from the lovely slickness between my legs to the way his scent fired every one of my receptors. "Oh, I will," I said against the hollow of his throat. "I will."

He laughed, a low, sexy growl, and kissed my forehead. "Then it's a promise. But for now, why don't we take care of something a little more immediate. Like the little matter of your very audible stomach."

No fooling; I was ready to stuff my gullet like nobody's

business. "Then lead on, lord of the manor. Let's sample the fruits of your efforts."

"I hate to tell you," he said as I took a seat at the little table, "but I haven't yet reached that evolutionary plane. For now, I'm still stuck at hunter-gatherer. Aside from the obvious, everything on these platters was left by my father."

Now was as good a time as any. "When did he die?" I asked, taking the wine he offered.

He smiled subtly, pouring his own. "First this," he said, clinking my glass as he bent to kiss me. "Good luck, Mrs. Devine."

His kiss was soft, lingering, sweet, so very different from our urgent clashing just minutes ago. I returned it with one of my own. "And to you, Mr. Devine. Or rather, as we've been so recently corrected to say, congratulations."

Andy kissed each of my cheeks before ending with one more against my mouth, a meandering meeting of lips and tongue that drew a sigh right up from my toes. "It should have been champagne, but as you'll find out soon enough, there's a lot of things around here that should've been, but aren't."

My God, he's such a good kisser . . . "I'm up to the challenge," I said, a bit dazed as I turned my attention to his little buffet. "You haven't scared me off. Not yet."

He raised his glass. "I'm glad to hear that, *ma petite*. I would very much like you to stick around awhile."

I would have to make a note in my journal later concerning what a number Andy's French asides did on me.

But for now, I'd blame my current sensory spike on the gustatory delights he was offering—his tomatoes were astounding—and get to the business at hand. "About your dad . . ."

He took a bite of cheese and bread, washing it down with a swallow of wine. "My father spent his final years here as a fisherman, farmer, and ersatz taxidermist before he died two months ago from liver failure. You see, his real talent lay in how liberally he could tip a bottle." His gaze shifted impassively to mine. "In other words, *mon père* was a drunk."

And he said it as if being a drunk was just another paternal characteristic like having blue eyes or being left-handed. "So I guess your childhood was pretty awful."

He shrugged. "Not exactly. I have memories of my father that are actually idyllic at times. You see, my parents' brand of contention was a bit more cerebral. Most of the time they did a good job of keeping it out of my earshot." He laughed, a short quick burst laced with irony. "It wasn't until after my mother took me back to Le Havre for good that things really got interesting."

This was potentially juicy stuff, but I had to appear curious, not eager. I turned the wine bottle, assessing the label, before I lifted it over my glass. "You said 'back to Le Havre.' I thought you were born right here?"

His thumb jutted toward the inside of the house. "I'm as American as you are. I was born right there in that bedroom. Though after I turned five my mother and I spent every summer in Le Havre until I was thirteen, and then we ended up staying."

I stopped, mid-pour. "Did you know that was going to happen when you left?"

"No. A few years earlier my father had taken to commercial fishing off Barnegat Light while we were away. That year he decided I should come with him. But my mother wanted just one more summer with me abroad, so he relented. Then in August she informed him we were staying and soon after he came over to try to get her to come home." He paused a minute, his face going hard. "It wasn't pretty. Two weeks later, I was enrolled in boarding school in Geneva."

"But did you want to stay there?" I finished my pour, then tilted the bottle toward him. "Didn't anyone ask you?"

He pushed his glass forward, his jaw tightening. "I was thirteen, the son of a French national. If she wanted me with her, that was the end of the argument."

"But what about your father? Didn't he—"

"It was nearly ten years before I saw him again." he said, making a cutting motion beside his glass. I set the bottle down. "After college I crewed for a year on a steamer. Then purely by chance I stumbled into him in a portside bar in Elizabeth. It wasn't a happy reunion. He was still bitter and I was a pretty angry young man. So, I never came back here and he never invited me." He lifted one shoulder in a shrug as he sipped more wine. "Ah, well."

"Is that why you had to have a plan? Because you're afraid our marriage will turn out like theirs?"

He looked up sharply. "It's as good a reason as any, don't you think?"

I let that lie for a moment before I asked, "So what happened to your mother? Did she ever remarry?"

"Yes." He swirled his wine and reached for another slice of cheese. "And she lived happily ever after."

I had an inkling now was not the time to examine that. "And your father?"

"No. But Jinks told me there were three or four women at his funeral looking way too mournful." His mouth crooked. "Anyway, I was at sea when I found out he was sick. By the time I was able to get here, he was already gone. Jinks said he went so quickly. He was planting his garden one day, and not long after he was dead."

"And since he left you this place," I said, "it proves he was still thinking of you. He couldn't have been all bad."

That seemed to surprise him. "You think I hated him, but really there was a lot I admired about him."

"Apparently." Because it led to a logical conclusion. I swept a hand over myself. "You left the life of a sailor, and brought me here."

He laughed, breaking the baguette and handing a piece to me. "Actually, I'm a marine engineer, and you're still a bit of a mystery." He leaned in, his arms across some very muscular thighs. "Tell me all about Julie Knott, Mrs. Devine."

"What's so mysterious?" I said, making little sandwiches out of fruit and cheese as I sipped some really excellent wine. "Anything worth telling's on videotape or digitalized. I grew up in Northeast Philly with a kid brother. Now he's a snotty ad exec for some boutique firm in New York. I talk to him twice a year. My parents live in Fort Lauderdale, and I see them even less."

"Not a close family," he said, polishing off the last of his wine.

"Not particularly. Though Mom was thrilled when I broke up with Richard."

"What do you think she'll say about this? Have you told her?"

I couldn't tell him it wouldn't last long enough to bother. "No. I'm letting a little time accumulate between you and Richard before I do. Because when I do tell her, she'll only be hurt that she never got to wear her mother-of-the-bride dress. My father will mail me a check."

"Which you'll mail right back. You don't need his money. I'm taking care of you now." He reached for my hand. "Come here. There's something I'd like to show you."

Apparently, the interview part of the evening was coming to a close. I swiveled around the table to his lap. "What is it?" I asked, sliding my arms around his neck.

"This," he said, his kiss ending any further interrogation.

My brain blanked, completely forgetting what we'd been talking about. Bad business, because we were just starting to get somewhere. But if I had to go off-topic, what better way to do it, his cabernet-scented self a double-whammy to my already-addled brain. I pressed against the expanse of his chest and breathed him in, his hair like dampened silk as I threaded it through my fingers.

"By the way," I said, "where did you go to get gussied up while I was hogging the bathroom? Jump in the lake?"

He kissed my neck, and I shivered. "Close. There's an outside shower behind the barn. Uses rainwater . . ." He kissed my collarbone. "Warmed by the sun."

"Really," I said, arching my neck, pulling him closer, his kisses trailing to the swell of my breasts. "I'd . . . I'd like to try that . . . sometime."

"No doubt you'll get the chance," he said, unbuttoning the bodice of my dress. A moment later his hand was covering my breast, his fingers kneading it with expert ease. "*Quels beaux seins,*" he murmured, his mouth falling to a nipple, his teeth grazing it through the lace.

What was my regret earlier? Something about missing the chance to flaunt my lingerie? Well, here it was, and all I could think of was how quickly I could get out of it. I squirmed, feeling a little swoony. It was bad enough Andy looked like a Greek god, but when he spoke French—*my goodness*—I wanted to rip my clothes off. I wanted to rip *his* clothes off.

"Andy?"

"Yes . . .?" He switched to the other breast, sucking, nipping through the lace while I quietly went out of my mind. "*Qu'est-ce qu'il y a?*"

I pulled away from him, his face between my hands. "Andy," I said breathlessly. "I think we need to go inside now."

He kissed me. Hard. "A very good idea." When he stood I was still in his arms.

"I'll grab the door." And just as I reached for it, the last sound I was looking for assaulted me.

"Bucky," he said, turning to the hellhound on

the steps, who was barking to wake the dead. When Andy looked at me, I knew what was coming. "Do you mind?"

A foregone conclusion. "Let him in," I said.

Andy set me onto my feet and opened the door to the yard; the collie loped in. He promptly sat down and, with his tongue lolling out the side of his mouth, commenced to give me the stare down.

"He really is a good dog," Andy said in his defense.

"An oxymoron," I told him. "The only good dog is someone else's."

"How about if he sleeps on the porch?"

"As long as we have a wall between us," I said, idly buttoning my dress.

Andy's eyes flared. "Hey, stop that." He looked to Bucky. "Dog—stay." Then, throwing the door open, he swept me up in his arms and swifted me inside.

The dusk had cast a glow over the room, gilding it in crisp ambers, the brass bed gleaming like a shiny Krugerrand. He set me beside it then faced me, unbuttoning the last of my dress before gently pulling it over my head. When I undid my bra and let it drop to the floor, I was naked, hoping the falling night would be kind enough to gild me, too.

Andy's gaze fell over me in waves as he stood silent, taking me in. "My God you're lovely . . ." he whispered, his hands skimming my shoulders and down my sides, resting lightly on my hips. From there he slowly drew me in, my belly pressing against the hardness beneath his jeans, my neck arching to meet his kiss.

My heart pounded in my ears. Not from fear—I was at last, past that—but from restless anticipation, an almost feral need to continue what had happened way too quickly just minutes ago. The realization nearly floored me. I'd always been so sensible! But with his scent all around me, his taste clean on my lips, all coherence vanished and I groaned, slipping my hands into the back of his jeans.

"Not yet," he said softly as he took a step back, going for his fly, still half undone from our first encounter. He unzipped then pulled out his shirt, unbuttoning it with torturous efficiency. I stared, transfixed, breathless with wanting him. When he slipped it off I got my first look at what I had lusted over every night since we met: his wide shoulders cascading to near perfect proportions, his chest taut, lightly tanned, and just hirsute enough to telegraph that this manly-man didn't much go in for trends. Then his thumbs slipped inside the waist of his jeans and down they went. As I should've surmised, he'd worn no shorts to land atop them. Because if he had, that would have meant he'd have to keep me waiting one split-second longer to look upon what I was openly gaping at.

Andy was one beautiful man.

"Come here," he said, holding out his arms.

I melted into him and he twisted us about until we fell on the bed, arms and legs weaving together as we rained kisses upon each other. I don't know how long it took, seconds only, before I felt myself rising, Andy's mouth on me sucking, nipping, driving me insane. I tried to hold on, keep his lips firmly on my own, but it was no use, he was everywhere, my skin alive, on fire. I dug my nails into his shoulders as he sunk lower and lower, his tongue trailing little stabs of lightning, my head arching into the quilt as the pleasure expanded and broke loose. When I could finally breathe again he turned me over, kissing my neck, the jut of a shoulder blade, the small of my back. Then he slipped lower, lower still, opening me to perform another small miracle. Before I could stop shaking he was atop me and I could feel his delicious heaviness, the drag of his chest across my back, his muscled leg twining mine, his hardness pulsing atop my bottom. He kissed my shoulder, my arm, his hands sliding under me to palm my breasts, but how much could one woman stand? I turned around in his arms, my sensitive nipples savoring the exquisite pressure, while the more immediate part of my body craved much more.

"Andy," I begged him, feeling him right at the entrance. "I can't stand much more."

He held my head between his hands. "Julie," he said softly, a bit gravely, "I didn't have time to say this to you before when we . . ." His gaze deepened, and he nipped my lower lip. "But I want to say it now, because it'll be true of every time we're together." He kissed me, so sweetly. "You honor me." Then he spread my legs with his and slipped inside me.

We both gasped, stilling. "*Julie*," he said, barely audibly. He kissed me, his forehead on mine. "Now we're truly married."

In another recent rendition of myself, the one more attuned to the ridiculous, the one who thought even the day before was passé, I would have heard those words just whispered and rolled my eyes, drolly opining, *if only he were real*. But at that moment, with my husband buried within me, his gaze languidly fixed on me, it was all I could do to keep my emotions in check. Even someone as jaded as me sometimes has hope, when my dissolute mind allows just enough slack to believe—*yes*, sometimes things actually lean in my direction. And because of that I reached up and pulled my husband to me, his kiss meeting mine with tenderness.

"Yes, Andy, we are," I answered, still barely believing it, fully realizing it'd never be 'til death do us part. And that's the line that kept me tethered in the real world, a line taut and unbreakable.

But for now I was in a place filled with natural rhythms, with a man strong and beautiful, filling me. So as he whispered words that sounded too achingly lovely, I let each thrust of his lovemaking remind me that sometimes nothing matters but the moment, and what's right in front of you.

He fell in even deeper, the sheen on his forehead matching mine as he pushed us even over the edge. As he spilled himself I kissed him, keeping everything.

Minutes later he lay back, his arm flung around me, his hand lost in my hair. I sprawled across his chest, listening to the slowing rhythm of his heart as he fell asleep. It was only after his breath deepened and he curled with me to his side that I eased away and crept into the bathroom, extricating the plastic bag containing my journal and the raft of birth control pills, from beneath the dresser drawer. So it was from there atop the toilet, with this stranger's remains still seeping from me, his grandmother's wedding ring encircling my finger, that I swallowed my insurance and rejoined my real purpose: recording mendacity, deep into the night.

Chapter Eight

Falling In

FROM JULIE KNOTT'S JOURNAL

30 August

Six days ago the only Andy Devine I ever heard of was a tubby, squeaky-voiced character actor who drove a stagecoach in a 1939 movie starring John Wayne. Yet, that afternoon I was to meet an identically-monikered twenty-first century version: an impossibly muscled, blue-eyed, dark-haired, and mythically gorgeous alpha male, advertising for a wife via a handwritten flyer on a utility pole, deep in the New Jersey Pine Barrens. As a feature reporter for WPHA Channel 8 News, Philadelphia, I went to cover the interviews this Victorian throwback was giving for potential brides at the local firehouse, all the while wondering why it was even nec-

*essary. But instead of covering the story, five days later
I became it.*

My manly-man's asleep now in the other room,
while I'm naked on the toilet writing in this journal.
I've stashed it under the linens dresser, in order to take
notes for a book I'm going to write about this adventure. But, because I intend to bare all (no pun intended)
and hold nothing back (except for one key point), I'd
like to keep my initial impressions to myself and away
from my new husband for a while.

Just this afternoon we were married posthaste at
Town Hall in Iron Bog, after which I was then driven
deep into the Pine Barrens, to what could only be
loosely construed as a "farm." Our reception consisted of midwifing the birth of Betsy the Jersey Cow's
yet unnamed calf; getting chased through a flock of
chickens and into a lake by Bucky, an obsessed Border
Collie; and nearly breaking my ankle confronting
Rocky the stuffed raccoon in the groom's landfill of a
living room. Afterward I was ultimately fed, wined
and unequivocally bedded by the stranger who's now
my husband.

The reasons why aren't very complicated: I've got
nothing to lose because I've already lost everything—
my job, my home, the man I was supposed to marry.
Not that I can go into detail at the moment; I can hear
Andy stirring, and I've maybe a minute to get back to
bed. And that's a part of this story one I can honestly
say merits further investigation.

I WOKE UP on my back in the chill bedroom, arms over my head, my body dampened from his warmth. And smiling. Good Lord, was I smiling.

With my eyes still closed I could picture him, lips soft and feathery against my breasts, his emerging beard deliciously abrading my skin as he traced from one nipple to the other. I squirmed, his tongue trailing down my belly to encircle my navel, his hands kneading my hips as he continued even lower, my hips rising with a jerk as he flicked the sweet spot, sending me aloft again.

"Oh *Andy* . . ." I purred, wrapping my legs around him.

"Jesus—*tu m'excites*," he growled and rising up, thrust into me.

I couldn't remember the last time I had this much sex, my randy Andy taking me with a masculine possessiveness that left me breathless and thoroughly overcome. Was it the third or fourth time? Or even fifth? I wasn't sure. Richard and I usually had sex every night when we were on vacation, but Andy set a whole new . . . *Richard*. My breath caught at the thought of him, luckily just as Andy nipped my earlobe, a definite precedent for that. I wouldn't think of Richard; I couldn't. Not in that way, at least. I would focus on my anger and his betrayal, and on the exquisite revenge this lusty adventure would grant me. But in the meantime . . .

Andy lowered himself to me, the soft hairs of his chest tickling my breasts as he slowly swivelled his hips, filling me like Richard could only dream of. I let my hands slide down the twin slopes of his rump, smooth to my fingers, flinching under my touch. I palmed them, squeezing.

His eyes flared. "Minx," he rasped, and biting my neck, thrust *hard*.

I almost shot through the roof. But I couldn't; I was thoroughly impaled. And enjoying it so much I allowed myself another orgasm. Andy did as well. I delighted in the way he went a little swoony, his eyes at half-mast, his exhale long and slow. I smiled with satiety and recovered confidence, firm in the resolve I could do this. And I was still smiling who knows how long later when I turned to curl next to him—only to find he was gone.

From outside I could hear a dog barking. Bucky, of course. "Andy," I called toward the bathroom as sunlight streamed through the windows. "I think the dog wants you." When he didn't answer, I raised up on my arm. "Andy?" I looked toward the screen door. "Andy—"

A gunshot reverberated from outside and I bolted from the bed. I was half-way to the door when I realized I was naked. Grabbing my robe, I barely tied it around me before I ran into the yard and around the house to the front. Not a hundred feet away I found Andy, shirtless and barefoot, his jeans half-zipped, a smoking rifle in his hand. Bucky was sniffing a mound of something most definitely dead in front of him.

"Bucky—stop," Andy said, nudging him away.

Okay, two things were running through my head, both alternately horrifying and eye-opening: how perversely sexy Andy looked with a rifle in his hand, and the bald fact there *was* a rifle in his hand.

"Andy! What the hell?" I said, coming up to him. I bent over a dead raccoon, its eyes bulging, its tongue hanging, a bullet hole neatly centered through its forehead. "Oh God," I whispered, recoiling.

He uncocked the rifle, half-opening it. "Bucky had him cornered, and he was ready to lunge, so I couldn't chance it. Especially since they trapped a rabid one not far from here last week."

"But how could you tell?" I asked, just as Bucky's head swivelled around to look at Andy. "Was he foaming at the mouth?" I glanced at the animal. "Doesn't look like it."

"Doesn't have to be. This one's a male, and they're not supposed to be out during the day. Females, maybe, looking for a meal for their kits, but this one should've been sleeping. Besides, he was skulking the chickens."

"Oh," I said, staring at the poor pathetic creature. Suddenly, and for whatever reason, I felt an affinity. "How dare he? Didn't he know it's our job to wring their necks?"

He eyed me wryly. "I detect a slight note of indignation."

"*Moi?*" I pointed to my chest. "*Non . . .*"

"*C'est Malin,*" he said, his mouth crooking. He set the rifle against a post. "Look, sometimes I'll have to kill things. It's not that I enjoy doing it, but when you're living this close to the wild, a lot of times you can't help it. Later on, I'll probably kill a deer so we'll have something to eat over the winter."

I laughed. "Kill a deer! Christ, Andy, haven't you ever heard of a place called a supermarket? They have all kinds of meat already dead for you."

"So it's better if they get so overbred they get hit by a car? Something's going to get them either way, you know. It might as well be—*no*, I said!" He yanked Bucky off the carcass again, the dog hunkering down with a whine. "That's the way it is here. You just do what you have to do."

The way he said it gave me a little chill. "I bet if there were lions out here you'd want to kill them, too."

"I don't think you're getting this," he said, his cheek twitching.

"Just never knew I married the Great White Hunter, is all."

"Trust me, when you catch a herd of them munching on the tomatoes you're about to harvest, you'll be yelling for the shotgun, too."

Now I was truly horrified. "So it's just blast away at anything trying to survive out here, right?" I looked around. "Why don't you show me where the salt licks are, then? Or your tree stand? Shall we rub ourselves with musk to get them all fired up, too?"

He cast a gaze up and down my body. "I don't think that'll be necessary."

I started to say something, then quickly demurred, my face going crimson. I gathered my robe closer around my neck.

He sighed. "Come here," he said, pulling me to him.

I laid my head against his chest, his richly masculine scent evidence for the logic of his conclusion. He ran his fingers through my hair.

"Sore?" he asked, kissing the top of my head.

I felt an erotic twinge at the bald intimacy of his question. "A little." I glanced at him, a bit abashed. "But I'm not complaining."

"That's good." He tipped my chin to him. "You're a beautiful woman, Julie, and as you may have already suspected, I find you pretty hard to resist."

"And here I was thinking it was my scathing wit."

"That came first. And then . . ." His hands slipped to my behind. "There was this."

I was struck by the irony. "Yet you didn't even so much as hold my hand until we were married."

"Yeah, well . . ." His fingers flexed against me. "I didn't want to influence your decision. I wanted the idea of our marriage to stand on its own merit."

I looked at him squarely. "*This*," I said, sliding my hands up and down his torso, "is pretty damn meritorious. You're one hot little package too, you know?"

He reddened slightly himself. "So . . . I guess we can pretty much agree we're attracted to each other."

God, he was so cute. "You can say that."

He leaned back against a post, taking me with him. "Even though we may have nothing in common?"

I pushed up on my toes, brushing my lips against his. "Seems like we'll have a lot of time to find out. We've already taken a big leap."

"By getting married," he concluded, kissing the corner of my mouth.

"By falling seriously in lust," I said, kissing him right back.

His arms tightened around me as he proceeded to set

every vein in my body on fire. I could feel him hardening beneath me, his breath coming short as he trailed
kisses down my jawline, my neck, toward my breasts. As
I arched back to allow him easier access, my addled mind
managed to fire a few pain synapses to my nether region,
reminding me that, amid all that heating up, I'd better
cool it down for a spell. As if on cue, Andy reacted.

"Jesus," he said, flushing, "I think we need a swim.
Come on."

I pulled back as he hauled me toward the lake. "Wait—
my suit's in the house."

He looked back, adding blithely, "You're joking right?"

Although it couldn't be much past six, whatever
morning chill there was had already dissipated, the day
rising warm and brilliantly sunny. Which only caused
me to realize: all the better for Andy to zone in on every
single flaw my body possessed. Now, I was no prude by
any stretch of the imagination, but and the thought of
being naked under the magnifying glass of full sunlight
was suddenly enough to make me want to hide under the
bed. Not that he'd give me a chance. As soon as we hit
the dock, so did his jeans. Andy stood stunningly naked
before me.

He reached for the tie of my robe. "C'mon."

I took a step back. "What if someone sees us?"

"Like who? We're in the middle of the woods. And
even if they could, who gives a damn?" He came closer. "I
sure as hell don't."

"If I looked like you I wouldn't give a damn either."

"If you looked like me," he said dryly, "you wouldn't

be standing here." He tugged the tie, the robe falling open. "Now come on. The swim will do you good."

I knew it would. And I knew I was being silly. So I tossed my hair over my shoulder and let my robe fall, Andy's gaze gliding down me as it slid to the dock.

"*Merde*," he breathed. He grabbed my hand and we jumped in.

The water was deep, over my head, though not so deep I didn't touch muck before shooting back through the chilly depths to the sun-warmed surface. Andy met me as I popped through the water, grasping my waist and pulling me toward him. Instinctively, my arms hooked around his neck, my skin goose-fleshy as it met the slipperiness of his chest. He lay back, paddling slowly as I lay atop him—my own personal raft.

"Now, that wasn't so bad, was it?" he said, his wet eyelashes sparkling in the sun.

"Freaking c-cold, I said, shivering.

He stopped. "Let's swim out to the float," he said, looking to it about fifty yards away. "You *can* swim, right?"

I thought of the thousands of laps I had clocked in the pool at the Y. "I can swim," I said, pushing off him. "And I won't even say anything as corny as 'Race you.'"

"A foregone conclusion," he said, diving in.

There's something to be said about swimming in the buff, about gliding through the water without the hindrance of Lycra or fashion statements. I felt liberated and decadent and slick as an eel, my body cutting through the lake like hot through cold. I was so enjoying the sensation, my normally competitive self didn't even care if

Andy was beating me, not that he made a big deal about it. Six feet from the float he cut behind me and once again clasped my waist.

"You swim well," he said, twisting me around to face him. "You damn near beat me."

"You're just saying that," I said, wrapping my legs around his waist. I lay back against the water to catch my breath. "Like I could beat a sailor."

"Not every sailor can swim," he said, his hand on my belly, his fingers swirling the little pool that had collected.

"Well, it's pretty damn obvious this one can," I said as he turned me about, one foot braced on the float's ladder, my body stretched out before him.

Off in the distance I could hear birds calling. The sky above me was clear blue and poofed with the occasional cumulous. Beside me the lake lapped against the wood, the top of it warm, slightly tea-colored, and fragrant with something I'd yet to identify. As I kept my gaze skyward, I was achingly aware of Andy's taut belly nudging my most intimate region, how his hand skimmed over me, past my black curls wavering like water rushes, around my hips and up my sides to my breasts, his fingers circling the hard peaks of my nipples.

"What do you want from me, Andy?" I asked, in spite of my own reasons.

He palmed my breasts, wet and bobbing, before he lifted me from the water onto the float. As I lay back atop it, the water draining from me down the slats, he hefted himself from the lake to my side, one arm flung over the other to cage me.

"I want you to be my wife," he answered, water dripping from his body to mine.

"How do I do that? How will I know what you want?"

He shifted, bracing himself on his elbows. "We'll work it out."

I sat up. "Do have any idea how ridiculous that sounds?" I wrapped my arms around my legs, dropping my head to my knees.

After a long moment, he said. "If you're saying my ideas are ridiculous, then you're saying I'm ridiculous. That's never a position I like finding myself in."

I lifted my head. He was looking toward the shore. I'd insulted him, something I figured didn't happen very often. "That's not what I meant. You could never be ridiculous. But your method does confuse me. Why did you pick a wife this way?"

He turned to me, impassive. "What you're really asking is why I picked you. That's simple. I wanted you."

Not really what I wanted to hear. "There has to be more to it than that."

"Not really. I took one look at you and saw everything I wanted, right then and that quickly." He shifted, his shoulders blocking the sun. "Call it desire, call it lust—call it whatever you want. But it didn't take a minute before I knew I wanted you on your back and myself inside you."

My mouth went dry; the only thing ridiculous now was the memory of his reticence. "But what about all that talk about partnership? About our marriage being a business relationship?"

"That hasn't changed. If anything, it's probably more important than ever. It forces me to look beyond the attraction to the long term." His eyes darkened. "And it gives me some protection if I can't."

I'm not sure I knew how to take this. "You mean after the spell breaks so you can get out?"

"Not only me. You too."

"And that's all there is?"

"Of course not, but—"

"*Huh.*" Was I really hearing this? "So all you really wanted to do was fuck me?"

He shrugged. "Well—*then.*"

"And now?" I asked, my hackles fully up.

He kissed my shoulder, grinning. "Now I'd much rather fuck with your head."

I slapped his chest. "Andy!"

"Okay! Okay!" He laughed, falling back. "I'm joking!"

"No you're not," I said, looming over him.

"You're right," he said, a finger trailing my jaw line, "I pretty much still want to fuck you, too."

Suddenly everything faded into the background, and there was only Andy and my hand pushing against him. He stretched back atop the float, his body still slick and gleaming, as I threw my leg over him and laid my body atop his. I savored his solidness, his arms around me in a seemingly unbreakable clutch. But I wouldn't kiss him. I lifted myself and slipped down, lower and lower, until I faced the obvious evidence of his admiration. I grasped it and took it fully down my throat.

He flinched, grunting, but I had just begun. I started

out slow, teasing, flicking and circling as he groaned, his fingers slipping through the slats to hold on. Then steadily I went faster until my speed was almost cruel, and he raised up, half-sitting, one leg arched, one stretched out beside me.

"Julie . . ." he groaned, his hand on my cheek. "Stop— let me take care of you." I could hear him heaving, his breath coming hard. "Stop or I'll—"

His hips jerked and his whole body spasmed, my mouth filling with warmth and salt and the most delicious sensation. I pulled on him, greedily swallowing, revelling in his release. When I finished, he stared at me wide-eyed. But before he could catch his breath I twisted off the float, diving into the water.

I swam no more than a few dozen feet before I heard the splash. I felt the turbulence from his powerful body when he came up behind me and twisted me around, opening my legs wide. But I wouldn't allow it, springing from his chest toward shore, my arms slicing through the water like a paddlewheel. By the time we reached the dock we were both panting.

"W-Why did you do t-that?" he heaved out, the water lapping against his chin.

I coughed, flinging my hair over my shoulder. "I have no idea what you're talking about." I reached for the ladder.

He caught my wrist. "Okay, look, I won't lie to you. I'm attracted to you. That's hardly an insult. And I do like you. As far as the rest, it's a bit complicated."

"Complicated . . ." I said, slipping my arm from his

grasp. "You said it was simple. You wanted me. Well, here I am. So tell me, what's next on the list?" I grasped the ladder and hauled myself up.

Within seconds, he was in front of me. "What's simple is my wanting you, but I'm well aware that my *keeping* you will be just short of miraculous. If you think I'm underestimating you, you're wrong, because as much as I want you . . ." He lightly brushed my cheek. ". . . If you didn't want me just as badly, you wouldn't be here."

He was right, but that was hardly what was so perplexing. It was having a man look at me the way Andy did just then, which didn't only have to do with my nakedness. It was more to do with how he made me acutely aware of my own femininity, and how that basic fact would always be as apparent and divergent from his own rampant masculinity as night was from day. Coming off of Richard's languid maleness, it was quite a shock to the system, but not something that was either unpleasant or unwanted. Just disconcertingly hard to get used to.

"You never answered my question," I said, slipping into the robe he held out for me. "What's next?"

He looked confused. "As in . . .?"

"I don't know . . . the farm, maybe?" I tightened the robe around myself. "Believe it or not, I am good for something else."

"Oh I'm *sure*." When he smiled, I felt the air lightening between us. "How about feeding, watering, and pasturing the cow? Mucking her stall? Feeding the chickens and gathering eggs, cleaning out their roosts? Hoeing and watering the garden, picking and sorting the vegetables, packing them for market? Checking the generator, the water levels, cutting back the blueberry bushes, picking peaches, turning the compost—"

"Hey, I didn't even get my coffee yet."

"And I barely even got started." He pulled on his jeans, and then pulled me into his arms. "Julie, I hardly know what I'm doing myself, so it's not only me and you that's a work in progress. I never said it would be easy, but in the end, I promise, it'll be worth it. That is, if you're not ready to sneak out of here in the middle of the night."

"No, not quite yet." Though it got me thinking about what it was that was so *complicated*.

I glanced back to the lake as we walked toward the farm, knowing there was a lot more than water running deep. I lay my head against Andy's shoulder, and he kissed it, wondering what it'd take to get inside his.

Chapter Nine

Shiny Objects

"AND THEN THERE'S the roof," Andy said, flicking a rotted cedar shake into a pile of trash.

"One question," I said, eyeing the porch, the rusty tools, the teeming barrels of who-knew-what, not to mention the miasma of filth and assorted desiccation that lay beyond the front door. "Why is the bedroom of this house straight out of *House and Garden*, and the rest of it so ghetto?"

He shook his head slowly. "And here I thought you had such a grasp of the obvious . . ."

I tied my robe tighter around me. "Silly of me to ask," I said, turning to the barking, squawking spectacle of Bucky chasing a hen into its coop. Then he stopped dead, turning to eye me menacingly, before he barked again and ran off.

"You know, that dog needs something else to do besides scaring the crap out of the chickens."

"Especially when we'll be collecting it later."

"The chickens?" I said, following him toward the barn.

"No—the crap."

I stopped him. "Excuse me?"

"I guess I haven't shown you the compost yet."

"You haven't shown me much of anything besides your—"

"It's behind the barn," he said smoothly, opening the door to it, "but first we have to . . ."

He didn't have to say anything more. The inside of the barn was humid with the scents of manure, dirt, and something definitely milkified. There stood Betsy the cow with her issue, munching hay while her calf suckled, her cartoonishly large eyes blinking obliviously at me. The two of them were so darned cute together, visions of Caldecott Medals danced in my head.

"Awww . . ." I said, scratching her behind the ear. "You know? We have to give the baby a name."

"Go ahead if you want to, but don't get too attached."

"Why? Are you planning veal scallopini for dinner?"

He tossed me a wry look, snapping a lead rope to the mama cow's halter as he inclined his head to the left. "Feed's inside that trash can over there. Dump a couple coffee cans into that bucket and bring it outside."

I opened the can to a rich scent of corn, oats, and what I suspected was molasses. I hadn't eaten anything since a bit of fruit and cheese the night before, and after all the sexual gymnastics, pouring some of that concoction down my gullet seemed entirely reasonable. I reached overhead to a neat row of coffee cans. When I pulled one out, something shiny and metal behind it reflected back, partially obscured by jars of liniment, vitamins, and more cans. I craned my neck, pushing up on my toes.

"Julie!" Andy called. "The feed?"

"I'm coming!" I yelled, dropping down. I scooped the feed into a bucket and went outside.

When I met up with Andy, he was letting Betsy and her calf into a fenced square of scrubby grass alongside the barn, hay, and what looked like food scraps shoved up in the corner. But my mind was distracted by shiny objects. Whatever they were, they didn't look like they belonged there, and something told me now wasn't the time to ask Andy about it. I'm sure his father had left many things lurking about, and Andy had barely scratched the surface of finding them. Perhaps I'd leave it to him to tell me. *Or*, as he came toward me, *not*.

He reached for the bucket dangling from my fingers. "I can't believe I'm standing here half-naked and barefoot, holding a bucket of cow food."

"Cow *feed*," he corrected me, pouring it into a rubber tub. "And you're the best looking farm wife I've ever seen."

"You've met how many at sea . . .?" I asked, taking the bucket from him.

He hoisted himself up and over the fence. "Now you know why you're the best." He grasped my waist, giving me a quick kiss. "Next, the chickens."

"Chickens? Andy!" I cried as he hauled me along. "I'm *starving*!"

"So are the chickens. But they eat before we do."

I sensed a distinct air of indifference to my visceral needs. But then again, it was hardly fair to demand special attention when he was in the same condition as me, his hair still dampened from the lake, his feet also bare (and probably bearing the residue of something dubious from the barn). And, using another of his appetites as a logical gauge, he was no doubt hungry enough to put any fair-sized animal within shooting range in jeopardy. I cast Betsy's calf a wary glance. Maybe veal scallopini wasn't so far-fetched after all.

"Here, take this," he said, handing me a well-worn straw basket.

"Don't tell me—for gathering eggs?"

He grinned. "Perceptive, isn't she?"

I slung it over my arm. "Shall I put on my milkmaid dress next?"

"We'll be leaving Betsy to her calf for the next few days, and since you asked," he winked slyly, "what you're wearing is working for me just fine."

"It would," I said, bending to peer into the henhouse. "So where are these eggs anyway?"

"They've been laying either in the coop or under these bushes around it." The wooden coop was about six feet long and about three feet wide, its two levels a little higher than my shoulder, built about three feet off the ground, hen-sized holes covered with plastic flaps at either end. It was clearly handmade, and probably pretty old, too, its weathered exterior soaking up many coats of whitewash over the years. Andy flicked back a latch then opened a windowed lid covering its front, revealing two straw-covered shelves. Several brown eggs were scattered here and there.

"Look at that," I said. "So that's where brown eggs come from. From brown chickens."

"Amazing, isn't it?" he said, plucking one out and depositing it into my basket. "Actually, they're New Hampshire Reds."

I fetched one myself, cradling the still-warm egg. "So why isn't it red?"

"Wouldn't that be just what you'd expect? Now, a couple dozen chickens should get you at least twenty eggs. Why don't you check under those bushes there."

I squatted to the low-lying shrub creeping alongside the weedy base of the coop. With the branches bent like over-reaching arms, it was a perfect refuge for an agoraphobic chicken. I leaned in and rooted around the dried leaves, fetching two eggs.

"Look!" I said, producing them. "Breakfast!"

He was decidedly unimpressed. "There should be at least two more. Look again."

I was just about to push aside a couple of rocks when something slithered over my hand. "Andy!" I cried, falling back, a flash of red and brown zipping through the brush.

"Oh, it's just a corn snake. They're harmless," he said. Its swath uncovered two more eggs. "Look what he found for you." He slipped his eggs into my basket and reached for the newly uncovered ones.

"*Ugh*, I hate snakes," I said, scrambling to stand.

"Ever eat them? Actually, they're not bad."

I grunted. "Well, if you're thinking about feeding them to me, you can forget it."

"I'm done feeding you, *ma petite*," he said. "I'll provide the raw materials, but as a proper farm wife, it's your job now."

The Julie of two weeks previous would've laughed out loud and opined *You're joking!* at such an old-school statement, especially with that mischievous twinkle in his eye. But he was right—I had to do *something* to prove my worth around this farm. And cooking was a good place to start.

As he lowered the lid of the chicken coop, I was well aware that'd be no simple task, especially considering I'd always been better at making reservations than I was at preparing anything past microwavable. But as starving as I was, I'd happily dip into my limited repertoire and concoct something. Good thing what I had at hand was within it. "How about I whip up an omelet?" I hefted the egg basket. "Though, we'll hardly need all these. Where's the refrigerator?"

Andy swiped his hands on his jeans. "No refrigerator. My father's wouldn't get below fifty degrees, so until I get a new one, we'll be eating fresh."

"You're joking." I thought of that little buffet Andy had set up the night before, right before we had . . . My stomach did a little flip. "What about that cheese we had last night? That must have been refrigerated."

"Refrigerate cheese?" His face squinched. "Spoken like a true American. A hard cheese doesn't have to be." He prodded the egg basket. "And neither do these. You just don't wash them until you use them. If you don't they'll keep for a couple of weeks."

"A couple of weeks!" I looked into the basket. "There's close to three dozen eggs here, and if you're getting them every day . . ."

"I've sold some to the store in town, but on Thursdays there's a farmers' market outside of Chatsworth. I was planning on going this week."

"But that's tomorrow," I said. I held out the basket. "You have to have more to take than just this?"

His face lit. "Exactly. Come and see what I've gathered so far."

We went to the far end of the barn, where we entered an airy, concrete-floored room with a drain, and lined with wooden bins groaning from all kinds of fruits and vegetables. "Right before my father died he had the pickers in for the peaches, and over the weekend I gathered what was left." He tapped two wooden bushel baskets stacked next to dozens of empty ones on the floor. "The rest of the stuff I got from the kitchen garden, but there's still more coming in, so much I can hardly catch up with it. And now the apples are just about ready to pick."

"Jesus . . ." I said, my gaze washing over a wealth of fruits and vegetables. "My God, look at all this stuff! You picked it all?"

He returned a couple of red potatoes that had rolled from the bin. "Yeah," he said, as if the very thought exhausted him. "What we can't sell or give away to the food bank, you'll can for the winter."

I thought of the lone, dusty can of olives that had been in what was, basically, a condiment larder in Philly. "Canning? I don't know anything about canning!"

"And what do I know about farming? Look, why don't we eat, and then I'll give you a dollar tour of the place, but first . . ." He reached for me. "Let's go clean up."

Clean up, of course, being a subjective term. "You mean the lake wasn't enough? Or do you just want to get me naked again?"

He lowered his gaze. "Is that a rhetorical question?" he said, tugging on the tie of my robe.

A few minutes later I found myself in an open-air shower, covered on just three sides, which his father had concocted from a barrel braced overhead. It was then fed through a rudimentary filter into a showerhead that looked straight out of the 1920s. With the sky above and Andy all around me, this normally mundane daily ritual seemed much more libertine than my *au natural* morning swim, especially with Andy swirling shampoo around my scalp. I slumped against him, nearly purring as he massaged the back of my head, faintly wondering if it was possible for my hair to have an orgasm.

"God, that feels good . . ." I moaned, his nails digging in.

"You have such beautiful long hair," he said, letting its soapy length unfurl down my back. He bent to kiss my neck. "Don't ever cut it."

I arched into the warm spray, the suds slipping down my breasts, my hips, my legs to the aged concrete pad below. "I wasn't planning on it. Though I have to pin it up in the summer, it gets so hot."

"What'll get me hot is pulling those pins out." He kissed my neck, my throat, trailing down to my breasts, his skin slickened by my own soapy remains. He took a nipple in his mouth, the morning stubble on his face scratching my already sensitive skin to hyper awareness. I curled my fingers around his shoulders as he fell to his haunches, his tongue tracing a torturous path down my belly. *"Si belle . . . si belle . . ."* he murmured, going lower, until we reached a happy parity from our earlier encounter on the raft, lifting me to the very tips of my toes. Before the last bit of suds had curled a path into the yard, he was carrying his thoroughly sated, yet very ravenous little woman into the house.

"You need a shave," I said, brushing the back of my hand against his jaw, his coarse stubble leaving a substantial impression against my fingers. *Such a manly man I married!* He set me to the floor in our bedroom.

"Which I plan on doing right now," he said, before pushing a teeshirt half into his pocket. "First, I have to switch tanks on the generator." He flicked an apparently dead light switch. "I should have done that last night, but we kind of got . . . sidetracked."

"Kinda," I said. I tried the switch myself. "Our electric comes from a generator?"

He sat on the bed, yanking on his boots. "You mean you didn't notice the distinct lack of power lines on the way in? Everything here works off a diesel generator—the electric, the water, the fridge will, once we get the kitchen cleaned out, that is." He stood. "For now, we'll have to cook on the grill in the yard. I'll get it going and you can make those omelettes. Frying pans and things are in the footlocker right outside the door."

"Got it," I said, trying to remember what was in the Western omelet I'd order at the Melrose Diner. "And please tell me you have coffee."

"*Ma petit poussin*, if the house were on fire and it came down to saving you or my coffeepot, I might be just a bit conflicted." At my gasp, he laughed, leaning in to kiss my cheek. "I'm joking! And oh—don't forget to put on your farmer's wife's clothes. After breakfast, we're going afield."

"Afield. Got it." I snapped him a proper salute. He laughed, waving me off.

I went to my suitcase. One of these days I was going to have to unpack, but for now I dug into my purse, needing to check my phone. I had told Denny and Brent I'd text them and here it was, almost twenty-four hours after I had left. Maybe the editor needed to contact me or the station had called about my resignation or maybe even—I swallowed significantly—maybe even Richard had … I sighed, pulling it out. Old habits died hard, and—"*What?!*" I nearly screeched, staring at the phone's face.

NO SERVICE.

I dropped the BlackBerry into my purse. *Damn*. Not that Andy hadn't warned me. But come on, mine was no flip phone. It was a state-of-the-art communications device, and this was New Jersey, for crying out loud. Maybe if I went outside. I dug it out again and went to the porch, but NO SERVICE still stared back at me. I went inside and fell back on the bed, disorientation rippling through me. It was one thing to be out in the woods with no electricity, running water or the fact I'd have to cook our rather rudimentary meals over a fire, but it. It was quite another to be without viable communications to the outside world. *Christ*, I thought, how can he stand it?

I ripped into my suitcase, past skimpy sundresses, skirts, t-shirts and shorts, lacy underwear and sandals, my running clothes and a pair of sneakers. I pulled out my Nikes and a wide cotton skirt and teeshirt. I was sure this wasn't what could be construed as farmer's wife's clothes, but it'd have to do for now. My stomach was growling from lack of my morning yogurt, my underarms were sweating from lack of air conditioning, my head was pounding for lack of a Mocha Latte Venti. I left for the porch and the footlocker.

What I found inside would surely make for a great campsite: cast-iron frying pan, sturdy-looking knives, plastic and jarred containers of what I assumed were food staples, a coffee pot. Alongside the locker was another old basket like the one I had gathered the eggs in. I piled into it stoneware plates, cutlery, a spatula, a can of coffee, a jar of sugar, a sharp knife, what remained of last evening's baguette. In the corner was a huge jar with something cloth-wrapped inside. I opened it to a strong smell of vinegar and cheese; I prodded the cloth back. Apparently this was the cheese we'd had the night before. Since it hadn't killed me yet, I closed the jar and slipped it into the basket.

Outside the door about fifty or so feet away I could

see the stone barbecue smoking away. Next to it was a wooden picnic table with the egg basket and some assorted vegetables, peppers, onions, tomatoes, a melon, plus a plate of melting butter, all atop a large wooden cutting board. On the barbecue, an old enameled dishpan sat atop a slate next to the fire grate. Behind it was a huge earthenware water jug with a spout at the bottom aimed over the edge. *Good Lord*, I thought, *so this is my kitchen*. Would I also need to go down to the lake and beat the dirty clothes on a rock? I set everything to the table, then ripped off a piece of baguette. I dipped it into the butter, my head fairly swimming from the infusion. I needed something to eat and quick. But first, the coffee. I lifted the tin pot.

I had a vague recollection of the enameled coffeepot that sat atop my grandmother's stove. Even though I was too young to drink from it, I couldn't forget the glorious scent it produced, even though I was pretty fuzzy on how she accomplished it. Now my coffee mostly came from someone else's carafe, but when I had made it in Richard's Technivorm Moccamaster, it was roughly a scoop and a cup of water for each serving. So I measured likewise into Andy's battered tin pot, setting it to the back of the fire grate. Next, the omelet. I hefted the cast-iron frying pan to the fire to let it heat up, knifing in butter. Then I washed the eggs the best I could from the water jug.

A bit of chopping and whisking later, I had enough veggies to toss into a six-egg omelet; all I needed as a bit of cheese. I opened the jar and upended it, the cloth-covered hunk sliding out. *Well, look at this.* I thought, *so this is where cheesecloth gets its name from!* I felt like I had discovered the secret to gravity. I shaved a bit off. Then, I dumped the vegetables into the pan and let them cook a bit before sliding in the eggs and sprinkling the cheese atop it.

While my omelet sizzled, I sliced the melon in two and deseeded it, recalling the casaba Andy and I had on our first and only date at the diner. That meeting seemed so innocent and ages ago, though it had only been five days, and it startled me a bit how intimate we'd become since then. But had we really? Did I know him any better? I almost laughed. Hardly any better that I knew myself. I looked to the coffeepot, now happily perking away. Who would have thought that of me a couple months earlier at the Daytime Emmy Awards, awash in Prada and walking the red carpet with Richard on my arm, his smile toothier than any of the plasticized people in attendance? I set a pair of plates on the picnic table and placed half a melon and half the baguette on each, with the cutlery atop the paper towels we'd use as napkins. I fingered one; quite a difference from the Bulgari scarf that had been in my swag bag at the Emmys.

I picked up the spatula and, holding my breath, folded the omelet; it complied perfectly. Eggs done, I shifted the pan to the slate, covering it with an extra plate. Then I poured an experimental sip of coffee and, tasting it, surprised myself. It wasn't half bad, so I filled it to the rim, then surprised myself again. I had no idea how Andy took his. Not that we had creamer anyway. With one look back at my first attempt at matrimonial domesticity, I went in search of my husband, his coffee in hand.

I had no idea where the generator was, but then again, he did mention he was going to shave. Since the only other sink I knew of was in the barn, I headed toward it. But just as I cleared the house, I spied him standing under a tree before a mirror, still shirtless, his face dappled with spots of soap, scraping something shiny against what looked like a long strap of leather. Once again a shiny object had transfixed me. Andy's back, the metal, the sun in my eyes, his muscled arms so rhythmic, all recalled a dozen old movies. Bucky, on his back at Andy's feet, saw me and flipped over with a bark.

Andy glanced over his shoulder, sunlight flashing off the dampened blade. "Oh, hello, wife." He nodded to the coffee. "Is that for me?"

As I stood there, fresh from cooking over an open fire, from showering under a barrel, from watching my bare-chested, vegetable-gathering, cow-birthing, woodchopping, 'coon-shooting husband strop a straight razor for his shave, a realization flooded me: this wasn't a farm. This was a detox from the twenty-first century.

"Yes," I said, going to him as Bucky shot past me.

"You're shaving with a straight razor under a tree," I stated the obvious. "Why? Did they run out of Bics at the Target?"

He took the coffee and after a sip, lifted my palm to his cheek. "Just feel that."

I gasped. It was cool and wet and—I slid my thumb

down his jaw—so smooth it nearly squeaked. "Andy! Like a baby's behind!"

"Learned from a merchant marine in Bremerhaven." He toweled his face, then slapped his cheeks with something out of a green bottle. "Nothing like those German blades," he said, snapping the razor closed. "Well, now, how goes it with breakfast?"

"Andy." I stood back. "I truly believe I've made the perfect omelet. And coffee and melon and maybe ..." I poked his stomach as he pulled his t-shirt over his head, "a few little surprises."

"Oh really?" he said, his arm slung over my shoulder as we walked to our *al fresco* dining room. "I can't wait." Then all at once his eyes narrowed. "Although I think I've figured out what the first surprise is."

I heard a clank of plate against metal, then looked to the barbecue just as Bucky jumped from it. "You little bastard!" I screeched, running toward him. The hellhound darted past me as my intended slap hit the air above him. When I got to my impromptu kitchen I found my perfect omelet mangled and half-eaten, the coffee pot on its side and hemorrhaging brew, the melons on the ground. I fell to a bench, whimpering.

"Don't worry, we'll make more," Andy said, squeezing my shoulder. "For what it's worth, your coffee was terrific. Now come on," he prodded me up by the elbows. "Practice makes perfect. And this time ..." He plopped onto a seat on the bench. "I want to watch—*hey!*"

I reached for another tomato. Holy cow, that man had good reflexes.

Chapter Ten

Wild Things

"SO HOW MUCH acreage comes with this place anyway?" I asked, closing the lid of the footlocker.

Andy banged one last nail into the gutter, dropping the hammer to the ground. "Oh, around six hundred, but most of it's wooded." He curled his hands under the aluminum and gave it a shake, testing for stability.

I leaned into the door jamb, smiling insularly; I truly believed I could watch his muscles flex all day. "Wow. Ever think of developing it?"

He looked at me as if I'd suddenly gone daft. "No. We've always come here to get away from people. Why would we want to bring more in?"

"Why would you want to own six hundred acres of woods?" I said, loping down the steps. "Seems kind of a waste."

"It's not waste if you leave the woods alone and let them go on doing what they'd do anyway without you." He tossed the hammer into an ancient wooden toolbox perched on the floor's overhang. "I think you'll understand a little better what I'm talking about after you actually have a look at it. Why don't you get ready?"

"This is about as ready as I'm going to get," I said, arms out at my sides, gesturing at my skirt, t-shirt, and sneakers.

"Hm." He eyed me. "I thought you were just dressing for breakfast."

"So maybe you're expecting black tie for dinner?"

His mouth crooked. "Hey, I don't care if you walk around naked as long as you're comfortable." And I believed he meant it. "I just figured you'd find jeans more appropriate for where we're going."

I thought of my hasty packing, and the fact I really didn't plan on staying much past the first frost. Not that I could tell him that. "I didn't bring any jeans."

"You didn't bring much of anything," he said ostensibly. "Not planning a very long visit?"

My hand flew to my chest. "Why would you say that!" *Because it's true?* I had to think fast. "How much do you think I could fit in a cab?"

He seemed to brush that off. "Then what did you do with the things you left?"

"There wasn't much," I said honestly. I'd never been much of a collector, always preferring to toss out the old for the new. My few things of value I shoved into two suitcases: original contract from the editor, a somewhat useless bankbook, my grandmother's emerald stud earrings, and enough clothes to last until the weather changed. "I left what household stuff I'd had with Richard, and my laptop, books and papers and the rest of my clothes with my friend, Denny."

He thought a moment. "The cameraman."

Then his gaze darkened. "*Richard*. That's your former fiancé, right?"

It was almost as if he were standing between us. "Yes."

"You leave anything with him you wish you'd taken?"

I felt like an insect pinned under a microscope. "Nothing I can't get later." *Say, around November.*

"So, nothing of particular importance."

I had to admit, "There was an antique tea table."

"Was it a family heirloom?"

"No." Richard had bought it for me during a trip to the Eastern shore of Maryland, back when we couldn't keep our hands off each other. I was ridiculously fond of it, and not for any particular reason connected to Richard, yet I felt a blush creep over me. "But I did like—"

"I'll buy you another one," he said quietly. "I'll buy you five more, if you want."

"That's not necessary," I said, taken aback. "I don't need you to buy me anything."

"Yet I would." He stared at me a moment before abruptly reaching for the toolbox. "Let me put this away. I'll be right back."

I watched him walk away, at a loss. What was *that* about? Was he actually jealous? Or was it something much more elemental? I didn't know, and at the moment I wasn't up to examining it. Not that he gave me much time to anyway. In short order he was striding toward me in heavy boots, the leather sheath on his belt unmistakably housing a large knife. Seeing that, my blood coursed a little hotter. Was it simply the Tarzanian implications, or had something fearful in me actually spiked? Either way, after the Rabid Raccoon Incident earlier that morning, I was happy he toted something that could inflict damage. Not that I relished the idea of his rolling around on the ground with some wild animal, but I set that image aside. His lordship and I were about to survey our dominion, and my stomach flipped with anticipation.

"Where first, Mr. Devine?" I said as he passed me, heading toward the back of the house.

He beckoned me to follow. "The kitchen garden, Mrs. Devine," he said, his smile an implication that whatever heaviness between us had eased. Funny how that ebbed and flowed; what was with him anyway? When we rounded the house I saw what twilight and a rim of bushes had obscured: at least a quarter acre of various crops, bursting past their obvious yield.

Andy stepped into a waist-high tomato patch, bright red-orange orbs dangling tenuously from their leafy vines. "Most of this garden isn't native to the area," he said, plucking an inordinately large beefsteak from within its wire cage. He rubbed it against his shirt. "Years ago, we had topsoil trucked in, as the soil's real sandy, which some crops like, mainly tomatoes." He bit into it before handing it to me. "We have your regular salad ones and some plums for sauce. Then there's cukes, eggplant, zucchini . . ." His finger bounced from crop to crop, pointing. "Lettuce, green beans, Brussels, carrots, potatoes, yams, radishes, onions, shallots, garlic, peppers . . ."

I took a bite of the tomato as he meandered through the rows, pushing aside lush overgrowth, the vegetables plump and ripe for picking. "And back there . . ." He flung his hand to a far corner of the patch, ". . . some sweet corn. And of course, an herb garden. Later on we'll get some winter vegetables, squash, pumpkin, cabbage, beets, cauliflower." He turned to look at me, eyeing me chewing tomato. "Good?"

I swiped my mouth and took another quick bite before handing it back. "Amazing," I said, meaning it. "So I expect we'll have some picking to do for the market tomorrow?"

He raised his palm to shade his eyes, looking past me. "In just a little bit. Before it gets too hot."

"Right," I said, already feeling the sweat collecting on my chest. I swatted at an encircling fly. "What time's the market tomorrow?"

"Crack of dawn—Bucky *come*!" he yelled, clapping his hands. I turned to follow his sightline: there was the hellhound, bounding toward us.

"Oh, why," I said, as the dog skittered to a barking halt before us. I bent to him. "I hate you, you canine catastrophe. Why don't you go terrorize some other farm?"

Andy dropped to his haunches to ruffle Bucky's fur as

the Border Collie licked his face. "You know, he really is a good dog."

"Every time you say that, he drops a new disaster on me. Perhaps I should have said '*He* hates me,' instead."

He scratched his fur a bit more then stood. "You know, my dad had him for three years before he died. From what Jinks told me, Bucky was his constant companion. I know he's acting a bit crazy now, but you think maybe it's because he's grieving? Do you think that's possible in a dog?"

I looked to Andy, the sun obscuring this big man before me. Instantly I imagined a boy running through the weeds, calling after his dad as his mother pulled him away. Growing up, my own family had always been around me, as constant as a hangnail. Yet as dismissive as we were to each other now, we had remained intact, touchstones of each other's collective memory. Maybe I couldn't possibly understand.

I touched his arm. "I'm sorry, Andy. Really, I am."

He looked down, his stance widening, as if covering more ground would make him appear too large, too overpowering for anything as elemental as grief. "For what?" he said, quietly gruff.

I slipped my arms around his waist, my head against the moist warmth of his chest, realizing perhaps he mourned more for the lost possibilities than for the actual man. He sighed, his chin brushing against my temple, and all at once the scents of the garden swirled around me,

"For nothing," I said.

He kissed my hair as something definitely furry slipped between our legs, sitting atop my feet. "Which will get you everything," he said.

PEOPLE WHO LIVE in cities are used to walking. Most often, it's simply easier to take to the sidewalk than to hail a cab or run after a bus or catch the subway. But that morning I had not only done more walking than I had attempted in weeks on a treadmill, I had walked with significantly more purpose: over creeks, up hillocks, down gullies, across savannahs, and through more trees and shrubs and wildlife than this urbanite has ever encountered out of an arboretum. In fact, we had covered so much sandy trail I was certain we'd walked every inch of Andy's six hundred acres until he casually informed me, two hours later, we had barely covered half of it.

"Next time we'll take the truck," he said as I teetered across a fallen tree over a stream.

"Thanks," I said, falling in.

But not before he'd taken me to his peach grove, forty short-trunked trees laid out in neat rows of five, the sandy road in between well-rutted from years of picking. Andy plucked one of the few that remained among the long leaves, branches he said were once laden with so much fruit they half-bent to the ground under the weight.

"Taste," Andy had said, taking a chomp out of a particularly monstrous one before holding it out for me.

I bit into it, succulent juice bleeding down his fingers and my chin, my mouth bursting with intense flavor. "Oh

God that's good . . ." I groaned, pulling his dripping hand back for another messy bite.

"This is what I call a leaner," he said, chomping more, spitting out the stone. "They're so juicy you have to lean over the sink."

"Cute," I said, snatching the last of it. "I'd be interested to know what you'd call a nice, dry Beaujolais."

He bent into me, licking a bit of juice from my lip. "With that, a piece of cheese, a loaf of bread and you . . . I'd call it dinner." He growled and I shivered. "*Délicieux.*"

As we skimmed the edge of the woods Andy pointed out another smaller grove of apple trees, and I suddenly thought it funny that in all the years I had driven through the Pines, I never imagined myself actually in them. They'd always been just an inert green corridor funneling me toward the Shore. As we crept past a herd of slumbering deer, hunkered down behind a wall of tangled vines and shrubs, I felt like a character in someone's documentary. Especially when we came across an expanse of squarish acre-wide trenches of red-tinged vines, each bordered by two-foot moats, with a large pond at the end in the distance.

"What's this?" I asked.

"Those . . ." he said, as if lost in memory. "They're cranberry bogs."

I fell to my haunches, peering into a trench, millions of red berries crowding each other. "So this is where cosmopolitans start. Are they yours?"

"No," he said, nearly laughing. "Cranberries were always beyond the scope of my family's ambitions. Remember the friend I mentioned, Ray?"

"You mean Ranger Rick?"

"I mean Ray who works for the Forest Fire Service."

"Right." I rose, looking across the expanse. I couldn't tell how much land the bogs encompassed. But it certainly looked like a football stadium and maybe even a bit of the parking lot would fit into it. "They're his?"

"His family's. Wait until you see this place next month. Nothing but a sea of red when they flood the bogs. It's a gorgeous sight."

It was one I knew I'd be around for. "Sounds awesome."

There was more, I'd soon find out, not that it didn't take us a bit more walking. We passed through more of the pitch-pined forest, the underbrush so sparse in places that dead needles were the only other thing crunching under our feet—before gnarly vines and laurel bushes took over. A bit more walking and then it opened up again to the ten-foot-high bushes of Andy's blueberry patch. Which was where I fell into the stream.

"I can't believe how much time I've spent getting soaked," I said as I sloshed to the streambank, splashed to the knees. "It's a good thing it's not freezing out or I'd be a Popsicle by now."

He smiled, pulling me to in. "I can't remember the last time I saw anything iced over . . . must have been five or six years now."

"Really?" I said, squishing my sneakers against a rock. "So where does Andy Devine winter?"

"Last year, Belize," he said, turning toward a blueberry bush. He stripped a few withered berries from a branch. "Too bad these are all gone. I picked the last of them right after I got here. Next June, unless the weather is terrible, we ought to get a pretty good crop out of them."

"Were you there all winter?" I said, flicking what remained of a bell-shaped bloom, now gone papery. "In Belize, I mean."

He flicked a few dead leaves from the bush. "For a healthy portion of it, I guess." He looked around. "Well, we've come full-circle. This stream feeds the lake by the house. See? There it is, past the bushes."

It was supremely interesting how Andy tossed out interesting asides about his nomadic lifestyle while actually telling me nothing. Then again, maybe he did. So far I learned he was a sort of a sailor, but the kind who could while away the winter in a tropical paradise? I came up beside him, sniffing a leaf. "You spent the winter in port?" I idly asked. "You don't sound much like a sailor to me."

He looked at me, eyebrow cocked. "And you're a TV reporter who doesn't even have a TV. I'd say we're both a little out of context."

I coughed; a perfect deflection. Good Lord, he was a master. And continually fascinating, I had to admit. I took a few squishy steps into the blueberry patch, aiming toward the house. "Come on, dear, I need to change my shoes and slip into a wetsuit. Would you like to help?"

"Only if I could talk you out of it," he said, pinching me into a squeal.

I SLOUGHED MY sundress to the bathroom floor and stared at my garden-abused body. We had picked I-don't-know-how-many pecks of tomatoes, cucumbers, zucchinis, green beans, and whatever else that was exploding in that ungodly fertile patch of earth, leaving me with a rash, a sunburn, and more bug bites than I could count—a veritable itching, scratching, burning trifecta of pain.

"Oww ..." I groaned, slipping a bra strap over my reddened shoulder, the contrast of my skin achingly apparent.

"Didn't I tell you to wear a shirt with long sleeves?" Andy asked me, unhooking me from behind. "Didn't I offer to rub you down with repellant?"

"But we were in the shade—*ooh*," I said, wincing as his hand brushed the baked skin leading up to my neck. Good thing I had worn a wide-brimmed hat while picking, or I don't think I would've have been able to turn my neck. "And how much sense does it make to slather olive oil on in the sun?"

"Eucalyptus in olive oil is a natural bug repellant." He held out his arms. "Look—not one bite. If you had covered up you wouldn't have gotten burned or bitten at all."

I tossed my bra to the corner. "I didn't think—"

"No, you didn't," he said, turning to the tub to twist the taps. "Get in the tub. I'll be right back."

"Yes sir," I said, kicking my dress away. Strange how he took such an authoritative tone with me. Maybe because the mirror was the only thing Richard had ever reigned supreme over. Maybe because it wasn't in my DNA to let someone take care of me on such a visceral level. Either way, at the moment, it felt good. I stepped out of my underwear and tested the quickly-filling tub, blissfully cool to my scraped fingers. A second later, Andy entered with a large, steaming pot. His gaze flicked over me.

"Turn it off," he said, a bit thickly, "and get in."

As I lowered my heated body it reacted as if I were sinking into the Arctic and I hissed, recoiling a bit as I clipped my disheveled hair atop my head. "Cold!" I said, shivering, even though the ceiling fan spun overhead, chopping the humid air with a languid thrum.

"Move your feet," Andy said as he tipped the pot over the tub, blackened water and teabags plopping out.

"Tea?" I said, instinctively kicking at the pods, churning the water brown. The couple of dozen or so bags bobbed around me as I slipped into the water up to my neck. "What's it supposed to do?"

"The tannins in the tea draw the burn out—here." He scooped up a few tea bags and molded them to my shoulders. Almost instantly, I could feel the pain easing.

"Aaaahh . . ." I said, my eyes fluttering in relief. "You're a genius, you know that?"

"Just an old sailor's remedy," he said, sitting on the edge of the tub. We idled there for a few minutes, saying nothing, Andy paddling the water with his fingers as it darkened obligingly. I closed my eyes, nearly dozing until Andy abruptly stood up. "I left some aloe for your bites on the sink."

"Why?" Was he leaving? "Where are you going?"

"I have to take that raccoon carcass to the police station so they can get it tested for rabies, so I'll—"

"Wait," I said, suddenly wanting him to stay very badly. A bit of pre-guilt, maybe, for the little deception

I'd commit while he was gone. "I . . . have a bite on my ankle I can't reach."

He sunk back to the edge of the tub, his hand skimming the water. "Where?"

I lifted my right leg, tea-water raining, exposing a particularly nasty greenhead chomp right above the anklebone. "There," I said, waggling my foot, causing the water to ripple back and forth against my breasts. He cupped his hand under my leg and scratched at it; it felt so good I nearly purred.

He set my foot back into the water, his gaze caressing me. "You know, no matter what I put you through, you never look anything less than perfect."

My goodness, the last thing I needed was another burn ripping through me. I pulled myself up, teabags plopping into the water as I leaned into him and curled my arm around his neck. "I'm just your poor comparison."

"No. Never." Andy's arm slipped into the water and he kissed me, my chest soaking the front of his shirt as he pulled me from the water. His kiss felt subtly contemplative, as if each pass of his lips was a study in exactly how to please me.

But I was after something more. I unzipped his fly and slid my hands into his jeans, sliding them down the smooth slope of his ass.

"Christ . . ." he said, deep and throaty as he yanked me from the tub and set me atop the sink. He opened my still-streaming thighs and drove himself in.

"*Ma femme*," he said softly.

"*Mon mari*," I answered, to his apparent surprise.

When he kissed me I could tell he was smiling, which let me tell you, only made me feel worse.

I WAS GETTING vegetables anyway. Which was how I'd justify snooping behind Andy's back. I dressed quickly and, grabbing a basket, hurried out to the barn. When I got there I perched on an overturned bucket and, pushing aside the coffee cans, came face-to-face with a satellite phone.

The reporters in my newsroom would use them when they'd go overseas, and Richard, of course, had to have one. I turned it over and back, knowing this particular one was state-of-the-art, probably worth at least a couple thousand dollars, leather-encased, water and dust resistant, and capable of reaching across continents. In the private world it was a rich man's toy, something I'm pretty sure Andy's dad didn't qualify for.

But what if it wasn't his; what if it was Andy's? This would explain why he didn't carry a cell phone. So why would he need this? And why in the world would he hide it from me?

"Julie?"

I jumped, teetering on the bucket until I landed hard on one leg. "Ow! Uh—

Andy!" I cried, the phone to my chest. "What are—"

"I forgot to bring tomatoes for Jinks," he said, staring at the phone he'd caught me with, red-handed. "Seems I kind of got distracted before I left."

I coughed. "Yeah, well, uh . . ." I straightened my skirt. "I was going—"

"My father's phone," he said, glancing from it to me. "I see you found it."

"No! I was just looking—" I sighed. "I'm afraid I'm not a very good liar. I got a glimpse of it this morning while getting Betsy's feed, but I didn't have time to look at it then."

"So you waited until I left to look at it now," he said, matter-of-factly.

"Yes—*no!*" I took exception. "You're acting like I'm lying to you."

"Are you?"

"Are *you?*" I countered, irked. I shoved the phone at him. "The cat's out of the bag—you have a sat phone. Big freaking deal." I brushed past him.

"Julie . . ." he said, catching my hand.

I turned, glaring.

He set the phone on a table. "I sent him the phone a year ago after Jinks wrote to me saying my father'd been diagnosed with liver cancer. Jinks had been trying to convince him to move to town, but he wouldn't budge. Since there's no service out here, I sent him this phone so he could call for help if he needed it."

"Really? He needed a two thousand dollar Iridium phone, capable of calling around the world, to reach five miles into town?"

Andy exhaled, shaking his head. "No. But I had the vague hope maybe he'd also use it to call his son at sea." He picked up the phone, staring at it. "I was wrong."

I wanted to dive back into the lake. "Oh, Andy. Now I get why you married me for my body. You certainly didn't do it for my brains." I brushed my hand down his arm. "I'm so sorry for being an ass. I should've figured."

"And I should've told you. Especially with no service out here, you'd need it in an emergency. I just wasn't thinking. Here." He handed it to me. "I'll have it installed in the house."

I looked to the wall; the charging station, though unplugged, was already set up. "No. It's fine out here. At least we know where it is."

He set it into the cradle, grasping me by my shoulders. "Forgive me?"

I laughed. "You're joking, right? I'm such an idiot I'm surprised you're not already looking for an annulment."

He took me in his arms, kissing my forehead. "Hmm . . . well, I think there'd be a slight issue concerning the consummation . . ."

Chapter Eleven

The Price of Infamy

1 September

The sun's barely up, and I've been awake and running around since four AM, putting into practice what I learned from my boots-on-the-ground tutorial on farmwifery yesterday. I've already fed the chickens and gathered their eggs, fed Betsy and her calf and led her out to pasture, picked more lettuce and tomatoes, as well as yanked out some rather persistent weedage from the herb garden I weeded just the day before. (Andy's "herb garden" is a continent away from the potted mint I had kept on our sink for Mojitos). While I did this, Andy hauled vegetables to the truck, as we're selling them at a farm market today, something we'll do for every Thursday through at least October, or as long as the vegetables hold out. This was after spending the previous day picking, separating, sorting and crating them (and getting my shoulders scorched, shame on me), and after Andy introduced me to a particularly vile concoction of manure, gypsum and food scraps known as a compost. Thank God, this will be something he'll take care of, at least at this stage, as it seems we'll be growing mushrooms in it, and the compost has to be turned with a pitchfork by hand. Since it's nearly ready, he hopes to move the process to the pasteurization stage by next week. I have no idea what that entails, but I'm figuring it has something to do with the nicest structure on the farm, a spotless, temperature-controlled shed next to the barn, which seems just the perfect place to cultivate a food grown in horseshit.

Like me, Andy's flying by the seat of his pants, and the thing I'd like to know is why. The more time I spend with him, the more I can see that although he seems accustomed to a bit of ruggedness, there's a definite worldliness about him that belies all this earthiness. For someone who's lived abroad and on the high seas, it just doesn't make sense why he'd want to hunker down on a farm in the woods. But that's what I'm here to find out, not that it's easy—I swear the man could win medals for caginess. I figure it has something to do with his parents, something he rarely talks about, perhaps when he moved with his mother to France, and the circumstances that led them to go there in the first place. I couldn't help but shake my head, thinking of the numerous ways that parents screw up their kids. At this point, I can't even judge how well he's done for himself, as I really have nothing to gauge him against. He's so tight-lipped about his past. Not like I'm not trying to wheedle it out of him.

Still, in spite of all my intentions and subterfuge, I can't help feeling like I've drawn the short straw. Here I am, hardly two days married, and who'd have ever thought I'd be feeding chickens and cows, aching in places I never knew existed, and sunburnt not from falling asleep outside the cabana, but from picking peppers and tomatoes? Gone are my civilized TV star pretentions: pedicure, facial, manicure, silk sheath, and Ferragamos, stripped by nature and all her basic imperatives. Who needs a good mineral salts scrub when my blooming calluses are so much more apropos?

But enough whining. It's time to get out of this bathroom and go rustle up some breakfast. More fruit and cheese, I'm suspecting, and right now I'd kill for a cup of joe. So I'm off to rub two sticks together and get the fire started. Ah, wilderness.

I FELT LIKE I was cheating on my husband.

Andy dropped off eggs for Uncle Jinks while I waited in the gas station's parking lot inside a truck packed with more of the same. I took out my phone and, finally getting service, texted Denny:

Hey wanted to let you know I'm ok out here in the stix!

Half a minute later I got back: *THK GOD! how r u? fukit im callin.*

Two seconds later my phone rang. "Christ, Jules, why haven't you called!"

Damn, it was good hearing Denny's voice. "I wanted to, but there's no service out at Andy's place. Plus I get the distinct impression he doesn't like cell phones." There wasn't any way I could explain it that would translate, especially after the sat phone incident the day before.

"Why? He doesn't have you chained in the basement or anything, does he?"

"As far as I know, he doesn't have a basement."

"Exactly where did he drag you off to?"

Good question. "Hard to say. It's out in the middle of the woods. If you need to get ahold of me you could always leave a message on my phone, and I'll pick it when I come into town. Or if it's really important call that gas station number I gave you. Uncle Jinks will give us the message."

"Uncle Jinks? Sound like a friggin' cartoon character. Why don't you just say to stop in Western Union and send a telegram? Or maybe get a homing pigeon and strap a message on its ass?"

"Denny, honestly, I'm fine. Andy has been more than . . ." I searched for the right word. ". . . *accommodating.*"

"Ohhh, now I've got it. You've just been too busy getting on it to call. I should've figured. After two years with that limpdick it's like leaving the convent. And what a dick he actually is. Wait'll I tell you what I heard."

A door slammed; Andy was coming. "Oh damn—look, I got to go. You take care, and I promise to stay in touch."

"Jules—what a minute—"

"Bye!" I rang off just as Andy opened the door.

He eyed the phone in my hand. "Letting them know you're still alive?"

"I was just telling Denny where to find the body." Damn; I was down to one bar. I dug into my purse for the changer. "Hey, you wouldn't mind if I charged my phone, would you?"

"Why would I mind?" He eyed me curiously. "And why would you have to ask?"

"Well . . ." I shrugged. "I know how you feel about phones."

"And how's that?" he said, starting the truck.

I tried for diplomacy. "That they're non-essentials. That you'd rather I didn't use mine."

"Really." He seemed amused. "Have I ever said that?"

"Actually . . . no. But it's the vibe I got."

"*Vibe.*" He pondered that a moment before he looked at me. "Julie, whichever way I feel, it applies to me, not to you. If you feel the need to stay connected with your people—for lack of a better descriptor—*back home*, go ahead. As for me . . ." He leaned over and, brushing his lips against my neck, whispered, "You're all I need."

I'd like to have melted into the seat. I dropped the phone back into my purse, my hand on his rock-hard thigh. "Well, when you put it *that* way . . ." I gave it a little squeeze. "Perhaps I'll worry about it later."

He gifted me with the barest of flinches. "The least of your worries, I'm sure."

Shameless, he was, giving me a look that smoldered. "So, how's Uncle Jinks?" I said, godawfully steady for someone ready to rip her clothes off.

Andy raked his hand through his hair. "Just fine. He says he has a surprise for us, a wedding present, but we won't get it until next week."

"Really? Did he say what it was?"

"Now what kind of surprise would it be if he had?" he said, pulling from the lot. "He did say it's supposed to be delivered next Friday."

"Hmm . . . *delivered*. Sounds big."

"Well, you'll have a week to speculate," he said as we drove out of town.

Which didn't take long. Iron Bog was no metropolis. We entered again into thick woods, the Pines enclosing us in dissipating early morning cool. I could tell it was going to be another hot one, but with Labor Day Weekend nearly upon us, I knew days like this wouldn't last for long. Not that in this pre-air conditioned world, I would mourn the sweat already collecting on my chest. Still, the breeze felt good through the opened windows, whipping my haphazardly clipped hair against my neck, the air currents ruffling my skirt. I put a hand to my thigh, staying the cotton from riding higher.

Andy's hand closed over it. "You look very pretty today," he said, squeezing my fingers. "But then I haven't noticed a day when you didn't."

I almost laughed. "Sunburnt, no make-up, hair a

wreck, covered in bites and starting to sweat—you sir, haven't the highest of standards."

"Beauty in the raw." He lifted my hand to his lips and kissed it. "I prefer it in its most unadulterated form. Plus . . ." His hand slid to my skirt, lightly skimming my inner thigh. "I know what lies beneath."

I shivered—trying to ignore the unintended metaphor. Better to focus on where his implication would trail to later. I caught his hand, lightly shuttling it away. "Down, boy—don't drive us off the road. And by the way, just where is this farm market?"

He flashed a portentous smile, so effortlessly sensual it was a wonder I didn't swoon. "On Route 70. A big market with lots of different farmers, where you rent a table by the day. My father had always gone on Thursdays, so they saved the same spot and day for him every week, and now for us. You'd think with the Shore traffic he would've gone more than one day, but . . ." He shrugged. "Guess it cut in on his drinking time."

"You say that so easily," I said, "but it's got to hurt."

He shrugged again. "Nothing I can do about it now. Anyway, it's a pretty busy market, even without the holiday Shore traffic, so we ought to do all right. Did so last week, at least."

Such a master at changing the subject, I once again noticed. So I would, too. "Anybody there you know?"

"A few, and the rest I've heard of. Ray should be there."

"The Fire warden." His mouth crooked. "Yeah, him. Selling the last of the blueberries, I guess. Plus his wife makes these incredible pies and jam. You'll like her. Celia's her name."

"Really." Visions of Ma Kettle danced in my head. "Maybe we could pull up the rocking chairs and swap recipes just like good farmers' wives."

Andy sniffed. "Maybe you could swap marketing strategies. 'Celia's Blues' has an output of eight hundred pies a day, and during harvest season her jamming operation takes on thirty employees."

I was properly chastised. "Well, spank *me*. Sorry for being so small-minded."

"Everyone's allowed a lapse now and then," he said, slowing for a light. "Never thought perfection was easy to maintain."

"You're too, too kind," I said. Not to mention a serial evader. I thought to give it another go. "Did you and Ray go to school together?"

"Sure, back in the Dark Ages. Practically grew up as brothers."

"Really. I supposed you missed him after you and your mother went to France."

"Yeah, I did." At that he winced. "We wrote each other for a while, then lost touch. Though he did come over one summer while we were in college to go hiking in the Pyrenees."

"You nature boys you. Can't keep you out of the woods, huh?"

"Oh, I didn't go. I was working and couldn't get away. Though he did stay with my mother a couple of days. Now, him, she liked."

"She didn't like any of your other friends?"

"Let's just say she had a thing about Americans in general."

"Yet she had married one." *Interesting.* "You know, I've heard so much about the weeks and weeks of vacation Europeans get, yet you weren't allowed a couple days off for a friend you hadn't seen since you were kids? That seems kind of harsh."

"Nothing I could do about it. I was at sea." He looked up ahead. "Hey—there's a Wawa. How about some coffee?"

A rhetorical question; he was already turning in. "Sure."

Evading again, but wasn't that just so like him. And realizing that made it odder still. As I waited while Andy ran in the convenience store, I couldn't help thinking how strange it was seeing him in so workaday a setting. Seeing him filling two cups with coffee, paying the cashier, scanning the headlines on the newspaper rack, holding the door opened for a woman with a stroller. So much more routine than see him birthing a cow or bringing down a rabid raccoon, crossing through his peach orchard or cutting a naked swath through the lake. I couldn't help marveling, in the few days I've known my husband, how fast the outsized had become mundane, and how even ordinary actions became fresh and mysterious and inordinately fascinating. When he came back to the truck and handed me a coffee, his fingers brushing mine, the memory of the night before returned in such a rush I was almost ashamed how much I wanted him. *How strange is that?* this wave of lust, this immediate craving I didn't know what to do with. Funnier still how I caught his gaze as we pulled back onto the road, and his eyes widened ever so slightly, almost as if he completely understood. Truth was he did, because all at once he veered off onto a smaller road, then onto one of the hundreds of sandy trails etching the Pines, traveling far enough to veer again into a clearing and behind an old shed, where he stopped and opening my door, pulled me into his arms.

"We *are* thinking the same thing," I whispered, baring my neck so he could kiss it. "How is it you could read my mind?"

"Like species seek out their own," he said, slipping my panties from me, opening his fly. I gripped his shoulders as he lifted me up.

I gasped like I always did. Yet with him inside me it seemed so natural. "Are you saying I'm just like you?"

"Yes," he said. *"Yes."* He gripped the rail of the truck bay and held me against it, my hand fisting a knot of his hair. I arched my back, pulling him in as his fingers dug into my hip, hoping he'd fall further and deeper inside me. Then I couldn't think anymore, my body alive and my mind spiraling, just as his was I'm sure, feeling his thrum inside me.

Later, our fingers curled around each other's as we set off down the road, not saying anything at first, just holding on, maybe a bit too tightly. After a few miles I sighed and lay my head against his shoulder, and we returned to our coffee, sipping it companionably. At a light he kissed my temple.

"You're good for me," he murmured.

That took me by surprise. Was I supposed to say something? I couldn't think of an answer. Then the light changed and we went on down the road.

Good as contrast to what? *For him to know*, a little voice said, *and for me to find out.*

THE FARMERS' MARKET was a joint venture of several local farms, and was comprised of a couple dozen long tables that carried any assortment of goods—grown, baked, bottled and sewn. Situated in a shady spot off busy Route 70, a popular Shore road in one direction, and toward Philadelphia on the other, it was barely six-thirty by the time we found our table under the umbrella of a big oak and proceeded to set up. The market also had a snack bar and frozen custard stand (and happily, a bath-room), so I was looking forward to lunching on some-thing beyond Andy's farm fare, even if it had to be a hot dog. Shortly after we hauled the last flat of tomatoes to the table another truck, this one all polished chrome and red paint, angled into the spot beside us.

"Andy!" a man called from the window of it.

A little while later I clasped hands with Ray, a tall, lithe cording of tan and muscle in a Fire Service uniform, and his blonde wife, Celia, so svelte and sophisticated I wondered if she just drove in from the Main Line.

"So this is the new Mrs. Devine," Ray said, his friendly gaze raking me. "No one could accuse Andy of dragging his feet." He gave my hand a hearty shake.

"Or settling for the girl next door," said Celia, placing her cheek to mine. "Welcome, Ms. Random Access." She leaned back, eyeing me inquisitively. "So, you didn't chase him out West after all?"

A chill shot down my spine. "What do you mean?"

"Sweetie, you're the talk of the town," she said, briefly turning to two workers unloading pies and preserves out of their truck, setting them atop a check-covered tablecloth trumpeting: *Celia's Blues*. "My sister does mornings for Prowler Traffic—maybe you heard of her? Barbie Coyle?"

Does mornings was apt. No one could banter double entendre with the deejays better than Barbie "Doll" Coyle, or "Bouncin' Barbie," as Richard had referred to her. I recalled the night we watched her strip off her bra atop the bar at a Delaware Avenue club. Of course, the next day he signed her.

But that hardly mattered at the moment. "Why? Did she say something about me?"

Andy shot me a warning look as she shuttled me aside. "The dish is your fiancé went back to his wife—you know, the one you stole him from?"

"*What?*" I cried. "He was never married. Where'd she hear that from?"

Her face screwed. "How long have you been off the grid?" She pulled out her phone and, tapping an app, brought up *phillyak*, a gutter gossip site Richard loved to troll. "Look at what Jake the Snake said yesterday."

I took it from her, aghast: *Where in the wide, wide world of sports is JK? How random is it if she left P-town for the Left Coast, to once again wrench the regal R from the arms of his once and future wife?*

"Jesus Christ," I said, handing it back, barely able to breathe. "It's so not true. It's just *gossip*."

"But that hardly matters now, does it?"

"Of course it does!" A few people looked in our direction, and we ducked behind the nearby frozen custard shack, an overhead cooling vent drowning extraneous conversation. "You have any idea what this'll do to my professional reputation?"

"And that should matter now because . . .?" She raised a tentative brow. "Didn't you give that all up when you married Andy?"

"Yes, of course, b-but—" Good Lord, I was practically sputtering. "But I never meant—"

"To give it all up forever? Hey sister, I hear you. No one knows that better than me." She glanced to her husband, enmeshed in conversation with Andy. It was a glance filled with resignation, and I actually felt for her, especially since I knew it was a portent that'd never apply to me.

"Look," she continued, "I spent years in public relations. Sometimes it makes no difference if it's true or not, and denying it only makes the lies more real. But you're in a good place now. Obviously your Richard's a shit, and well worth getting out of your life, but if you have to bide your time until it all blows over?" She placed a hand on my arm and dropped her gaze dramatically. "Honey, I could think of worse men to bide time with than Andy."

I couldn't speak; I was absolutely comatose. When

would it stop? This damage Richard had wrought. How much of a mess would he have to make of my life until his demolition of me was complete? Married? Had he been? Why hadn't he ever told me? It made so much more sense now, how he couldn't ever break his hold on Annika. All at once my head was splitting. I looked beyond the farm stand, wanting to bury myself deep in the woods where no one would ever find me. And then it hit me: *wasn't that what I was already doing?*

"Uh-oh, look there," Celia said, pointing to the two buses pulling into the parking lot. "Here come two busloads of little old ladies with lots of daughters to buy jam for. And who all need peaches to help them poop tomorrow morning." She tugged my arm. "Come on, let's get to work. There's Social Security dollars to be snatched out of those pocketbooks."

So I went. The rest of the day went by in a flurry of fruits, vegetables, and lots of sweat and car exhaust, and since I was still in the metro-Philadelphia viewing area, I had donned a big straw hat and sunglasses to keep my recognition down to a minimum. Although Andy's eyes were questioning, we never had the time to talk beyond some pretty utilitarian conversation. Then late in the afternoon, I headed to the bathroom and, taking out my phone, trolled the local news sites until my one bar faded away and my irritation level kicked up to four.

Both Richard and Annika were keeping mum about the marriage thing, but that didn't stop the gossip mavens from getting to the bottom of it. One had unearthed the six-year-old Maryland marriage license from which Richard and Annika had been married, when Annika was barely eighteen. Three weeks later, her parents had had it annulled. I blew up the image and nearly fell to my knees: it was the same signature I had seen gracing his cards, our checks, my contract. Then another site said they had never divorced and he was still married, leading to another headline that painted him a potential bigamist, which of course, had me looking the perfect fool. What kind of journalist could I be if I couldn't even get the dirt on my own life?

The "official" story the station was floating was that I had left on sabbatical, saving them the embarrassment of admitting they had kicked me out first. Other sources said I was in Seattle chasing down Richard, while an anonymous source said my bank account had been frozen by my former fiancé, leaving me homeless and penniless. (Gee, I wonder who *that* was?) All of this seemed to attract either sympathy or scorn, depending on whether one backed Team Richard or Team Julie, but one thing was certain. The general consensus was I had left my faithful viewership high and dry, and that was an offense past forgiveness. The whole thing made me so ill I came *this close* to tossing the BlackBerry in the trash. Turned out I didn't have to when it died. As I came out of the bathroom there was Andy, waiting for me.

"Ready to go home?" he said.

"They hate me," I said, trudging past him to slump atop a picnic table.

"Who?"

I waved my phone in futility. "All of Philadelphia, it seems."

He fell to his haunches before me. "Are you in Philadelphia now?"

"No," I said, glaring at him. "But it also encompasses South Jersey and all of Delaware, and if you're streaming, then maybe worldwide, too." I laughed. "Every news site has me either as a victim or an idiot, and I have to tell you, neither is very flattering. I dropped my head to my hands. "Julie Knott's Random Access is now Julie Knott—Random *Ass*."

He sighed. A moment later my hands were in his. "Or how about something else? It's yours if you want it." He lifted my chin. "How about Mrs. Andy Devine?"

Somehow a tear had weaseled its way down my face, and I swiped it away. "Yeah, there is that."

"Julie, I told you I'd never let anything happen to you, that I'd always take care of you. Do you believe me?"

On some fantasy level, I did. "Of course."

"Then who cares what they think, what they're saying? That was then, and what we have here . . ." He kissed my hand. "Is now."

He was right, of course. And deep down, I knew that someday I'd prove them all wrong. But to do that then, I had to do *this* now. I snuffled away another tear. "Then get me out of here."

He rose with me. "The truck is packed. Let's go home."

And for now, I did.

Chapter Twelve

Lesser Homes & Gardens

So I RETREATED to the woods, to hide and to heal, and to make a temporary go at this happy home thing. I desperately needed to keep from dwelling on my imploding life and keep my eyes on the prize; I had work to do, after all. And although Andy was generally the best diversion a girl could ever hope for, there was still the ghetto rest of our house, which we absolutely had to do something about and fast. I could put up with the rusty barrels, a broken-down tractor, rotting lumber, and other assorted remains from the estate's glory days, but neither of us could abide a living room that'd bring on an asthma attack every time we entered it, and I was really tired of eating cold or off the grill every day. What I wouldn't give for baked chicken or a mango smoothie, not that I could get either until a refrigerator and a working stove materialized. Until then it'd take a lot of hefting and hauling, some twelve-hour days, and of course, a forty-yard Dumpster.

"Rocky's going, right?" I said, covering my nose as the front door swung open, the taxidermied raccoon wavering from the ceiling, where it hung upside-down. I recoiled from its malevolent, glassy-eyed glare. "Somehow this place attracts bad raccoon karma, and the sooner he's gone the better."

"No shit," Andy said, his gloved hands yanking it down. "I'll bury it in the woods." Bucky followed, barking his head off all the way. I imagined he thought he cornered another of its rabid peeps, and no way was he letting this one go without a fight.

While Andy attended to Rocky's internment, I took a few ginger steps into the living room. Andy had already ripped down the ratty curtains and dropped a sheet of plywood over the spot in the floor I had fallen through, but I wasn't taking any chances. Although he had also removed most of the piles of various crap, he'd left me to decide which of the dozens of pieces of furniture in this much-abused room we'd keep. One thing it did have going for it, beside a gorgeous stone fireplace, was its wealth of windows, and I threw open every one of them on my way to the kitchen at the back.

Again, lots of windows, and like the rest of the house, full of junk. But at least it was sunny and there was, much to my surprise, another bathroom off to the side, with not only a sink and a toilet, but a washer and dryer. A serviceable utility closet lay just outside it, and along the back wall, a gas stove, a stainless steel sink, and a long countertop that bent with the wall to end at a space for a refrigerator. Opposite the closet sat what looked a sturdy wooden table, chairs, and a hutch. At least that's what I could see under piles and piles of newspapers, old mail, flattened food boxes and, in a plastic milk crate, innumerable bottles of pills and vitamins. Then, underneath it all, I found a photo.

It was in color, but severely faded, so I took it to the window for a better look. What I saw was an elegant man dressed in a white blazer and a stunning woman, sitting at a table in most likely a café. Spent mussel shells lay on a plate at her elbow, a cocktail glass and cigarette in her fingers. And even with the aged fading, her eyes, cat-like and decidedly wary, shone a vibrant blue.

She had to be Andy's mother. I turned the photograph over. *Viviane Fontaine* was typed on the back. *Marseille-1983. Typed.* How very odd.

"Where'd you find that?" Andy said over my shoulder, an unreadable expression on his face.

"In this pile of junk. Is that your mother?"

He set down the wheelbarrow he'd brought in for the trash, taking the photo from me. He turned it over and back. "Yes."

He seemed transfixed; who wouldn't be? She was to rampant femininity what her stallion of a son was to male prowess. "She's gorgeous."

"She still is," he said dryly. "My mother's looks are simply part of her toolbox. As essential to what she does as a camera used to be to you."

"I take it that's not much of a compliment."

He sniffed. "Take it as you want. It's simply a statement of fact." He flipped the photo to the counter.

"Who's the guy? Your dad?"

"No," he said flatly.

I took another look at the man; where Andy was raw masculinity polished at the edges, this man appeared the bon vivant, a hipster Mr. Smoothie perennially popular with the ladies. Much, it irked me to think, like Richard.

"Is he the ship's captain?"

He peered at me, almost as if he were loath to say. "Right. The ship's captain."

"Do you want to tell me about it? Like, how they met?"

"They met in a bar. She met my father in a bar. Actually, it's pretty commonplace. I've met a few ladies in bars myself." When he finished with the table, he pushed the wheelbarrow to the counter, tilting it up to scoop more papers into it. I snatched the photo from him just in time.

"But did you ever think *I* might want to find out a little more about the family I married into? I think I have a right to know where you came from."

That got his attention. He set the wheelbarrow down and looked at me. "What do you want to know?"

"How should I know? Every time I ask about your family you're either vague or you change the subject."

"Maybe because I don't find them as fascinating as you do." His eyes narrowed. "Or as interesting a topic for your book."

"Sorry to disappoint you, but the book is supposed to be about *my* experience, not about your crazy family."

"And what would that experience be without me?"

"What a colossal ego! If I didn't know better I'd say you set this whole mess up for plot!"

He stretched his arm across the doorway. "But you *don't* know better, do you? And if it's not about my family, then why do you keep asking about them?"

"Are you saying I have an ulterior motive?"

"I don't know." He leaned in. "Do you?"

Damn; I didn't have a logical thing to answer with beside a frustrated, *"Ooooh!"* I shoved an armful of junk mail into the barrow.

After a few moments of this he intercepted. "Julie, stop," he said, his hand staying my arm. "Stop—listen to me."

"What?" I said, shooting him my iciest glare.

He pulled me to him and I hardly resisted, the warmth of his chest like some burly siren song. I breathed him in, no longer conscious of clutter and dust, but only of his scent, becoming as familiar as my own. I sighed, closing my eyes.

"It's just that I don't know what to tell you," he said. "Except for that bar in Elizabeth, I haven't seen my father since I was thirteen. I mean, you can ask me what you want, but I don't know if I can help you. He's pretty much a stranger to me."

"Which is a shame, because you should know where your roots are." Lord knew I heard enough about my own. "You should know where you come from."

"I come from here. And after I left . . ." He paused. "It's like I didn't exist here anymore. Anyway, if I need any more roots, I'll grow them with you. Now." He kissed my forehead, letting me go. "Is there anything else you need to know?"

How could I answer that? My head swirled with a thousand more questions. All of which I'd probably have to figure out on my own. "Hey, I thought you said you didn't do the whole 'meet chicks in bars' thing."

"Well, not for a potential wife anyway."

"Then for what?"

He eyed me, as if obvious. "What do you think?"

I dropped my jaw, feigning outrage. "You *slut!*" I cried, flashing a breast.

He laughed out loud. "*Tu es méchant!*"

"I have no idea how that translates, but if it means—"

"It means back to work." He twirled me around, sending me on my way with a slap to my behind. "I'll be bringing in a load of lumber from the truck."

"As if I need more wood," I said, rubbing my rump. Andy snorted over his shoulder as he tromped into the yard.

By THE END of the afternoon we managed to clear the living room, kitchen, and a bit of the second bedroom (which seemed to serve as dump for most of Iron Bog) of the surfeit of trash, recyclables, dead appliances and furniture left in the house. As for what I'd keep, the dining set in the kitchen seemed fine, if not crusted with years of neglect, much like the grease-coated knotty pine and wallpaper that covered most of the walls. Andy assured me the set was solid maple and nothing Murphy's Oil Soap and a good polishing wouldn't cure. Much to my absolute delight the stove fired right up, but the bottled gas that fueled it ran out as soon as it proved its worth. Andy'd replace it on the next run into town. Of course, being adverse to *E. coli*, I'd have to scrub free the ossified pasta, indefinable vegetables and meats, and the bubbled remains of several failed attempts at baking before I could use it.

At least the water worked, both hot and cold, though the sink itself was barely recognizable as stainless steel with all the food gunk, grease, bugs, and bottles crowded together with POISON! XXX marked on them. Hands gloved, I cautiously pinched them out, letting Andy haul them off to wherever one disposed of chemicals that were not only toxic but HIGHLY COMBUSTIBLE! or carried the warning, USE ONLY WITH PROPER VENTING! or the graphic of a hand being eaten away by acid. Needless to say, I didn't argue the advice, DO NOT DRINK!

The water also worked in the sink in the half-bathroom off to the side. The toilet, though, was clogged with something that appeared ... *furry*. Ever since the raccoon's burial, Bucky had attached himself to my hip, and after spying whatever occupied the toilet bowl, he went into a barking frenzy. I quickly dropped the lid, but he kept on barking.

"It's okay, boy," I said, tentatively petting his head, "Andy will get rid of it—okay? Now, quiet. Quiet, boy . . ." I scratched him behind the ear and he whined, giving me that toothy doggie-smile before he licked his chops and sat, pressing against my leg. It surprised me how soft his fur really was, and how happy my petting seemed to make him. Maybe he really liked me. Or maybe he was just hoping I'd fry another omelet for him to steal. I turned back to the washer and dryer, Bucky rising to follow.

The kitchen cabinets I left for last, where I was rewarded with some decidedly new-looking crockery. After I waded through a five year supply of tea, coffee, and condiments, I found some rather dusty Emile Henry plates, bowls, and cups, a simple, everyday pattern in a perky yellow shade. Surprisingly, not a single piece was cracked, chipped, or stained, which amazed me since mostly everything else showed at least a modicum of hard use. There were place settings for eight and upon further inspection I even found serving pieces, including a lovely soup tureen which Andy caught me examining.

"Last thing I'd expect to find here," I said, thumbing off a bit of film to reveal a shine beneath. The effect made me feel like a kid on Christmas morning. "Will you look at this, Andy? Just like new! I must say, your father had the oddest taste."

"These were my mother's," he said, lifting a plate. "From what I remember, we only used them on special occasions. Not that there were lots of them." He set it back with a tiny *clink*.

I found some little dishes shaped like scallop shells. "Why? No holidays in the deep Piney woods?"

"Sure, but it's not so much the deep woods as the deep woodsmen." He took my hand. "Come on, I want to ask you something."

I followed him into the living room and nearly lost my breath. I'd been so immersed in the warren that was the kitchen, I didn't pay attention to what Andy had accomplished. With the curtains gone and the bright light streaming in, unencumbered by greasy rugs, fishing gear, and stuffed raccoons, I could almost see what the living room truly was—a sunny, rustic space full of possibilities. Except, of course, for the myriad broken and filthy furniture.

"I've divided it into three camps," Andy said as I regarded the three groupings. "Keep, repair and Dumpster."

I eyed the keep pile: two pine end tables and a matching coffee table, dirty but relatively scratch-free; a freestanding lamp and a table lamp; a short, square stool that fit near the hearth. The next group consisted of an overstuffed sofa with clawfoot legs, one of which was lay on the cushions which left it leveled by a cinderblock; a carved rocking chair missing a rail; and a corner china cabinet stuffed to the gills, whose front glass had cracked. The last contained something that had once been a recliner, but now resembled a chaise lounge; a pair of very uneasy-looking chairs; a half-dozen tables, folding and otherwise; and some completely unidentifiable stuff.

"Anything you don't agree with?" Andy asked.

"No . . . I think you did a pretty good job. Though I think even the "keep" camp is wishful thinking."

He slapped his hand into the sofa's blue embroidered cushion; a plume of dust wafted out. "Look at that etching around the top. Top quality, and probably an antique." Then he gave the arm a punch; it resounded with a deep *thunk.* "See? Solid. Celia told me about an upholsterer over at Dulles Corner who does really nice work. We can have it restuffed and get the leg fixed. Then a good shampooing and it'd be like new."

I eyed it dubiously; I had a feeling Celia also had champagne taste. "If you say so." I looked to the scuffed and filthy wooden floor. "I'm glad you got rid of the rugs, but what about this? It's falling through."

He stomped it, hard. "This is oak planking. The only reason you fell through was because my father chose that spot to set up his taxidermy studio, and the constant runoff ate through the floorboards. Three or four new planks ought to fix it right up. Then we can sand it down and varnish it and it'll be good as new." He turned toward the stone fireplace, fingers framing it. "Maybe a nice hearth rug right there and, with a roaring fire on a cold winter's night, well . . ." He looked to me with a definite smolder. "Ought to be downright cozy."

It ought to be; it even seemed like it right then. So much so, I was already feeling the heat. Or maybe it was just the way he looked at me, warming me down to my toes. I gave the front of my t-shirt a flap, feeling the sweat trickling down between my breasts, the scent of a full day's worth of tugging, hauling and tossing making itself apparent. An unlikely remedy came to mind. Unlikely for me, anyhow.

I turned toward the door. "Will you excuse me?" I said, thumbing the hem of my t-shirt as I headed outside.

Bucky followed, and so did Andy, though not trotting beside me as the Collie did, but slowly, a dozen yards behind. To make it easier for him, I left a breadcrumb trail of my clothes to the lake, first a shirt, then each sneaker, shorts, my bra, and just before I reached the dock, a tortoiseshell clasp, where I slowly let my hair unfurl. It was there he stopped, maybe to watch it sway across my back as I stepped onto the planking, or slide over my shoulder as I stripped away my panties, just before I pushed up on my toes and dove into the lake.

Did I hear a hiss as the water hit my skin? Sure felt like it, the contrast of cool and heat puckering each pore into gooseflesh, cooling me instantly. I glided under the surface like an arrow just shot, as slinky as an eel. I felt swift and reckless and decadent, never more conscious of my body and how lethal its effects were. He wanted me—oh boy, did he ever—and even if my mind had not yet enraptured him, his desire for me was irrefutable, and that alone made me invincible. No matter how this escapade would play out, I'd always remember this small slice of time when what I *was* was just enough, and suddenly my arms became electric, propelling me with superhuman strength through the murk, my lungs nearly giving out before I broke the surface to the bright sky overhead. When I looked toward the shore I saw Andy on the dock, simply watching. I took a deep breath and swam toward him.

He was indistinct at first; maybe it was the water in my eyes. Or maybe I was half-blinded by the westing sun, as it sank closer to the treetops past the house. Then Bucky started to bark and Andy wasn't looking at me anymore, but toward the water to my right. I kept swimming, aiming for the dock.

I was maybe fifteen feet from it when I stopped, treading water. "Hey, sailor," I said, visoring my eyes, "why don't you come on in?"

"Julie," he said, preternaturally calm, "move back very—"

Something pierced my breast and I screamed, and all at once, Bucky was airborne.

Chapter Thirteen

Down on the Farm

I CLUTCHED MY breast, blood spilling through my fingers, the water turning a bright red. Before I could scream again a splash rained over me and Bucky appeared out of nowhere, teeth bared, snatching something out of the water as it whipped my shoulder with a loud *thuk!* I yelped, arms pinwheeling as the dog flung something long and wiry into the air to splash into the lake yards away. I took it as my cue to get far away as fast as I could and kicked frantically for the dock. Andy was already in the water, and within seconds he pulled me onto the dock.

"Don't move," he said, laying me back, and stripping off his t-shirt, he pressed it hard against my bleeding breast.

"It's not stopping!" I cried, watching the white cotton quickly turning crimson. Suddenly I felt sick and I closed my eyes, the dock starting to spin.

"Open your eyes," Andy ordered. "Look at me." They fluttered open, and I did. "You got snakebit, but it's a harmless water snake. It only looks worse because of the water and their spit's anti-coagulants."

Snakebit! Telling me that didn't help much; I felt the bile rising up my throat. "Anti—what do you mean?"

He turned the shirt around, pressing again. "Means whatever's in the bite slows the blood from clotting. But it's not poisonous. You're not going to bleed to death, and the only way you're going to get sick is if you let it get infected."

I didn't care what he said; I closed my eyes anyway. "Why didn't you tell me there's snakes in this lake?"

"There's snakes in every lake. The trick is to get out of their way when they're swimming. Usually they get out of yours, but you must have crossed its path. Good thing Bucky snatched it off, because these snakes have a pretty prickly temper, and it would've bit you over and over again."

"Oh my God—Bucky!" I bolted upright, frantically scanning the lake. "Where is he? Is he okay?"

"He's fine," Andy said, looking a bit surprised at my concern. Just then the dog loped up the lake bank, giving himself a good shake before he trotted around to the dock. He sat down a few feet from me, flashing his toothy grin, his tongue lolling.

"My hero," I said, reaching out to scratch him under the chin. He licked his chops and barked and shook again, water raining over us in doggie-scented droplets, making me aware Andy was the only one dressed among us. Bucky remedied that by promptly climbing into my lap.

I hugged him, pressing my cheek to his neck. "Oh dear, I guess this means we've bonded." He twisted his head and licked my nose, and all at once I was laughing, bare naked and sopping and so very satisfied with my new canine friend I didn't even notice I'd dropped my compress.

Good thing Andy did. He scritched Bucky behind the ear then nudged him off me, lifting the bloodied t-shirt from where it had fallen on the dock. He cocked his head, eyeing my breast. "Well, there you go. It's stopped bleeding." He stood and, grabbing my hand, pulled me to my feet. "We'd better clean it out."

Self-conscious, I crossed my arms over me and looked around for my clothes. They were still where I had left them, strewn across the yard, veritable stepping stones to the front door.

"We'll get them later," Andy said, lifting me into his arms. "You know, this is getting to be a habit, carrying you from the lake."

"All part of the plan," I said, waggling my feet. "Delicate insoles, you know."

"I'm not saying I mind," he said, "but it does set a dangerous precedent."

"Oh really? Why?"

He kissed my forehead and smiled a bit too lethally. "I could get very used to it."

A few minutes later we were both in the shower, doing a very good job of cleaning mostly everything out. Afterward, as I applied Neosporin to two angry-looking pin-holes, Andy was stepping into his jeans, leaving me to wonder why I was still languishing in my robe. "Going somewhere?" I said.

"Into town," he said, sitting on the side of the bed as he strapped on his sandals. "I won't be long."

"I'll take that as a non-invitation," I said, coming around to sit beside him. "Care to tell me why?"

He turned, pressing me back to the bed. "Because you'll be busy," he said, lightly kissing my neck. "Getting ready for me and the surprise I'll be bringing back."

"I love surprises," I said, pushing a bit of damp hair behind his ear. It was getting late, almost twilight, and his eyes shone a crystalline blue. "Except it better involve eating. I'm absolutely *starving*."

"Oh, it'll definitely involve eating," he said, untying my robe to bare my breasts. "Now let's take a look at that bite."

Which would be fine if all he did was *look*. But he didn't. He had to skim his fingers to the underside of my breast and lift it ever so delicately, his thumb rubbing in the bit of antiseptic cream I'd missed, the pad of his hand lightly abrading my nipple as he did. My brain told me it was a gesture innocent of any sexual implications, yet my body responded with a large, shivering sigh. He lifted his eyes to mine, his hand sliding to the flat of my belly.

My God—it never took much. How did he do it, this instant arousal by just quirking an eyebrow? Odd how I was always ready for him, stranger still how he always wanted me. I raised my head and nipped the side of his mouth, tracing my lips across his. They felt cool, soft, tasting of mint and longing, like a bit of little-boy-happiness at getting the birthday present of his dreams. But how could that be? I couldn't imagine him not getting anything he ever wanted. Such as me, it embarrassed me to think. He wanted me, and there I was . . .

His mouth opened and his tongue met mine before it closed in the deepest kiss I could imagine. This had to be more than just lust. But I also knew it was so much less than love. I wasn't quite sure *what* it was, except that it always baffled me,

"*C'est pour toi que je vive,*" he murmured, kissing my ear. "I'll never let anything happen to you . . . you do know that, don't you?"

Why the urgency in his voice? "Yes, of course, Andy." He kissed my neck. "Of course I do."

He growled something indiscernible and kept kissing me, my shoulder, my collarbone, each breast, and lower. Soon his hands were at my hips and he was spreading my legs, his tongue tracing the inside of my thigh, running higher and higher until it was on me, and I arched from the mattress in surprise.

There had never been a question of how much Andy excited me. He was a strong, sensuous man, a man who seemed only too aware of his sexual prowess and the power it held. But he didn't wield it maliciously as he genuinely seemed to appreciate women. Yet, as much as he did, there was no question he was used to being on top, metaphorically or otherwise. And it wasn't even because it was his preference; it just seemed he'd come to

expect it because his women did, too. I'd seen it in all the
faces of those he interviewed. I heard it in all their voices.
The funny part in my—or any woman—realizing that
was that it was the most devastating part of his allure.
He *needed* us to need him, and we were only too happy to
table whatever strengths we had accumulated to bask in
his unwavering desire. Quite a heady notion to consider.
Even harder to accept. Except we all had accepted it read-
ily. And if I had, what did that say of me?

At the moment it didn't matter; I was coming, swiftly
and violently. And if that was the sole perk of this alli-
ance, then it made me more than happy. Mainly because
it was the only thing I'd ever take from him, or any man,
ever again.

FROM JULIE KNOTT'S JOURNAL . . .

6 September

*Tonight I baked a chicken! No kidding, we finally have a
working kitchen that's actually NOT al fresco! Granted,
there's still a bit of scraping and painting and sanding
and refurbishing to do (not only to the kitchen, but to
the rest of this sorry house), and we still don't have a
fridge (which should be delivered Thursday, a wedding
present from Uncle Jinks), but for the first time in a
week—I've been MARRIED a week?!—I had the luxury
of cooking and eating without the imminent threat of
bird crap landing in our food. We took our first meal at
our newly cleaned and polished kitchen table, enjoying
said chicken stuffed with fresh herbs and tomatoes with*

*a basil vinaigrette, green beans, roasted corn, and the
requisite bread and cheese (a must, I have learned, for
every one of Andy's dinners), plus a nice pinot grigio
(wine, another requirement, not that I'm complaining).
For dessert, I tossed together a peach and blueberry
crisp. For the first time in a week, I'm full!*

9 September

*Today we drove all the way to Hammonton (inciden-
tally, the Blueberry Capital of the World) to stock our
new fridge and cleaned-out cupboards from a real, live
supermarket. Remarkable how many things you don't
need when you're eating off the land. I, for one, bought
five cases of Mason jars as well as several boxes of Hefty
Bags and Rubbermaid plastic containers for all the veggies and fruits and whatnot I'll be canning and freezing
(I'm really up for this, no kidding.) I even bought some
yeast, as I'm determined to make crusty baguettes for
Andy, even if it'll take all day. (I Googled a recipe I saved
on my notepad.) By the way, while I was shopping Andy
took off for Home Depot. At an hour and a half, it's the
longest we've been separated since we married. A hell of
a long time to pick up paint, but then again, I've always
considered it a men's Disneyland. I'm such a sexist pig.*

12 September

*Andy removed the calf from the farm today. I knew it
had to be done, so it wasn't a surprise, especially since*

he said he kept her way longer than he should have. She screamed all the way out of the yard, and Betsy mooed like someone was beating the crap out of her. It was all very sad. Andy assured me she's going to be raised as a dairy cow, and she wasn't going for veal. I hope he's right. Of course, this means that Betsy will have to be milked twice a day (he has an electric milker, thank God), but we also will be getting some freaking delicious milk. I've tasted it; unbelievable! Andy also said we're going to make our own brie.

20 September

The rest of the house is finally fully habitable. It's far from finished, but it's relatively crap-free. The washer and dryer work, the other toilet's been de-rodent-ed, we're growing mushrooms, the apples are ready to pick. And last night we snuggled on a blanket in front of our unlit fireplace. Even Bucky has found a place to sleep on the hearth. It really is quite nice. Also, I found another photo of the man Andy had previously referred to as "the ship's captain" bookmarking a page in an old Joy of Cooking. I was looking up a recipe for pickles when I came across the photo. The name "Daniel Mercier" was typed on the back, in the same way it had been for Andy's mother. Didn't take much to deduce these pictures probably came courtesy of a private detective. The funny part was when I noticed what page it was marking: how to roast a pig on a spit.

27 September

Ray has asked Andy to help with his cranberry harvest next week. He has fifteen acres of bogs, so it'll take a few days, though he doesn't have to be there for all of it. Andy suggested having Ray and Celia for dinner after it's over, a little post-harvest celebration and a chance to show off our newly-refurbished house. We had Uncle Jinks to dinner the night before last, and he said it already looks like another world. And oh yeah, this morning I got my period. Andy will most certainly find out tonight.

I HUNG RED check café curtains in the kitchen, and sage green floor-length ones in the living room, which we could open during the day with brass pull backs. Not that there was anyone around to peek in, but I liked having the option. Options were always handy to have around.

What a difference nearly a month had made on the farm. The chickens were producing at least a eighteen eggs a day; we always had fresh milk; I was well on my way to freezing and canning enough produce to (theoretically) last us through the winter; I had a nice stock of herbs drying in the barn; the apples had been harvested (both by us to eat, cook, and sell, and by a week's worth of pick-your-own-ers who had stripped us bare); we had a tidy sum in our coffers from our summer fruits and veggies, and the first crops of fall and winter vegetables were almost ready; the house and grounds were cleaned up and cleared out and all finally felt like home. Most days I worked from sun-up to sunset, but I had never been in better shape, both mentally and physically, especially since in all that time I hadn't touched a computer, watched a TV, used a microwave, GPS, food processor, air conditioner or hair dryer, nor had a manicure, pedicure, wax, or haircut. But I honestly think I never looked better. As a matter of fact, I had eschewed most implements of modern life for convenience or entertainment, relying instead on conversation, watching the stars, reading, and writing in my journal. And, of course, something else that probably predated any of it.

Which led to the dilemma I now faced. As had been our habit we ate dinner late, then lingered over it, taking coffee and dessert outside on the front porch where we talked endlessly about nothing and everything. I learned silly little things about Andy, that he loved those round caramels with the white gunk inside, he always brushed his teeth as soon as he got up, and although he'd been all over the world by train and sea, he'd probably only flown a dozen times. From me he learned I passed out when I got my ears pierced at fifteen, I put ketchup on fried chicken, and I'd never once had stage fright. As the sky above us blazed with starlight, the world between us got a little smaller, and I was sure I saw a side of Andy he saved just for me. All the more reason why I was feeling a little traitorous about our bargain just then, even though I was quite certain my compliance would have been beyond comprehension.

He set his coffee down and, reaching over, pulled

me into his lap. I settled into it, looping my arm around his neck. As always, he showered before dinner, and he smelled of French-milled *savon* and wintergreen shaving soap. I leaned in, taking a heady whiff. He looked up and smiled.

"The nights are starting to get cool," I opined.

He nodded, looking toward the lake. "One thing I remember about this place is the way it looked in winter, the snow covering the pine trees, the frozen-over lake, the deer coming right up to the house. You see lots of hawks then, too. Once I even saw a bobcat."

"A bobcat?" I cringed. "Oh, nice. Why didn't you tell me there were wild animals here?"

He laughed. "Aren't all animals wild? Well, except for Bucky." He reached to the dog, lying next to the chair, and scratched his ruff. Bucky whined appreciatively, rubbing his head against my dangling leg. There's an odd thing: I didn't even mind.

"Anyway, you hardly ever see them," he added. "Most scientists believe they're extinct in the East, that they were killed off a long time ago. But every now and then someone sees one, which actually, isn't surprising. There's no shortage of deer to eat. It's not like they have to go around stealing babies anymore."

Cue Julie. I pulled back to look at him. "Andy, there's something I have to tell you. You might be a bit disappointed."

With the moon nearly gone and with only a dim light from the kitchen, it was hard to read his expression. "Really? About what?"

No sense mincing words. "I got my period this morning." I waited a few beats, and when he didn't say anything, I continued. "I know our agreement is contingent on my getting pregnant, but you have to know, it's not for lack of trying. Maybe we'll have better luck next month, so I wouldn't read too much into this. I've had friends who've waited much longer to get pregnant, one of them who had to—"

"Julie." He pressed his finger to my lips. "I'm under no illusion we're ready for the fertility clinic just yet. It's only been a month. Calm down."

I slid his finger away. "I *am* calm." And I was, too, even mouthing these bald-faced lies. Because even if they were grounded in the inherent logic of our union, I couldn't help feeling removed. As if there were almost two Julies now, and that one wasn't logical at all. "It's just that I know how badly you want children."

"And I do. And I'm sure they'll come eventually. But until then . . ." He eased me off his lap and we stood up. "There's me and you, and that's all right for now." He took my hand. "Let's go to bed."

Which promised to be odd, to say the least. There hadn't been a night since we'd been married that we hadn't had sex. I often wondered whether that was abnormal, but I'd given up caring. I was enjoying myself too much. And because of that . . .

"Andy," I said, turning to him as we walked into our room, the big bed looming before us. I traced my finger down his jaw and kissed him lightly, brushing my hip against his. "I know we can't . . . *you know*, tonight, but that doesn't mean I can't take . . ."

He stopped me with his kiss, as deeply romantic as any ever attempted cinematically. "You know what I've wanted to do ever since we were married?"

"What . . .?" I answered, breathless.

He kissed me again, his fingers kneading the small of my back, and with the monthly ache laying low against it, I nearly purred with contentment. "Just hold you in my arms all night. Do you think we could do that? Would you mind?"

I couldn't help but laugh. "What are you—some kind of everywoman's dream? Real men just don't act like you!"

"Because men like that aren't real men," he said, lifting my dress over my head. "And they wouldn't deserve you."

Though men wanting babies as badly as you said you did would be a lot less cavalier. And, although I was relieved, why did it give me pause?

Chapter Fourteen

What Lies Beneath

3 October

Andy's been working the cranberry harvest at Ray's farm all week. He took me there Sunday to watch the flooding of the first bog, where I also got my first lesson in the berry's cultivation. I never knew cranberries grew on vines that could be generations old, and they grow in acre-wide pits that are filled with about eighteen inches of water to harvest. Seems the berries are hollow and float to the top once they're shaken off the vines with a machine called a beater. It's a pretty gorgeous site, this sea of red berries, which are then corralled with a boom before being sucked up a tube and into a truck. Looks so easy it's hard to imagine dozens of workers used to pick them by hand.

But with Andy gone all week, I've had the farm to myself, which also includes all the work. I've become pretty proficient at this milking-thing, and pretty addicted to Betsy's unpasteurized milk. I'm sorry, but drinking it with the cream intact is my answer to crack—I just can't get enough. The brie we made should be ready by the weekend, so we can schmear it on my homemade baguettes when we have Ray and Celia over for dinner on Sunday. I have a feeling it's going to take at least that to impress Celia . . .

I HAD BECOME one of the Iron Bog Free Library's best patrons, taking out at least seven books a week, on anything from the latest fiction to recipes to the care and feeding of chickens. Normally, Andy and I would both go on Saturday mornings, but this being the last day of the berry harvest, I didn't expect him until dinnertime. I had just renewed Julia Child's cookbook, picked up a handful of Patrick O'Briens for Andy and the two latest Lisa Scottolines for me. As I slid them into my tote I saw a familiar face: Mrs. DeForest, the town archivist, who had stood up for us at our wedding. She was on her way out of an apparent meeting when I noticed her and waved. Her face lit with recognition and she came right over.

"Mrs. Devine! How are you?" she said, clasping my hand. "As well as a newlywed can be, I'm guessing!"

"I'm just fine." The woman had quite a grip for an octogenarian. I noted the sign by the room she had just exited. "I see you're on the Historical Committee."

"What would a town archivist be without one?" She readjusted an overstuffed folder she held against her. "They just gave me a brand-new batch of documents. I'll be scanning and cataloguing for a week."

I tapped the folder. "That's quite a load. I guess that's proof enough of what Andy had said—you *must* know everything."

She laughed, but I could see the truth of it behind those eagle eyes. "How is that husband of yours? Could've knocked me over with a feather when I saw it was him."

"Yes, it's been quite a few years, hasn't it? But I guess he had to come back sooner or later."

"Maybe, but after it happened, there wasn't anyone here who thought they'd ever see him again."

I stared at her. "After *what* happened?"

"Oh dear ..." she sighed, "you must forgive me. I should never assume."

And neither should I. "I'm missing something here." I placed my hand on her arm. "I think you're just the person to clue me in."

Consternation crossed her face. "Mrs. Devine—"

"—Julie."

"Julie." She stiffened almost imperceptibly. "If you need to know something about your husband, you should be asking him, not me."

There was no way I was letting this woman go. "True, but unfortunately my husband prefers to let the past stay buried, while I'm operating under the impression there's something about him everyone knows except me. I'm a reporter, Mrs. DeForest. You know I'll find out whatever it is eventually. But I'd really rather keep it close to home, you know what I mean?"

Her gaze never left mine. "I believe so."

"Then please, if you could just talk with me for a bit, I'd be so grateful. Is there someplace we can go to for coffee?"

She looked honestly cornered, readjusting the heavy folder again. "There's the Cranberry Café."

I glanced at my watch. "Then it looks like I'm buying you lunch." I slipped the folder from her hands. "Here, let me carry that for you. Our truck's out front."

"I'd rather walk. It's just down the street."

"Are you sure?"

She squared her shoulders. "Absolutely."

THE CRANBERRY CAFÉ was a quaint little place, a country throwback with rustic wood, lace curtains and plenty of antique glass, but nouveau enough to include decadent-looking Italian pastry and Wi-Fi. Turns out this all made sense as some serious business went on this time of year, with the cranberry cooperative's huge receiving station located just out of town. The place was loaded with farmers and co-op execs, all chattering about the business of berries. We managed to bypass them all to the sunny veranda out back, and an umbrellaed table facing a pond. Mrs. DeForest took a seat across from me, still looking a bit wary.

"Mrs. DeForest, I feel like I've strong-armed you into coming, but truly, that wasn't my intention. It's not that

Andy hiding something from me, but I'm sure you're well aware how time can color perspective, and he was young when he left. Plus it always helps to get an independent point of view."

My spin seemed to be working (so relieved I could still work it) until she smiled wryly and said, "All right, Julie, you can stop selling and relax. I'm here. So let's start by your calling me Lila."

"Lila—I like that. I have a friend who named her daughter Lila Rose."

"Not Madison or Peyton or Brooklyn? Nowadays it seems every little girl's name ought to have a Zip Code attached to it."

"That's so true! Well, I've always been one for the classics. I thought if I ever had a daughter, I'd like to name her Alice."

"Really. From *Alice in Wonderland*? Or perhaps *Alice'sRestaurant*? Alice Cooper?" Her eyes raked me. "Alice in Chains?"

I laughed out loud. "I see you're up on your pop culture references."

"Because I lived through them."

There was nothing I could put over this woman. "Actually I was thinking of Alice Roosevelt."

"Well, now there's one whose heyday even predates me. But I did always like 'If you haven't got anything nice to say about anybody come sit next to me.'"

"I've always liked her style. And yours, too." I folded my arms atop the table. "There's nothing like being honest and forthcoming."

Just then the server came for our order, and I could sense Lila gauging. We both decided on chicken salad with walnuts, grapes and dried cranberries, as it seemed appropriate, and salad was always easier to talk around. As soon as the server left, she jumped right in.

"I'm going to assume he told you something about his mother," she said, squeezing lemon into her iced tea.

"That she was French, that she was nineteen when she married his father, and she was—"

"Pregnant? Yes, I knew. I was township clerk at the time, and as in all small towns, well . . ." She shrugged. "Anyway, you should have seen them back then. Andy's dad was so . . ." She shook her head, smiling in remembrance. "He wasn't as exotic-looking as his son, but oh boy—the apple doesn't fall far from the tree. And her! I don't think one day went by I didn't see that woman in three-inch heels, even when she was so pregnant you'd think she was ready to burst. Always perfectly put together, hair and make-up like a fashion model."

"Viviane . . ." I said idly, and I didn't know why.

"That's her name," said Lila. "Is she still living? Do you know?"

"Yes, in France. And still beautiful, Andy says. Remarried to a ship's captain."

"To a ship's captain? Really. The old man never said. But it makes sense." She seemed to draw into herself a moment. "I was married once in my life, widowed ten years ago, but as the township clerk I'd issued licenses for I can't tell you how many couples, young and old. And just from that, I could get a pretty good idea whose marriages would last and whose would go bust and, truth be told, I was usually on the mark. Now those two?" She shook her head. "Like dead men walking."

She laughed. "Oh, *he* was in love, all right. He mooned over her like a teenager, giving her anything she wanted. But to me, she always seemed to be looking for the exit. Didn't help, either, she was just a kid."

"And really far from home," I added. "Plus being in the woods is hardly like living in a bustling port by the sea."

"Which was why I guess he moved them to the lake house after the fire."

"Okay," I said, "this is the part where I'm supposed to say, 'What fire?'"

"In which I'll answer, 'Did you know Andy's parents lived in another house before he was born?' in which you'll say—"

"'No, tell me about it.'"

We both laughed over that one, though she quickly returned to business. "They first lived closer to the main road in a big, old house that used be a tavern. Back when the trail was a post road to Camden." She paused, digging into the burgeoning file. "I think I have—ah, here it is. An old photograph from the thirties."

It was a big clapboarded building with dark shutters, several out buildings and four bricked chimneys. "You mean those old ruins?" I peered closer. "We pass it going in and out of town. Andy mentioned his family owned it, though he never said his parents lived there."

"Maybe because it wasn't for very long. I guess they had visions of fixing it up and making it grand again, as they applied to the township to see if they could get it historical status. But a month or so after they arrived, it caught on fire. Now, fires are common in the Pines, they're even part of their ecosystem. But it's the woods that usually catch fire and spread to the houses, not the other way around. When they don't, mostly it's kitchen fires, but this one started in the bedroom."

"Well, that's easy—smoking in bed. They both did smoke, apparently."

"But the investigation proved the fire had started in the middle of the night in an overstuffed chair. When the fire companies arrived, she was out in the yard, and he was still in bed. They had to bust through the walls to pull him out. He was stone drunk. After the investigation they could've fixed the house up, could've even gotten those federal funds for a historical site, but they held an auction and sold anything of value, even the cedar shakes on the roof, before they knocked it down. After that they moved to what had been Andy's grandfather's house by the lake. After Andy was born she mostly kept to herself. No one thought her very friendly. If there was something going on at Andy's school, she'd make an appearance, but that was about it."

I took another look at the photo. "Would you mind if I kept this?"

"Go ahead. It was probably his dad's anyway. It was found in an old file from the investigation."

I turned it over; a county stamp was on the back. "But this happened before Andy was born. So how could it involve him?"

Again, the timing worked in Lila's favor as right then our salads arrived. After the server left Lila plucked a roll from the basket, splitting it with her thumbs. "There was another fire."

"Oh? When?"

"The spring before Viviane and Andy left. This time it was the barn. Burned right to the ground."

I thought a moment. "Which would explain the relative newness of the barn compared to the house. "What was the explanation for that?"

"Kerosene heater. Rumor had it the old man was living in there. He was burned over thirty percent of his body. The investigation showed his cot caught fire, but he said he got burned from trying to put out a blanket that had fallen from his bed."

Andy never told me this, but then again, why should he? He hardly talked about his father at all. Suddenly I became distinctly aware of how little I really knew my husband.

I picked at my salad. "Maybe he'd been drinking?"

"It's a possibility." Lila eyed me, no doubt aware of the bomb she'd just dropped. "But two weeks before, he had gotten out of the drunk tank. Word was he was determined to quit drinking. There was no trace of alcohol found in or near the barn, but he could've done his drinking someplace else. A couple days later Viviane and Andy left for France."

"So what does this all mean?"

"There were rumors she tried to kill him."

"I figured you'd say that. Did you believe them?"

Lila sighed. "Who knows what really goes on between a man and a woman? Certainly there were things my husband and I never discussed with anyone." She stabbed a tomato, twirling it a bit on her fork. "Think of marriage as a storefront. There's a lot you can see from the street, but the real business goes on in the backroom. Maybe theirs was doomed from the start. I certainly thought so."

Boy, was she ever right about the backroom. "So what do you think of ours?"

"You and Andy?" She smiled, waving me off. "Why, you two are in it for the long haul. Anyone can see that."

I smiled back. After all, I was all about a convincing argument, whether I believed it or not.

WAS IT POSSIBLE to love a house? Because I certainly did. After a month of beating it into submission, Andy's broken-down, ghetto-envious shack had gone from calamitous to cozy, all cedar-shaked glory in polished wood planking and shiny knotty pine, from a braided rug before the fireplace to cheery curtains blowing in the breeze. There were field flowers on the coffee table and mantel, and in the kitchen, fresh baguettes, a bottle of burgundy, and coq au vin for our dinner, simmering atop the stove. It was nearly seven o'clock and all the chores were done, and I, freshly showered, stood in the doorway awaiting my husband, his faithful dog—who, since the "snake incident" had become my constant companion—at my heel.

"Did you like that, boy?" I said, rubbing his silky ear. "Was that good?"

Bucky licked his chops, his paw on my foot, wagging his tail appreciatively. Lately, he'd become quite proficient at playing me, having just scored chicken livers and gizzards atop his kibble. It's not that I was ever averse to cooking; I just never had the time or energy. But having been forced into it out of necessity (Iron Bog was hardly an epicenter of eateries), I found I enjoyed it immensely, even more so when Andy (and Bucky) enthusiastically approved. So I was especially looking forward to tonight's meal, as it'd been the first time I attempted such a quintessentially *français* dish, and I desperately wanted to get it right. Especially since there were a couple of things I intended to discuss with Andy over it.

After having lived in the city so long, I was still getting used to being out in the big bad woods by myself, not so much during the day, but after sunset, when it seemed to have a million voices. With the weather still relatively warm, the insects continued their symphony every night, along with the hoot owls, the nightingales, the frogs, and whatever else out there I wasn't curious enough to identify. Bucky, though, was an immense help, a protective presence. Nothing could get past him. Even so, as the beauty of the Pines wrapped itself around me during the day, I couldn't help feeling its shadowy aloofness at night, one that dissipated like a fog the second the lights of Ray's truck lit the yard, bringing Andy home.

"Hello Ray!" I called to him, opening the screen door.

Bucky shot out in a frenzy of joyful yaps for his alpha. "Don't forget—tomorrow night at six!"

"I'd never forget a free meal! See you then!" he called back, turning the truck around. He waved to Andy, yelling "Thanks, again!" before shooting up the back trail toward the bogs.

"Well, hello, you cranberry cutie," I said, spying Andy, looking slightly worn around the edges.

"Mmmuph," he grunted, his jeans wet up to the thighs, his t-shirt stained and sweaty, his hair a ruffled mess under his cap. He trod past me to the laundry room, where, as was his habit after work, he stripped bare, unceremoniously dropping his filthy clothes in the hamper.

"Guess what?" I said, following him into the kitchen. "You might be happy to know I'm good to go again."

He stopped, eyeing me over his shoulder. "What?"

"I said . . ." I shifted my hips, affecting my most potent come-hither look. "I *said* I'm *good* to *go*."

He sniffed, saying, "Wait five minutes—and bring the wine," then left for our room.

Five minutes later I sat on the bed, a glass of wine in each hand. Andy emerged from the bathroom in a burst of steam, naked and rubbing his wet head with a towel.

"Wine?" I offered, holding up a glass.

"Thanks," he said, tossing the towel to the floor. He took the glass as I sipped mine demurely, downing the wine in one gulp. "*Ahh* . . ." he growled, placing the glass to the dresser before turning his simmering gaze to me.

"This won't take long," he said. "Do you mind?"

I considered that a moment. "Will you pay me back later?"

Andy set my wineglass aside and, easing me back, removed my panties in one seemingly seamless movement. "With interest, *ma belle*, you can bank on it." And just like that he was inside me.

Ten minutes later we were in the kitchen, tucking into the chicken. "Absolute truth," he said, looking relaxed and sated, "this is the best damn chicken I've ever had."

Had the lights been out I would've glowed in the dark. "Really? You think so?"

He reached for my hand, smacking a kiss on it. "Probably because I can still taste you on my lips. Now pass the platter, *ma petite*, I'm starving."

Later on, over fruit and cheese, I divulged a less pressing bit of news. "Guess who I had lunch with today? Mrs. DeForest."

He was balancing a grape atop a piece of Beaufort. "Really? Where'd you run into her? At the market?"

"At the library. And oh, I picked up those Patrick O'Briens you wanted. She had just come from a meeting of the Historical Society. We started chatting, and since it was lunchtime, I invited her." I reached into my pocket and placed the photo on the table. "She had a big packet of old photos, and one of them was this."

He eyed it from where it sat, then slid it over without comment. After a few moments he said, "No one's sure what really happened, you know." He looked up. "Including me."

"You mean the fire."

"*Fires.* I'm sure she mentioned both." He took a double sip of wine. "But if you had to hear it from anyone, I suppose she's the most impartial."

"If I had to hear it from anyone . . ." I met his gaze directly. "It should've been you."

He sat back, thumb and forefinger bracing his chin, his eyes coolly washing me. "You're right. I should have told you. But I thought I'd let you get to know me better before I did. Because I wanted you to know the whole story, not just the rumors, as close to the truth as I can get it. Especially about the second fire."

I could feel my heart pounding in my ears. "Why?"

"Because my father believed until the day he died I set it."

Chapter Fifteen

Combustibles

"Dɪᴅ ʏᴏᴜ?" I asked.

An old rage smoldered behind those eyes, and a bruising from tamping it down too long. "No," he said, dropping the cheese and grape back to the plate, reaching for the wine instead. "There were a lot of things I didn't like about my father, and even more he didn't like about me. But I'd never do something like that, no matter what anyone said."

"Exactly what did they say?"

"That if I had, it would've been justified."

"Why? Did your father beat you and your mother?"

He poured more wine, taking a healthy swallow. "No. Though she always played the victim very well. She let everyone think he did." He glowered at me. "What those rumormongers didn't know was had he been violent, it only would have been reactionary."

When he looked away I figured it was the end of his disclosure, but it was only for a sip of wine before he continued. "My mother's a hard woman to live with. If she wants something, she goes after it. She never learned to compromise. But then she's always been able to scheme her way out of any situation so I suppose she's never had to. Maybe people like that should never be married, because what's marriage *but* compromise? She used my father's passion for her as a weapon against him, and he was so crazed by it he let her ruin his life. He let it drive him over the edge." There was a steely cast to his face now, an undercurrent of bitterness to his voice. "It didn't make any sense to me when I was growing up, but it makes perfect sense now."

"You mean as far as your parents are concerned," I said.

"As far as anyone's concerned. Whatever my father was or did, the only thing his passions accomplished was to make everyone around him miserable."

"So you think his love for her was the cause of all their problems?" I refilled my wine. "So if passion makes for bad marriages, then logically speaking, to have a model marriage, you need to keep passion out of it. Hmm . . ." I said, a bit tartly, "are you suggesting all the passion between us is a mistake?"

The smolder returned, though wholly different. "Is that the impression you get?"

I stood, leaning against the counter. He was getting me angry, and I needed the distance. "So passionate *sex* is okay, but it can't go beyond that. You can be passionate for my *body*, but it can't go any deeper, because going deeper equals going nuts."

"No," he said, a bit condescendingly. "What I'm saying is when you lose yourself to another person you're surrendering control of yourself. It's only logical."

"So what's wrong with losing control of yourself? What greater tribute can you pay to another person than to trust them completely? To trust them enough to believe they'd make the right decisions for you, that they'd take care of you, that they'd never let anything happen to you? Didn't you say those things to me? Didn't you even put it in writing?"

His cheek twitched. "It's because I put it in writing that you can trust me."

"But why would you have to? Isn't that what marriage implies anyway?"

"An implication isn't a guarantee."

"But in this case, isn't it? And if it's not, why don't you say what you really think? That logic and passion can't coexist. But to be passionate about something is to defy logic and do it anyway."

"Logic is the basis of everything," he said. "To think otherwise is ridiculous."

"Oh really? I know writers who write without ever making any money, artists who paint for years before they ever sell a painting. I know a runner who dropped sixty pounds, fought asthma and diabetes, and trained for three years through snow, ice, and heat before she was fit enough to get into the Boston Marathon. Then, a week before, she broke her leg. As soon as she was out of the cast she started training again, and a year after that, she finally ran it. Now you tell me, what's the logic in that?"

He was unmoved. "The logic is train hard and you'll get into the Boston Marathon."

"But if she didn't have a passion for running, she wouldn't have accomplished it."

"That's talent, not passion."

"You're missing my point."

"You're not making one."

My God, he was exasperating. "Then what's yours?"

He rose, coming toward me. "I'm not saying there's no place for passion, but not if it rules you. Better to think things through."

I laughed. "Like I did? For all of five days?"

"You can always change your mind."

"Oh—that's right." I could feel my neck heating. "We're a work-in-progress. Thank you for reminding me. I feel so much better now."

That little muscle on the side of his jaw was twitching again. "That's not what I meant. Our contract gives you security, with or without me."

"Is that what we're calling it—security? Let me tell you something, six weeks ago I learned a hard lesson in what *security* with a man really means, and there's no such thing, contract or not." I left for the living room, slugging wine as I dropped to the sofa.

"Where did that come from?" he said, following me. "What happened to you makes our contract even *more* important."

"But why was it even necessary? Why couldn't we just date and get engaged like normal people?"

"Please remind me how well that worked out for you."

"Yeah, well fifty grand's one hell of a booty call if it doesn't work out for *you*."

The color rose in his face. "Then why did you sign it and marry me? Just for the book?" He scanned my face; I was hard-pressed to mask it. "You'd really marry me for a stupid goddamned *story*?"

I wouldn't answer; I wouldn't give him the ammunition. I crossed my arms, turning away. "Go to hell."

His eyes flared and he yanked me to my feet. *"Mon Dieu—je perds mon temps avec toi!"* All at once Bucky sprung to my flank and growled, surprising Andy so he jerked back. *"Non! Couché!"* he cried to the dog. I wrenched away, falling back to the sofa. The dog leaped into my lap.

Andy's gaze shot from his hands to me, as if suddenly wondering where I'd gone. "Jesus," he uttered, looking horrified, "I'm so sorry, I didn't mean ... oh *hell*." He shook his head and left for the bedroom, slamming the door.

I buried my face in the dog's ruff, waiting for Andy to quiet before I went to the kitchen. I grabbed a bottle of burgundy. But as soon as I opened it I knew I hadn't the stomach for more. Instead I cleaned up, mechanically doing all the things I'd been contracted to do. Truth be told, I was surprised we hadn't had this argument earlier. Men were all the same; it's only their *modus operandi* that varied. When I finished I went back to the sofa and lay down. With the windows still opened, an early autumn chill crept over the room. It matched what I felt inside. I grabbed a pillow, hugging it.

Sometime later, I heard the bedroom door open, the floor creaking to the foot of the sofa. From the light of the half-moon I could make out his shape but I felt it more, remembering his weight atop me, a delicious heaviness. I had gotten so used to it, its absence was painful. But the memory wasn't enough. What he'd said hurt more than I imagined, even more so considering it was true. I shifted around, turning my face into the cushions. Bucky moved with me to settle his head on my thigh. Again the floor creaked and I could hear Andy moving toward the front door and out, his footsteps disappearing into the yard. After that I couldn't think anymore. I covered my head, falling dreamlessly asleep.

WHEN I WOKE up Andy was gone, at least from the general vicinity of the house. The truck was still there, so he hadn't gone far, but before he left, apparently he'd been pretty busy. The eggs were collected, Betsy had been milked, the garden watered, the mushrooms tended, a big basket of yams dug up and on the porch, the hanging latch on the gatepost fixed, and a half-dozen other chores that needed attention were accomplished. I, on the other hand, had spent a fitful night on the sofa and rose two hours later than I usually did at the scandalously late hour of eight AM. As I dragged myself around the yard, still dressed in the skirt and t-shirt I had worn the night before, it was a wonder I'd been able to string together two coherent thoughts at all. I'd never felt so wretched.

I wasn't even sure what we fought about, or why I had gotten so angry. Andy had started out baring his soul, and I had turned it against him. Which was dangerously close to what his mother had done to his father, I'm sure. I dropped to the front porch, contemplating that. Was that how he was seeing it? Was our contract really nothing more than a guarantee against falling in love with me? It's not that I wanted him to anyway. As a matter of fact, I was counting on that he wouldn't. So why did it irk me so?

Maybe because an opt-out clause was much easier to take when it was my own idea, and not one of his contracted options. Maybe it hurt to think I was that expendable, even though he had given me no indication I was. Maybe I was beginning to get a bit too comfortable with this whole arrangement, and the reality of a life afterward was getting a little too close. I had already passed the halfway mark; it was all downhill from there.

I shuffled inside and went to the bathroom, washing my face and brushing my teeth, but as I wandered into the kitchen, I hadn't the barest appetite. The dishes from the night before were still in the drainer, our empty wine bottles still on the counter. And under the table, the sandals Andy had worn to dinner after making love to me so furiously I could still smell him on my skin. I picked them up, holding them out. He was so big, so outsized, so . . . well, I wasn't sure I knew. Which made me feel even worse. I set them by the fireplace. Because now I wanted to know everything.

I fed Bucky, dropping kibble in a dish outside the door. As I watched him eat, his black fur as shiny as a seal's, I thought of those first few days when he scared the hell out of me. Now he trailed after me and slept at my feet every night. I could hardly imagine what it'd be like without him. But sooner than later, I'd have to. I dropped to the porch steps, my arm slung around him.

Where was Andy? But then, where was I? And where in hell was I going? If this was a precursor to what my life would be like later on, then I'd better get used to it. Damn reckless of me not to see what lay down the road, naïve of me to think it would be easy. And shame on me for thinking I could come out the other end the same.

WHEREVER ANDY HAD gone, I hoped he'd be back soon as we still had Ray and Celia coming over for dinner, and I had no way to cancel. What would I say if I did? So I went about the preparations for the dinner party as if nothing had happened, making dough for Quiche Lorraine and baguettes, gathering herbs, salad greens and beans from the garden, mixing a vinaigrette dressing, and stopping at Jinks' to pick up fresh scallops, just dug from of Barnegat Bay that morning. As I pulled into the gas station without Andy, Uncle Jinks' radar immediately switched on.

"Oh no," he said, eyeing me flying solo, "Where's Andy?"

"He's busy," I said, trying to sound chipper. "So much going on now."

"Okay." One bushy-gray brow shot up. "Now tell me what really happened."

"Nothing," I said, reaching for my purse. "He just had some fence to fix or whatever. How much do I owe you for those scallops? Hope they're big."

He swiped his hands on a rag. "As big as the whopper I'm sure you're telling me. Be right back." He left for inside.

I felt awful lying, but then again, I just plain felt awful, which I was sure was how I looked, and that had to have been his first clue. My mood matched the day, which was growing steadily more oppressive, an unseasonal humidity hovering in the air like a blanket. A minute or so later Jinks returned, a plastic bag of shucked scallops dangling from his hand.

"Andy owes me apples," he said, passing me the bag. "Let me have them and we'll call it even." He craned his neck toward the truck's bay. "Are they in the back?"

"No," I said, "I guess he forgot. But you can get them when you come to dinner tomorrow. Maybe I'll even toss in a pie."

"No, don't bother. I'm sure you have better things to do than make pies. Oh—one more thing." He reached in his back pocket, handing me a brown envelope. "Lila DeForest dropped this off for you. Said she would've given it to you the other day if she'd known she'd run into you."

I ripped into it, then swallowed hard. It was the snapshot she'd taken of Andy and me on our wedding day. "Look," I said, showing it to him.

"Ha!" he laughed. "You both look ready to shit your pants."

I stared at it. Jinks was right, yet in a way, Andy never looked more beautiful. I shoved it in my purse. "Thanks, Jinks. See you soon." He waved me off as I pulled out.

I turned down the road to the farm, barely out of first gear, letting the woods swallow me. Here and there the pines oaks were browning, the Scarlets going their moni-kered red as other deciduous trees showed bits of orange and yellow. Already the drying undergrowth was littered with acorns, and I knew in the next few weeks the forest would explode with color. I don't think I realized until then how much I longed for it. Or as I drove the wooden bridge across a cedar marsh, how much I'd like to see it frozen over, deer tracks pocking the snow. In fact, all the things Andy had told me about—harvest moon hikes, tundra swans, gathering pinecones and holly for Christmas wreathes—I prematurely mourned, knowing his stories would always be just that.

I pulled over when I reached the site of the old tavern, its ruins more visible as the summer vines and ferns withered away. I wondered what it would've been like had Andy grown up there, if he had taken me home to it instead of the farm. I wondered if the lack of the familiar would've weighed as heavily as it did his mother, her gen-tility smothered between the branches and undergrowth. With a new husband in a strange country, bursting with baby and closed in by these woods, she must have been suffocating, and maybe right then I understood, if only a little, before I drove on.

I FOUND ANDY sitting on the front steps when I returned, unshaven and wearing the same clothes from the night before. He looked to me, droopy-eyed and miserable, as I parked the truck and came up to him.

"Where've you been?" I said.

He didn't answer, just extended his hand, and when I took it he guided me to a spot beside him. After I sat, he pulled my fist to his mouth and kissed it, then, unfurling my fingers, pressed his lips to the soft pad of my hand.

"I don't care why you married me," he whispered into my palm. "If it was only for the story, then you did what you had to do." He looked up, his eyes bright and blue. "I'm just happy you did."

"Oh, Andy . . ." I choked out, the night, the morning, the reality of the afternoon and what would follow all descending. "I'm glad I did, too."

Andy cradled my face. "*Je t'adore . . . Mais tu me fais craquer, tu sais?*" He kissed me, a kiss so beautifully consuming I was breathless. I curled my arm around his neck and pulled him in.

Andy trailed his lips to my temple. "I didn't sleep at all last night. I just lay there, so cold without you. I thought of all the work you've done on the farm, your cleaning, your cooking and putting up with me and never complaining . . ." He held my face in his hands. "Then to see you lying in the dark on the sofa, not wanting to be with me, well . . ." He buried his face in my neck. "I couldn't stand it. I did what work I had to do and then I started to walk, trying to get you out of my head, but nothing worked because all I could think of, *chérie* . . ." I pulled away, looking up at him, "was holding you again." He brushed his finger down my face. "I'm an idiot, right?"

"Of course," I said, feeling so much better. "Idiotic to worry about an idiot like me. I don't deserve *you*."

"Maybe," he said, and I poked him. "But I'm what you have, so get used to it."

"I'll certainly try." We sat there in companionable silence for a few moments, the weight of so much unsaid between us. But neither did we want to ruffle the delicate détente of the last few minutes. So I diverted to the mundane, reaching into my purse. "Look what Mrs. DeForest left for us at Uncle Jinks."

He slid the photo from the envelope. "Oh, look at that."

I laughed. "I know. It's awful, isn't it?"

He kissed my cheek. "No. You look lovely."

"I wouldn't a few minutes from then, would I?"

"Ha! After you jumped in the lake!" He shrugged. "Ah, well. At least she captured the moment."

We laughed again, Andy flapping his shirt. He looked to the clouds thickening in the east. "Man, it's humid. It's getting hard to breathe out here."

"I know. Like the air's made of wool or something."

"Leave it to a writer to think of that." He kissed my cheek. "I'll be in the barn."

And I'd be in the house. I smiled, rising toward it. All was right with the world.

"OH MY GOD, Julie—this brie is *incredible*," Celia gushed, spreading her fourth smear atop a hunk of baguette. She looked to Andy. "Now, how would you say that in French?"

"*Incroyable*," he said, taking a bite of salad. He winked at me, clearly amused.

"Imagine that," Ray opined. "It's almost like you're speaking the same language."

"Ray! Tell Andy he simply must teach us how to make brie. If anything, we're taking some of that milk home." She turned to me. "It's the hottest thing now, unpasteurized milk. You know how hard it is to get? At some Philly stores they sell it in the back alley." She took another bite, rolling her eyes in bliss. "Oh Jesus . . . I believe you've outdone yourself, Julie. I'm having a food orgasm . . ."

"Shall we have dessert and coffee on the porch?" I said. "It's so warm out; we're probably not going to get many more like this." As I gathered up the cheese plate I nodded to Celia. "Why don't you and Ray go on out? We'll join you in just a bit."

A few minutes later, Andy held the tray as I piled on the dessert and coffee. He leaned in to kiss me. "Everything was fabulous, Julie—the food, the table, the wines. You did an incredible job." His mouth crooked. "*Incroyable*."

"Either one will do," I said, kissing him back. Suddenly a rumble shook the room. "Andy, did you just make the earth move, or was that—"

"Thunder. Maybe it's finally going to rain." He thought a moment, leaving for the porch. "You know, I can't think of the last time it did."

"Not in a week, at least," I said, holding out the door.

"Eleven days," said Ray on his feet, peering out over the lake as the clouds rumbled and flashed. "We've been on high alert for two days now."

I gripped Andy's shoulder as he set down the tray. "What's that mean, Ray?"

"Means if there's a fire, he gets to play cowboy," Celia said, taking the baked apple and whipped cream I offered. "He lives for these things."

"I'd rather live without them," he said. "But what're you going to do?" He took a cup of coffee, turning back to the yard.

As the sky flashed again, I asked, "Do you think there's a chance of a fire, Ray?"

He shrugged. "There's always a chance when the Pines are dry for this long, but you're pretty far from the tree line. You should be fine."

"I'll tell you what's fine," Celia said. "These apples." She pointed her spoon in my direction. "Julie, darling, I'll be doing eight hour days at the gym for the next month thanks to you." She took another bite and nearly swooned. "My God . . ."

Andy had joined Ray at the door, the screens rattling with each rainless boom. It was getting closer, or maybe just more powerful, and that had me sipping more wine than coffee. Then Ray's phone rang.

"Yeah?" he said, stepping into the yard. "Where?" A few seconds later, he turned to us. "Lightning strike in Fall's Corner, around mile marker twenty-two. Hit a patch of old growth." He yanked the door opened. "Celia, we got to go."

"Yeah, yeah, I know the drill," she said, taking one more bite of apple.

"Christ, that's less than five miles from here," said Andy.

"Better get prepped. It's always the best thing." Ray downed his coffee, handing me the cup. "Thanks for the wonderful dinner. I have a feeling it's the last food I'm getting for a while."

As we watched them pull out I said to Andy, "What do you think?"

He put his arm around me and smiled. "We'll handle it. Don't worry."

I sighed. Not what I wanted to hear.

Chapter Sixteen

Surf 'n Turf

ANDY'S DAD HAD kept an old police scanner in the barn, and we set it up in the living room, listening late into the night. There had been a few more lightning strikes in the general vicinity of Fall's Corner and all with very little rain, hitting mostly wilderness with lots of dead timber for fuel. By two PM we heard two hundred and fifty acres had burned, and you could smell the smoke in the yard. By three, it was close to four hundred acres and you could see it, a gray fog wisping through the trees and over the lake, filling the air with a choking thickness, making it hard to breathe. By three-thirty, even though the house was closed tight you could still smell it inside, and by four we climbed to the roof, seeing flames for the first time, the sky above it a sickly orange. By the time we climbed down, Uncle Jinks, a longtime volunteer fireman, was pulling into the yard.

"Twelve hundred acres, so far," he said, stepping out of his truck. "They've managed to contain it at Fall's Corner, but six houses caught damage outside of Sheffield Township, most of them with no firebreaks."

"How about the ones *with* firebreaks?" I asked, coughing. Already it was hard to breathe.

He didn't have to answer; the hot gust of wind that blew across the yard did it for him. "Anyway, I've been sent to tell you to evacuate. Unless the wind shifts, you've got an hour, maybe two, before both roads out of here won't be passable. We're bringing a pumper truck in to start wetting down the woods from your lake. You can go on over to my house. It's still smoky, but nowhere near as bad."

"Julie will go," Andy said, "but I'm staying to help."

"No!" I said, clutching Andy's arm. Whether it was my reporter's radar or I'd become more attached to this place than I realized, I wasn't about to leave either. "I want to help just as much as you."

"Which both add up to nothing," Jinks said, adamant. "Look, you can hardly breathe now around this smoke, and in a little while we're all going to need masks if we want to breathe at all. If you're worried about your house and barn, you have a real good firebreak, and I'll make sure everything gets soaked down, which we can do a whole hell of a lot better and faster than with that garden pisser you've got there. Now, go on and get out of here while you still can."

Andy opened his mouth to argue, then apparently thought it pointless. With the smoke rolling in over the lake, there really wasn't much he could argue about. Not that he appeared to like it.

"Okay, you win," he said. "Julie, why don't you pack an overnight bag for the both of us. I'll go get the truck and round up Bucky."

"You'd better hurry," said Jinks. "The smoke's getting pretty bad, pretty fast."

I didn't need him to tell me that; already my eyes were stinging so badly it was hard to keep them open. Smoke had even seeped through the floorboards and roof and into the house, a gray pall and stench wafting through it. I grabbed my overnighter from underneath the bed and stuffed it with underwear and t-shirts and anything else I could think of, panic gripping me as I gasped for air. I remembered an old story I heard and wet two linen dishtowels down and threw them in a plastic bag. The reek of smoke was like a chokehold on my throat, even worse when I opened the front door and realized the contrast. I couldn't see ten feet past the front porch. I stumbled down the steps, almost blinded, the hem of my t-shirt over my nose as I searched the fog for Andy.

"Andy!" I cried into the murk.

Almost immediately the truck pulled out in front. "Hurry—get in." Before I did I checked the seat and back. "Where's Bucky?"

"He wasn't in the house?"

"No!" I yelled. "Andy, we can't leave him."

"I don't want to, but how can we find him in this soup?"

"Bucky!" I screamed into the yard. "Bucky!" I turned to Andy. "If he doesn't burn up, he'll suffocate—we just can't leave him here! We can't!"

Andy whistled and yelled, but it was impossible to see past the immediate, our own voices seeming to end in a dull thud. Then Jinks came up alongside. I tried not to panic when I saw the breathing mask in his hand.

"If you're looking for the dog," he said, "I saw him running across the road as I pulled in the yard."

I clutched Andy's arm. "He's probably disoriented by the smoke. Oh, Andy, we'll never find him now."

He looked at his uncle. "Will you watch out for him?"

"I just saw him not ten minutes ago; he's fine. When he shows up I'll take him with me. Now go on, get out of here." Jinks looked to me. "I have your number, and you have mine. I'll keep you posted. Like I said, it's the smoke that's worse than the fire."

"What about Betsy?" I said. "And the chickens?"

Andy laughed, which I took as a good sign. "The chickens will just have to fend for themselves, but Betsy's safe in the barn."

"And I'm the one who showed you how to work that milking contraption," said Jinks. "She won't burst. Now, go on get out of here before you won't be able to see at all. The pumper should be here any—well, speak of the—!"

Just then a fire truck rumbled into the yard. At least I thought it was a fire truck as the smoke momentarily stirred, followed by a couple pick-ups containing men and equipment.

"Okay, now I feel better," Andy said, shifting the truck

into gear. He looked to his Uncle Jinks. "You be careful, *mon oncle*," he said, clasping his hand. "There's lots of food and coffee in the house for you and the men, so help yourself."

"Thanks, don't think we won't. Now go on and get that wife of yours out of here." Andy waved, pulling out of the yard.

Driving through the smoky woods was a nerve-wracking exercise in patience, made even worse by the cover of night. You wanted to go fast but you couldn't see, as without the painted lines of an asphalt road to guide you, all you had was sugar sand and the claustrophobic fencing of trees and undergrowth. With the headlights reflecting back glare, I believed we could've gone faster crawling. At one point it was so thick we apparently drove right into the smoke's trajectory. With wet dishtowels over our mouths and noses, Andy had to crack the window so he could hear the road as we couldn't see it, the air outside so black and viscous it would've been easier breathing from the bottom of the lake. My throat scorched and my eyes streaming, the interior of the truck like an oven, I broke out in a sweat, gasping for air through the damp cloth.

Andy rubbed my neck. "Just a little bit longer."

Wishful thinking, I knew, when all of a sudden it brightened and a herd of deer thundered across the trail, leaping madly into the woods. Ahead flames licked the trees on the other side of the road, burning as fast as a match struck to paper.

Andy stomped on the brake, his face frozen, his fingers whitening around the steering wheel. "Andy . . .?" I said but he didn't answer. "Andy!"

In the microsecond it took me to shake his arm he reacted with a jolt. As the flames climbed and licked, I swore I could see that boy from all those years before, finding his father on fire. "Andy!" I cried, shaking him.

He whipped his head toward me, as if suddenly discovering I was there. He clenched his eyes and, turning, refocused on the road. "Hold on," he said, squeezing my hand. Then he stepped on the gas and roared forward.

I coughed, holding on, my heart in my throat.

The burning branches arced around us like a fiery tunnel, snapping and whirring. I never knew fire was so noisy, but it crackled, rumbled and howled, screeching pitifully as the wind blew through it, crashing when it took down a limb. Andy bore through the conflagration like a guided missile, his head up, his body forward, his eyes dead ahead, while I clawed my nails into the dashboard, terrified, coughing and in awe. With the fire lighting the inside like a thousand-watt bulb Andy was beyond illuminated, a study in incandescent tenacity.

"Just hold on," he said. "We're almost through."

"I-I'm okay," I said, and just like that, I was. Suddenly the flames receded, and within the next hundred feet the fog lifted, at least enough we could see the trail again. By the time Andy idled at the stop sign on Main Street, the smoke had thinned into a haze, three more fire trucks turning onto the trail to get into it. A few more feet and we hit tar. I was so happy I wanted to get out and kiss the ground. Instead I kissed Andy's cheek.

"Thank you for getting me out of there," I said.

He looked wired, relieved and oh-so-grateful. "Thank you for trusting me enough to do it."

"Oh Andy," I said, kissing his cheek again, "I want to say I'd trust you with my life, but it looks like I just did."

He leaned in, but whatever moment there was to be between us was suddenly broken by a bark.

We both turned at once and saw Bucky yapping his head off from the bay of the truck. "Bucky!" I yelled.

"He must have jumped in as we were going through the smoke," Andy said. He opened his door and immediately the dog hopped out of the back and in between us.

"Bucky! You bad boy!" I cried, hugging his smoky ruff. "Damn, if you don't smell like a barbecue. The first thing we're all doing at Uncle Jinks' is take a shower, you included." I coughed. "It's even up my nose."

Andy turned onto Main Street. "Sorry, but you're going to have to wait a little longer," he said, just as Jinks' house appeared in the rear window.

"Hey! You passed Uncle—say . . ." I peered at him. Where're you going?"

"It's a surprise. We should be there in an hour."

"And where's that?" I said as he veered a sharp left. "Wait, I know this road. It goes to Tuckerton. We're going to Tuckerton?"

"Sure. It's where we pick up Route Nine."

"Why're we going to Route Nine?" The last thing I was in the mood for was a surprise when I was exhausted, smelly, and badly in need of coffee. "Andy! I'm tired and filthy and I can hardly breathe. Where in hell are you taking me?"

He smiled again, nudging me back to the seat. "I'm taking you as far away from all this smoke and fire as we can get. Now relax and close your eyes. I'll wake you up when we get there. And open your window." He rolled down his. "The air's already clearer."

I hadn't the strength to argue. I rolled down the window, the cool air hitting my lungs like an infusion. I sucked it in, my head clearing enough to tell the rest of my body that at a quarter past five AM all was well, and no one would mind, least of all me, if it shut down for a little while. I closed my eyes and promptly complied.

THE TRUCK BOUNCED and my eyes opened, my head lolling against the headrest as Bucky lifted his head from my lap. Ahead lay an expanse of bridge and water, the sky lightening over land in the distance.

"W-Where are we?" I said, momentarily disoriented, every bone in my body aching.

Andy's arm stretched across the back of the seat, his fingers kneading my neck. I sighed, feeling the vertebrae pop. "Long Beach Island, coming up."

"Long Beach—?" I reached through the fog of memory. "You have a house on Long Beach Island?"

"Well, it's more like a cottage."

"Cottage is fine," I said. Bucky hopped up and stuck his head out the window, and recognizing a good idea when I saw one, I did too, the air salty and crisp, snapping me awake. As we bumped from islet to islet over the causeway, the bay slipped like mercury beneath us, and I felt a tingling which had nothing to do with hunger and exhaustion. "Are we spending the day?"

He squeezed my hand. "Or two. How's that sound?" A shimmer of ocean became visible for a split-second as we topped the highest bridge. Since I was little, there wasn't anything I loved more than the Shore, becoming the seasonal Jersey Girl for at least two weeks every summer, three, if my father could manage it. "Sounds too good to be true. But what about the farm? Does Uncle Jinks know?"

"He knows," Andy said, steering the truck off the bridge. At the Boulevard he turned right, and through the waning night and with hardly a word, we drove nearly to the tail of the long barrier island, past storefronts and houses already shuttered for the off season, through the larger village of Beach Haven and to where the island narrowed to just the boulevard and interspersed houses, ocean dunes on one side and bay reeds on the other. With the end of it in view he made a left into a driveway, and up a rise to a small blue-shuttered, clapboard house, bordered by dune grass and holly. Andy picked through his key ring and we went inside.

When Andy flicked on a light I could see it was at least half the size of the farmhouse, with white wainscoted walls and wood floors and a brick fireplace in the living room on the left, which stretched into a kitchen the width of the house, and on the right, two tiny bedrooms and a miniscule bathroom. Bucky trotted in and settled by the hearth. But I only noticed it in passing as I went directly to the door at the other end, which opened to a small covered porch, and a berm of dune, and a soft, undulating roar.

A second later I was at the railing, taking in beach and ocean and a faint pinking on the horizon, the breeze ruffling my hair and pebbling my skin, promising a last taste of summer. I closed my eyes, breathing deeply, letting the salt eat away at the smoke and stifle, the unobstructed expanse of sea and sky such an antidote for the last twelve hours I felt giddy, and oh-so-grateful.

"Oh, Andy," I said, wrapping my arms around him, "thanks for bringing me here. I couldn't ask for any better place."

"Good. Because for the next couple of days I'm making it the honeymoon I never gave you." He slung his arm around me and we looked out on the darkened beach, stars fading behind the coming dawn. "You know, I did a lot of thinking yesterday, some of which made me realize how badly I've treated you."

"What?" I said, pulling away. "You never—"

"Julie," he said, a finger against my mouth. "Let me finish. When I do there's a good chance you'll agree with me."

"Okay." I settled against him.

"Anyway . . ." He sighed, glancing to the ocean. I knew whatever he was trying to tell me wasn't easy, and that scared me a bit. "When I thought about how quickly you jumped into this marriage, barely knowing me, and how busy we've been ever since, not to mention how hard you had to work since the day—almost since the very minute—we got married, well ... I think it was pretty unfair of me to expect you'd just go along with what you signed up for without first being a bride, because like the bastard I am, I never treated you as one."

Now he was just confusing me. "Andy—what the hell are you talking about?"

He turned us toward the beach and the red line of illumination to the east. "I'm like the father who tosses his kid into the water to see if she'll sink or swim. And that's unfair, because who was I to assume you'd think the deal I offered would be enough? Yet there I was, taking advantage, thinking my grand promise on paper would suffice. But it couldn't, no matter how much it'd eventually amount to. Because it could never show just how much you mean to me." He let me go, taking from his pocket a little wooden box. "I was going to give this to you last night after everyone left, but we sort of got ..." He laughed softly. ". . . sidetracked."

When he opened it my heart clenched; inside was a diamond ring in the same style as my wedding band, carved platinum with a setting of about a carat. "Oh Andy . . ." I said, barely breathing it.

He took the ring from the box and slid it on my finger; it fell into place like it was molded. "I've been carrying this around since the day we were married. I should've given it to you then, but I wasn't sure you'd take it."

I couldn't help but laugh at the irony. "My dear, no matter how self-sufficient I may be, diamonds still are a girl's best friend."

"No doubt." And then he went very quiet. "But this ring is different. Where the wedding band was a symbol of our contract, this diamond's more a symbol of . . ."

"The heart than the mind." When he smiled, I placed my hands to his chest. "You're right. I probably wouldn't have taken it then. But now?" Now everything seemed changed, altered. Although I wasn't sure how it happened, I knew it had. "I don't know how I lived without it. Thank you, Andy. It's perfect."

"And so are you." He kissed me and we turned toward the rising sun, its trail burning a reddish path from horizon to shore. Had I been burdened with an ordinary sensibility, I would've harkened it as a portent, but that was way too easy. So I took it for what it was—beautiful, like my husband before me, strong and lusty and carrying me inside, the world rising around us.

Chapter Seventeen

Paradise Island

ANDY LAY BENEATH me, clasped between my legs, his cock deep inside me. I loosened my smoky-scented hair, my breasts lifting as I plucked out clips and pins, his hips slowly undulating as his fingers circled, kneaded, tormented my areola. I swiveled likewise, once, twice, three times, then lifting up, let my hair fall, a curl catching on a nipple before it swooped to the underside of my breast and I came down, damp flesh meeting damp flesh, charged beyond electric. He hissed, jolted, and I reached back and under, my fingers just skimming before I cupped their weight in my hands, rolling them like Ben Wa. He hissed again, cursing softly, grabbing my wrists to pull me against him.

"*Merde. Tu te comportes comme une chienne en chaleur . . .*" he whispered against my mouth, "*mais, oh . . . t'es un sacré bon coup.*"

"You know . . ." I said, nipping the side of his mouth, "I'm going to have to learn French if I ever want to understand what you say when you fuck me. I suspect . . ." I nipped him again. "It's very saucy."

"You're saucy," he said. *"Coquin."* His eyes glittering, he clasped my behind in his big hands, and squeezed. "What do you want to know? That I live to fuck you? That you're the best fuck I ever had? Well, there it is, I've said it."

He punctuated that with a few well-delivered thrusts, and before I knew it he had me on my back, my leg slung over his arm. He thrust again and I moaned. *"Oh, oui, oui,* that's it . . . *ma chérie . . . ma belle . . ."* He leaned down, his lips just gracing mine before he opened them with his tongue and kissing me deeply, took my breath away.

"Ma femme . . ." he whispered, just soft enough to break my heart.

My God, wasn't it bad enough he was gorgeous with the most perfect body and blue eyes and that lovely accent which could swallow me whole? Wasn't it enough he knew exactly how to touch me—just as he did then and I bit my lip, mewling—his warm breath in my ear, whispering words whose translation worked more from emotion than meaning? But did he also have to be so smart and kind? Now *that* was my undoing. I writhed beneath him as he thrust so deliberately, winding me higher and higher and higher still. Then I saw his face, every angle chiseled by morning sun as he raised up, and throwing his head back, I could tell—by the burgeoning muscles in his arms, the tautness in his chest, how he roared when everything inside him poured into me and I spasmed with bliss—I was beyond it all.

He kissed my eyes, my cheeks, my lips, smiling with the ruddy glow of a sated man. "You're wonderful," he said, his finger trailing down my jaw "*Je t'adore.*" He kissed me again. "*Je t'adore.*"

I was falling, falling.

I AWOKE TO a sound I used to know as well as my own voice—my phone ringing—whose vocal irregularity now relegated it to another lifetime. Yet it was enough to send me bolting from within Andy's slumbering embrace, to wonder where the hell its blare was coming from. For lack of anything better I grabbed the bedspread from the floor and wrapped it around me, closing the door as I left for the living room. Almost immediately I found it; there was Bucky, growling at my purse from where it sat on the sofa.

"Good boy," I said, and patting his head, dug out it out. Thank God—it was Uncle Jinks. "Burned to the ground?" I said, my whole body clenching.

"Sorry, but no," he said, laughing. "Though we did wet the house down just in case. Gave it a good soaking, so if anything, it's spanky-clean. The guys are just pulling out now. They thank you for the couple pots of coffee your hospitality made them." "So is it all out?"

"Around here, at least, since the wind shifted and it started raining, but there's still a few hot spots. I expect we'll get them all contained before night hits, if not sooner. It's still smoky as hell though, so stay put."

"It's not raining here yet, but it's sure looking like it." Not exactly what I wanted in a beach holiday, but ... I smiled inwardly ... the indoor activity wasn't so bad, either.

"It will, don't worry, but it shouldn't last long. So enjoy yourself. Everything here is fine."

"Is that Jinks?"

Andy emerged from the bedroom, yawning, naked, and I must say, somewhat formidable-looking. "Hold on, Uncle Jinks. Andy wants to talk to you."

When I handed him the phone he pulled me back against his chest, caging me with his arm. "Morning," he whispered, kissing my neck. "Uncle Jinks! So how is it?"

I swore the man had a double-jointed personality. As he listened and offered particulars to his uncle in an oh-so-businesslike manner, he slowly undid the toga I had made of the bedspread while hardening most deliciously against my hip.

"Uh-huh, uh-huh, okay," he said as Jinks jabbered, kissing his way down my neck to my shoulder, the bedspread now a puddle on the floor. Not to be outdone, I whirled around and, falling to my knees, began to meet him halfway.

"Uh!" he croaked.

"What?" I heard Jinks say.

"Nothing Uncle!" he said, half an octave higher. "You just do what you think—is best, and I'll talk to you—

tomorrow! 'Bye!" He rang off and tossed the phone to the sofa. "Dammit Julie!"

"Done talking?" I said, after two quick licks.

He grasped me by the shoulders and pulled me upright. "I was talking to Jinks."

"And I was giving you a—"

"I'm well aware what you were doing, but I was on the phone—"

"When you should be *on me*."

He arched a brow. "Really?"

"Well, you started it."

"You're right." He eased me back into the sofa. "Which means I'll finish it." Then he spread my legs and lowered his mouth to me.

It took four-point-five seconds, I shivered, shook and screamed, and then he was inside me, so efficient, my sixty-minute man. But wasn't that the best part, my being in his arms, staring up into those eyes, his taste in my mouth? He came and called my name, the sound of it like poetry, and after it was over we held each other for just a few moments more, nuzzling, whispering, his heart beating against mine.

I said against his neck, "You're scrumptious, Andy, but I'm about to die of starvation."

He looked around. "What time is it anyway?"

"Look at my phone." I arched my neck backward; it was wedged in the cushions. He reached past me and grabbed it. "Eleven-forty-two."

Bucky whined, pressing against Andy's leg. "When's the last time he was let out?" I asked.

Andy winced. "The last time he let himself out." He kissed my shoulder, pulling himself from me. "Why don't you catch a shower, and I'll go find us something to eat. There's a deli just down the road. I'll walk Bucky along the way."

"Sounds excellent." So a few minutes later, with Bucky leashed by a length of clothesline (both of us forgot his real one), Andy left, leaving me to face the cottage, the beach, and the ocean on my own. I pulled on a nightshirt and threw open the back door.

If rain was on its way, it hadn't hit yet, and I went to the railing, surveying my domain. The beach was all but deserted, except for a lone fisherman about a quarter mile to my left, and no one in the other direction. The morning was a bit cloudy and somewhat sultry, and I expected a hell of a downpour soon, but for now I wanted to take every advantage. I took the long flight of stairs down to the beach and, sinking my feet into the rumpled sand, trotted straight for the ocean.

I stopped at the shoreline. I'd soon find out if what I always heard was true about the New Jersey water, that it was warmer in fall than in summer. I tentatively inched toward it until the surf washed over my toes. I sighed; it was true. The waves rolled toward me in gentle folds. I glanced up and down the beach: still pretty much vacant. So there was a good chance no one'd notice I was dressed only in a thin, yellow nightshirt that barely reached my knees. Not that I cared. After living in the woods for six weeks, cooking over open fires and copulating like a rabbit, surely swimming practically naked in public could hardly matter when my norms went to extremes. So I took a deep breath and, stepping into the surf, dove right in.

I wasn't about to press my luck; I'd been around water long enough to know you shouldn't swim alone, especially when certain local denizens had no qualms against eating me alive. But damn if it didn't feel so good, slinking like an eel underwater. When I popped to the surface I felt all traces of the smoky night slough away, my skin and hair awash with salt and clean. I looked around me: endless ocean and sky above, a long strand of white sand, Andy's cottage dead ahead looking so pert and independent and—it suddenly struck me—*safe*. I contemplated that tiny revelation and the little house: *safe*. As much as I was growing to love Andy's farm in the woods, this place seemed different, exposed to even more brutal elements, but a refuge all the same. I felt an affinity, and I didn't know why. But somehow I knew if there ever again came a time like those horrible first days after Richard left me, I would want a place like this to come to. Not that I'd let that happen again. A wave crashed at my back, pushing me forward. Because this time I'd do the leaving.

I swam toward shore, a rumble of thunder in the distance.

By THE TIME Andy returned, I had showered and set the table, finding and washing the same style of French crockery as we had at the farm. I also got my first good look at the house. The furnishings appeared utilitarian yet not without style, a sturdy painted wood table and chairs, a small matching hutch, a Danish modern living room set, all vintage, but still looking good. Things were hardly dusty, as I suspected the place had been given a good cleaning lately, and although the beds weren't made up, there were recently-laundered towels and sheets in the linen closet. Which made me think: had Andy been planning this romantic little hideaway? Had he just been waiting for the right moment? I held my hand out, admiring the diamond ring he had given me the night before. Coming here and getting this just couldn't be a coincidence. So when Andy and Bucky returned with the rudiments of breakfast and a bag of kibble, I asked him.

"Correct me if I'm wrong," I said later, slicing a corn muffin just as Andy emerged freshly showered from the bathroom, "but this honeymoon wasn't exactly an impromptu decision, was it?"

He sat down, opening the local newspaper. "Why do you say that?"

"Not that I'm complaining, but you must have planned it. This place doesn't exactly look uninhabited."

"That's because it wasn't. My father had it rented out for the summer. The cleaning service was just in to close it up for the winter."

I don't know why that deflated me, but it did. "Oh," I said simply, picking bits off the corn muffin.

Andy sighed, folding his arms atop the paper. "Something wrong?"

I shrugged. "I don't know. I just thought . . ." I popped a bit of muffin in my mouth. "Nothing. Forget it."

"No. Hey." He pulled my hand toward him. "What is it?"

I shrugged again. God, I hated being petulant, but this was bothering me. "Maybe I just don't like the idea of being an afterthought."

"What?" He pulled back, looking positively pinched. "You think *I* think—"

"Oh, forget it," I said, feeling stupid. I slipped out of my chair and into his lap. "I'm sorry," I said, looping my arms around his neck. "I'm just happy I'm here. For whatever reason."

"Julie, you could never be an afterthought, but remember—we had to contend with birthing a heifer, chickens, a trashed house, overflowing vegetables, and a myriad of other things that needed immediate attention. And this house wasn't even empty until a few days ago." He bounced me on his knees a few beats. "*Tu comprends?*"

"All right, I get it." I kissed him, and we sat in companionable silence for a bit, Andy sipping coffee and reading the newspaper. "So . . . what do you want to do now?"

He kissed me, smiling wickedly.

"Again? Come on, there's more to a honeymoon than just *that*."

"Like what? It's raining!"

What began as a downpour now seemed to be easing. "Even with the rain."

He sighed, slowly shaking his head. "Jesus, you're such an American."

"So are you, but every now and then your Frenchiness

precedes you. Come on, get up." I slid from his lap. "We're going out."

"Where? It's hardly a beach day."

"But we're not going on the beach. We're going shopping."

"Shopping!" My manly-man gaped at me as if I just suggested he don a pink tutu. "Why?"

I pinched the front of his shirt. Here—smell this. We still stink like smoke. If we're going out tonight we each need to get a new outfit. And we *are* going out tonight, aren't we?"

Andy sniffed his collar. "Okay, you're right. Let's go."

"Just let me get my shoes."

As I trotted to the bedroom, he mumbled, *"Frenchiness?"*

WE WALKED HAND-IN-HAND from the restaurant to the bayside, looking strangely enough like a couple on their honeymoon. As the water lapped against the pilings, the half-moon rising behind us, Andy slipped his arms around my waist and pulled me to him, his forehead against mine.

"Forgive me yet?" he said, most contritely, kissing my hand.

I tossed my hair, wearing it loose that night, thinking about whether or not I should absolve him of his most egregious transgression. "I'm still thinking . . ." I slipped my hand to the back of his neck. "Kiss me, and I'll let you know."

That afternoon, we had left our rather vacated end of the island for Beach Haven a few miles away, rambling in and out of the shops that were still open, buying a dress, a rather sexy bra set, and four inch heels for me, a polo and a pair of khakis for Andy, and swim suits for each of us. Soon after the rain stopped and the day became sunny and warm, we headed to an outdoor café for coffee, sharing a bread bowl of lobster bisque. Then we took a walk along the docks, mainly so Andy could impress me by talking nautical shop with a couple of captains. One of them was kind enough to not only give us a tour of his boat, but to also engage Andy in a rather spirited discussion about his engine's compression. Only after I was thoroughly dazzled by talk of twin MTU 600 horse-power diesel engines did Andy spirit me back to the cottage. I squeezed into my new bikini and Andy into his swim trunks, and we ran down to the water. The clear sky had brought out some fishermen, though they were a bit down the beach on either side.

"I must tell you," I said as my feet hit the surf, "it's been years since I've worn a bikini." I repositioned the top, my girls nearly boiling over. But what did I want for ten bucks? "I can't believe you talked me into it."

Andy raked me with his gaze, smiling appreciatively. "Why? You have the figure for it. You look gorgeous. *Fantastique.*"

"But it'll be hard to swim in." I picked at it. "I feel like I'm falling out."

He came up to me, running his thumbs over the rim of the cups. "Then take it off. European women go topless at the beach. It's no big thing." His hand trailed to the clasp in between, his finger looping under it.

My eyes widened. "Don't you dare . . ."

"Do . . . what?" He leaned down to kiss me, distracting me with his well-placed tongue. Suddenly the bikini top popped apart, slipping down my arms to the water. I gasped, palming my boobs while he snatched it from the surf a split-second before the next wave took it.

"Give me that you bastard!" I yelled. Andy promptly shoved it down his trunks and dove into the water.

"Son of a bitch!" I screamed, diving after him.

By the time I hit air he was in front of me, laughing hysterically and hauling me to him. "You bastard!" I cried, pummeling his chest, which only made him tweak my high-beam nips and laugh harder. So hard a minute later I was joining him, jumping in and out of the waves with my new-found freedom.

"See?" he said. "Isn't it easier to swim without worrying if your top will fall off?"

"Yeah," I said, up to my neck in the water, "but how the hell am I supposed to walk out?" I stuck out my hand. "Fork it over, buster."

"You sure?" His eyes dropped to my buoyant boobage. "You look terrific."

I waggled my fingers. "Absolutely. Give it here."

"Okay . . ." He sighed dramatically, reaching into his trunks. His face went blank.

"Don't tell me . . ." I shoved my hand down his shorts, rummaging through every square inch. He leaned back, grinning. I looked up in horror, snatching my hand out.

"How could you!" I cried. "At a time like this!"

"For Christ's sake—you had your hand down my pants! What did you expect!"

I looked away. *I will not laugh. I will not laugh.* "Where is it!"

"I don't know! There's netting in this suit, it must have slipped out somehow. Maybe there's a hole?"

The perils of cheap suits. The wind had kicked up, the water now warmer than the air, and I was starting to freeze. I crossed my arms in front of me. With evening prime fishing time, more fishermen had set up on the beach, these ones within viewing distance. The longer I waited, the worse it would get. "I'm getting out."

Andy slung his arm over my shoulder. "Stay close to me and no one will know the difference." And just like that, we ambled from the surf, where just before we hit dry sand, we looked down and there, washed up on the shore, was my elusive top.

"Well, look at that," Andy said.

I looked at it a moment then, stepping away from him, turned and in full frontal fishermen position dropped my arms. "Get it for me, darling, will you?"

Just before I turned to stroll back to the cottage, I could have sworn a fisherman or two dropped their poles. But then again, I'm sure plenty others were raising theirs.

After that, I fully intended to torture Andy. I showered with the door wide and the shower curtain half open, slowly slathering myself with soap and shampoo until I was sudsy and shiny, arching each leg on the rim of the tub to shave. As he worked his razor across his own beard, I could see him swallowing hard, so I tried to make it even worse when I slipped into my new champagne lace underwear, the boy shorts giving him a tantalizing glimpse of my bottom. And I'm sure the boned bra piqued his ardor much more than any naked boobs could've that afternoon.

But the *pièce de résistance* had to be the four-inch sandals I bought—spiky, strappy little things I swear were designed to bring him down. When I walked out of the bedroom, a slip of lace just peeking from the deep cleavage of my white wrap dress, my newly acquired height now elevating my charms for easier viewing, Andy's eyes nearly popped out of his head, his mouth so dry I needed a drink of water.

"Ready?" he rasped, gaping at me.

"Am I ever," I said, licking my lips. I squeezed past him, brushing my hip against his on the way to the door.

Dinner was no better. I did my best *Tom Jones* imitation while nipping shrimp cocktail and crab legs. At one point Andy reached under the table to furtively caress my knee. I coldly crossed my legs, shifting.

"*Chienne,*" he whispered, pouring another glass of wine.

So when he broke our kiss there at the bayside after dinner, Andy was one supremely frustrated man. "Well? Will you still make me suffer?"

I tossed my head—and my hair—looking upward, thinking. "I don't know," I said, biting my lip as I caught his smoldering gaze. "Why don't you take me home and find out."

He grabbed my hand and we were off.

I don't think I've ever ridden so fast down a residential street in my life. Andy peeled down the boulevard, pulling sideways into the driveway. He jammed the truck into park then pulled me out his side, leaving the door half-opened as he fumbled for his key and threw open the front door. I went right for the back porch, where I pertly half-perched on the railing.

"Well?" he said, raking a hand through his already well-raked hair.

I leaned against a post, my breasts arching sweetly, and with a bit of a pouty lip, said, "I guess I'm just not in the mood." I shrugged. "Sorry." I hopped off the railing, heading inside. "I'm tired. Good night."

I wasn't halfway to the door when his hand caught my arm. A moment later I was back atop the railing, Andy firmly between my spread legs. "Where do you think you're going?" he growled, his eyes like blue crystals in the moonlight.

"I-I was going to bed," I said, barely able to speak.

"Really?" He slid my dress up my legs. "Did you actually think you'd get there without me?" Two fingers slipped to my crotch; I immediately went wet. "Or without this first?" He slid a finger inside me.

I threw my head back as his thumb worked its magic, grasping his shoulders for support. Before a minute was out he had my satin boy shorts on the porch and I was coming so violently I shook in his hands. When I came back to earth, my fingers were at his zipper.

"Fuck me, Andy," I said, fumbling with it. "Fuck me—*please*."

"How about—*no*," he said, slapping my hand away. "How about—*I'm* tired?"

I grabbed at his cock; he pinned my hands behind my back, biting my lip before shoving his tongue between my swollen lips. I had just come, but I was already wanting more, panting against his mouth, my hips writhing as he pressed his pelvis into mine.

"Andy ... Andy ..." I panted, never wanting him more.

"How does it feel, *ma petite*, to want something ..." He kissed me savagely. "Want something so badly you can't have?"

I fought against his grasp, but he only tightened it. "Andy ..." I kissed him hard, tasting blood. "I'll do anything if you only—"

"Anything?" He laughed. "Oh, *ma chérie* ... you just said the magic words." He freed himself, and within a second he was inside me.

I felt a million things imploding—my mind spinning out of control as he was everywhere: in me, above me, around me, his scent like sexual adrenaline. We grasped at each other, panting, heaving, Andy pounding me so hard I felt each thrust like a beat of my heart. Then suddenly he lifted me up and we were spinning around, Andy slipping from me only long enough to carry me inside. We fell to the bed, all arms and legs and kisses, and then miraculously he was inside me again, rising above me, his gaze firm when he bent to kiss me, his mouth so soft against mine.

"You're mine," he said, "my wife, *ma femme*. They can

look all they want, appreciate you like I do, but they can never have you. You're mine, wife. *Mine.*" Then he took us both over the moon.

For a little while, I fell asleep in his arms, and as was my habit, I eased away and slipped into the bathroom. After I flicked on the light, I caught myself in the mirror where all at once it hit me. "Oh, shit . . ." I murmured, breaking into a sweat.

I wrenched on the cold tap, slapping my face with freezing water, my heart pounding. I grasped the sink, trying to steady myself, but it was no use. There was no denying the reality slowly seeping down the inside of my thigh.

I was fucked—metaphorically and otherwise.

Chapter Eighteen

Reentry

I HAD FORGOTTEN my birth control pills.

I plopped down on the toilet, my head in my hands. Not only had I forgotten my pills, but because of our argument and the confusion over the fire, I hadn't started a new pack Saturday night, which meant, because of a lapse for my period, I last took a dose nine days ago. Which led me to think the unthinkable.

I could be pregnant.

"Jesus Christ ..." I groaned, how could I have been so incredibly stupid! I counted the times we had sex: once Saturday night, not at all on Sunday, but once early this morning, then around noon, then just a few ... " Jesus ..." *Four times.* Three, just today. I couldn't have done better if his spunk and my eggs had partied in a Petrie dish.

I got up, splashed my face again with cold water.

Think. Think, I told myself, grappling for a towel. People have had sex from time immemorial, and they couldn't have gotten pregnant every single time. How did they avoid it?

I could've been practical and run down the local drugstore for a morning-after pill. But how would I've gotten that past Andy, especially since it would bring on my period, and didn't I just get over it? *Scratch that.* I recalled reading a book where a whore douched with— *No*, I thought, cringing. *Get serious.* Then I remembered something from my high school health class, about the Rhythm Method of birth control. That a woman's safest time to have sex was right after and right before her period, since ovulation usually occurred in the middle of her month. I breathed a sigh of relief. Until I remembered this method was statistically unreliable because there were too many variables. *Like how being on the pill skewed ovulation.* Damn. *Think, think . . .*

About what? I could hear Andy stirring in the other room. Not having any more sex was pretty much out of the equation, especially since . . . I shivered. I couldn't trust myself to resist him. Each time we were together I couldn't wait for the next. And then there was the elephant in the room.

He *wanted* to get me pregnant.

And I wanted him to keep wanting me. Against my better judgment, I wanted him desperately. I picked up my toothbrush and scrubbed. *Good Lord*, how I wanted him. If anything, this honeymoon was only making it worse, Denny's skepticism becoming more believable every day.

*And what if he falls in love with you? Or worse, you fall
in love with him?"*

I shot him my iciest glare. *"After Richard's screwing,
I'm never falling in love again."*

He laughed. *"As if you ever have a choice."*

"I always have before."

*"Then you've never been in love. Because when you are,
there is no choice."*

"Julie?" Andy said, knocking.

I opened the door, toothbrush in my mouth. "Mmmph?"

He came in, removed the toothbrush and, pressing his
hand to the small of my back, kissed me deeply before
sliding my toothbrush into his mouth.

"The heels add a whole new dimension," he said with a
wink. He reached past me to the toothpaste, and squeezing an inch onto the bristles, stuck the brush back into
his mouth.

I leaned back against the sink. "I was using that."

He brushed a bit more, then spit, rinsed, kissed me
again. "Here." He handed it to me and glanced to my shoes.
"Leave them on." Then he left, unbuttoning his shirt.

I stood there, numbed, a quivering deep inside me. I
guess I had no choice but to place my faith in the Method.

Jesus Christ, I was so sunk.

THE NEXT DAY we didn't do much of anything, just slept,
ate and enjoyed each other, ending up on the beach by
early afternoon. A storage shed next to the porch had
yielded a cache of beach chairs and umbrellas, and adding

to that a blanket and a bottle of wine, we stretched out on the sand in the sun. I was on my back as Andy, on his belly, lay next to me.

He pushed up on his elbows. "More sunscreen?"

I yawned, raising my arms over my head. "You've already put enough on me to last a week." I tilted my sunglasses to peer at him. "I suspect it's just a ruse to rub me down in public."

He slipped off his. "Why do you think I'm lying on my stomach?"

I nearly blushed. "You're insatiable, you know that?"

"You make it easy," he said, one finger trailing the half-moons of my breasts.

He kissed along the periphery of my mouth, tiny little kisses that made me sigh, before his arm half-caged me and his lips opened to mine. He tasted of salt and surf and Beaujolais, a wet curl drooping from his hair to swipe my cheek, his fingers caressing my chin ever so lightly. When he raised up and opened his eyes I caught my reflection in their blue shimmer, my heart clenching from his impossible beauty. He wasn't real, this man, neither the way he looked nor the way he made me feel, and I knew it was only a matter of time. I kissed him once more then closed my eyes, drifting away to dream.

AGAINST ALL LOGIC, I was falling for my husband. No matter how much I could blame Andy, it was nobody's fault but my own.

The evening had begun rather innocently. After the

beach we showered and changed, then drove to Kubel's for dinner at the other end of the island in Barnegat Light. With a half hour until sunset, we went to the lighthouse and took a stroll on the walkway, nearly reaching the end before I made my fatal error. We were both leaning against the railing, facing Island Beach State Park across the inlet, when I posed a question I never should've asked.

"Andy," I said, the breeze blowing my hair from my clip, "why did you do it?"

He looked at me, instantly understanding. "You mean the advertisement?"

"Yes." I tried to put it delicately. "I mean, you did give me your reasons that day at the firehouse, but—"

"Yes, I did." He stiffened a bit. "And you thought it so outrageous you didn't believe me?"

I almost laughed at the irony. "Look, no one knows better than me how truth is so much stranger than fiction, but I've always had a feeling there's more to it."

"There always is, isn't there? And you won't be able to start that book until you find out, right?" He looked down at the black boulders rimming the shoreline. "Always the reporter, eh?"

"That's so harsh," I said, bristling more than I deserved to.

"Sorry," he said, somewhat admonished, "I didn't mean to be. But it's the truth, isn't it?"

More than you know. Which made the whole thing look a bit sordid. "I'm not asking because of the book. I'm asking as your wife."

He straightened, looking as taken aback by hearing

that as I did by saying it. "What difference does it make now? It led me to you, didn't it?"

"Purely by accident. If my editor hadn't seen your sign, and I wasn't—"

"Julie, stop." His eyes softened, yet he seemed conflicted. "However odd you think my method, it worked, didn't it? Here you are, and I couldn't be happier."

"You say that now, but what about in the future?" My God, did I hear myself? I had no idea why I was saying this, but somehow I couldn't stop. "I've been here before, and I ended up on the street."

That muscle on the side of his face twitched, the way it always did when he was peeved. How funny was it I knew that now?

"No, you haven't been here before," he said. "Because if you had, you would've been with me, and you would've known the difference." I tried to pull away, but he held on. "Julie, I've told you before I'm not him. You can believe me when I say I'll always take care of you. What do I have to do so you will?"

Say you love me. I wanted to hear it, I *needed* to hear it, against all rationality, defying my best laid plans. I knew it wasn't right, because if Andy was sincere—and I had no reason to doubt he wasn't— and he knew what I'd done and why, he'd only end up hating me. And what would become of me then?

So I said nothing; I just pushed up on my heels and kissed him. I kissed Andy Devine with everything in me, knowing I would never feel this way about another man, because no man would ever make me feel like I always felt with him: *that I was worth it*. He held me in his arms, lifting me off my feet.

"Let's go home," he said, and within the hour we were there.

There was no preamble, no attempt at seduction, just me and Andy and what, by now, came as naturally as breathing. I never thought I'd find someone so intrinsically in tune with me, but there he was, sloughing off what was left of my clothing, leaving it with his by the bed as he took me into his arms. How was it I never tired of him, shuddered each time like the first? Because every time was a small implosion, sparks flying. They were as real as I'd ever felt them. I buried my face in his neck, breathing him in.

As he moved inside me, as he whispered into my hair, I fell deeper and deeper, and I'd never been so afraid. I knew it was illogical; didn't he say he cared? But did he love me? Oh God—if he did, I'd never get out of here. The man would kill me for sure. But how could I stop it?

Maybe if he hadn't kissed me. Maybe if his eyes hadn't looked at me the way they did, so swimmingly languid, so lost in me I was gone. With him buried deep inside me, with his scent dizzying my brain, my heart swelled with such a rush of emotion I couldn't hold it back any longer.

"I love you, Andy," I whispered, finding release in the words. "I love you with all my heart."

His eyes widened and he fell to his side, taking me with him, his leg over my thigh, his hand at my hip. Except for our joining we lay a foot apart, his eyes falling to half-mast as he began to move again. He slid his hand down on me, circling slowly, and when it came we came together, my fingers tightening against the swell of his chest as his breath hissed through his teeth, the force of it draining what color I could discern from his face. When he finished he slid himself from me and rolled over, falling asleep soon after.

What did I do?

When I awoke the moon was up. I could see it from the bedroom window, high and bright, shining on Andy's face from where he watched me, propped up on his elbow. Whatever had been in his eyes before was now replaced by passiveness, his hand insistently running up and down my back until I turned on my belly. With an arm on either side of me he rose up and spreading my legs apart, drove himself in from behind.

All at once he became a force, pounding, pounding, his fingers digging into my neck, my teeth rattling from the impact. There'd been times when I'd crave such an encounter, moaning and groaning until I'd push back with equal gravity, but this wasn't one of them; something was terribly wrong. "Andy . . .?" I said and suddenly he pulled out, falling to his side, his back to me.

"Andy . . .?" I whispered, pushing up. "What was that?"

"Go to sleep," he said, pulling the sheet over him.

"And you go to hell." I shoved my arms into my robe and left for outside, slamming the door.

My eyes stung, but I wouldn't give in to crying. The air was cool yet sultry, like the eastern edge of a hurricane before it moved out to sea, and wasn't that fitting?

I had the feeling I'd just come blindly through a storm, feeling its rage without ever seeing what it's about. With most of the houses were dark and the sky was bright and clear. I looked out over the water, the horizon dotted with twinklings of boats and barges. I gathered my robe and headed toward them, wondering why I continually wore my heart on my sleeve. Maybe I needed that bit of abruptness. It'd reminded me that Andy was no different from any other man after all. I hiked up my robe and waded into the warm surf, my gaze tossed up to the stars, the Milky Way spread like smoke.

You just had to go and say it, didn't you?

A few moments later Andy joined me, his hands in the pockets of his jeans, panic all over his face. "I'm sorry," he said. "I treated you like a whore just now."

"Yeah, you did," I said tightly. "What exactly did I do?"

"Nothing. Why would you think that?"

I turned on him. "Then what did *you* do that'd make you do it?"

He sighed, looking down as the water swirled around his ankles. "I've done many things, Julie, horrible things to women I could never tell you about—I'm too ashamed." When I gasped he looked up sharply, holding his hand out. "Oh no—not like that. I swear I never have and never would physically hurt a woman and dear God . . ." He grimaced. "On my life I would never hurt you. But in the past? I'll just say a cold heart can do infinitely more damage. I should know." He laughed softly. "I've seen my wreckage."

He scrubbed his face, then looked at me. "Be patient

with me, *ma chérie*. Please believe me, it's nothing you did. Maybe I've just been at sea too long. Maybe I've just never learned how to treat a real woman." He took a step closer. "Which you are, more than any woman I've ever known. When you left I thought you'd leave me for sure."

"Ha!" I laughed sharply. "Where would I go?"

It was a throwaway line but where, in fact, *would* I go? Back in my real life I had no home, nor much of anything else. Only a promise of a book and nothing to anchor me anywhere. I looked up. Except . . .

"Here. The cottage." he said. "I want to give it to you."

"What?" I was stunned. "You can't be serious."

"Well, I am. It was never meant to be mine anyway." He looked out toward the horizon. "My father bought it for my mother so she could imagine France on the other side. He thought maybe if she could she wouldn't feel so homesick, then maybe she'd care for him a little more." He turned to me. "Julie, you can say what you want, but I know you were desperate when you married me that you felt you had no choice."

"If I was, I certainly don't feel that way now."

"But who knows how it'll be later? When I said I'd take care of you, part of that was knowing you'd always have a place to go, no matter what happens between us."

Why didn't I like the sound of that? "Why? Are you planning on leaving?"

"Leaving's not the point. The point is you'll have something of your own, a place you can always go to for whatever reason."

"But I don't want to go anywhere," I said, the thought

coming to me like a revelation. "I want to be wherever you are."

He brought my hand to his lips and kissed it. "Which is exactly what I want to hear, but knowing you have a choice will only make it sweeter." He reached into his pocket and retrieved a key, pressing it into my palm. "Tomorrow I'll work on getting the deed changed to your name only. Consider it my wedding present to you."

I was completely overwhelmed. "Andy, I appreciate the gesture, but it's really not necessary. Put it in both our names if you want, but you don't have to do this." I thought of our contract, staring at the key in my hand. "Aren't we supposed to share everything?"

"Everything but this," he said, dropping the key into the top pocket of my robe. He buttoned a flap over it. "It's yours."

I pressed my hand to it. "I don't know what to say."

He lifted my chin. "Say thank you, and say you . . ." He kissed me.

He didn't have to finish; the words were on the tip of my tongue. *"Je t'aime,"* I whispered as he gathered me into his arms. *"Je t'aime de tout mon cœur."* I kissed his neck, his breast. *"J'ai envie de passer le reste de ma vie avec toi."*

Andy groaned, cradling my face in his hands. "Did you learn that for me?" He kissed me again. "Do you know what that does to me? *Je pourrais mourir."*

I didn't understand, but I filed it away for later, as I always did with Andy, in a spare chamber of my heart. So I told him I loved him, and although I didn't hear it back, I couldn't think about it now, not with the water lapping around us, my fingers in his hair, my body lost in sensation. All I could think of was Andy carrying me to the sand, Andy opening my robe and his jeans, Andy driving deep inside me.

The moonlight was on his face, his lips a breath from mine. "You have no idea what you mean to me—what you'll always mean to me, what you've done for me, and for that, I adore you." He kissed me, moving achingly slow within me, his heart beating against mine.

I slid my arms around him, Andy's kissing so passionate yet so ephemeral I couldn't decipher it and wouldn't try. I loved him, and whether he loved me back didn't matter. A happiness spread through me I never thought I'd feel. Maybe it was selfish. If it was, I didn't care.

That night he held me in his arms, our bodies so entwined we didn't need a blanket, waking before the light crept through the windows. Once more we made love, Andy against the headboard as I straddled him, his head nuzzling my neck, murmuring nothing and everything. "No one's ever made me feel as I do with you," he said. "You're my heart, my life." He kissed a trail down my breast, taking a nipple in his mouth, his tongue encircling it as jolt wracked through me. "If I could climb inside you, I would," he whispered, pressing me back against the mattress.

"Julie . . ." he murmured, like a man deep in fever, "I do care for you, you do realize that, don't you? But I'm . . ." He clenched his eyes, opening them with a quiet desperation. "Julie, you've changed everything. Please stay with me, make a life with me. How I'd want my child—*our* child—

to have a piece everything we've had together. Would you want that?" He raised up, dropping his hand to my belly, almost reverently. "Would you do that with me?"

Why was he saying this? Wasn't it everything we were about? Or did he know? Had he somehow found out? Didn't matter. Because if he could read my mind now he wouldn't bother to ask.

"Yes," I said, meaning it more than I've ever meant anything in my life. "Yes." I grasped his hips, rising up to meet each thrust, drunk on the possibility. He bore down and throwing his head back, buried his seed deep inside me. I closed my eyes, keeping everything, so much in love. So ridiculously in love.

BEFORE WE LEFT we shut off the water and drained the pipes in case we didn't make it back before the first freeze. As if autumn had moved in overnight, it was suddenly sweater weather, punctuated by Bucky's head out the car window, his tongue lolling in the breeze. I slipped one over my shoulders as we pulled out of the driveway.

I laid my head against Andy, feeling a little sad. "I couldn't have asked for a better honeymoon," I said. "Thank you for bringing me here."

He kissed my temple. "Thank you for coming with me. I'm afraid the farm's going to be a little dull for you after this."

"I doubt it," I said. "I don't think anything could be dull as long as you're around." Then I laughed. "Jesus, listen to us. We sound like a bad 'B' movie."

Andy grinned. "After acting like an 'X' for the past two days, I suppose we could use the change of pace."

We stopped for lunch at a diner on the way home, lingering over coffee and a shared lemon meringue, neither of us wanting to break the spell. But in the same sense I couldn't help feeling a bit excited, like a page had turned and I was beginning a whole new phase of my life. I had left the farm literally choking on what it once had been, and now I felt alive with anticipation. For the first time in years I had a place where I belonged, and no one was going to take that away from me. I looked across the table to Andy: strong, virile, my protector. Nothing could happen to us now.

The effects of the fire became more apparent the deeper we drove into the Pines. Because of all the smoke and darkness we hadn't really noticed how much of it had burned, my skin prickling when we hit the charred patch we had driven though when the fire jumped the road. By the time we closed in on the farm the evidence had all but disappeared, the scent of smoke tamped down considerably by rain and three days distance, but still drifting through the air like an aftertaste. As we pulled into the yard we could see the ruts left by the pumper truck, deep digs into the mud now dried and molded into place by the sun, the firefighters' muddy footprints trailing up the porch to the front door.

"Can't wait to see what the inside looks like," I said.

Thankfully, it appeared they had shed their boots before they went in. Everything looked fine until I noticed a water ring and a bit of sagging seam tape on the kitchen ceiling. I dragged a chair over to it and climbed up to look.

"Andy!" I called, poking the damp spot. "It looks like the roof is leaking into the kitchen!"

"The fire hose must've loosened some shingles when they wet down the house!" he called back. I could hear his inspection had already led him into our bathroom. "It leaked in here, too!" he added, over the sound of something scraping across the floor.

I looked down to where the leak led, right atop the kitchen counter and not two inches from the sink. "Would you believe this?" I called out. "It couldn't leak just two more inches to the right? It would've landed in the sink! That's our luck, isn't it? Is it leaking above the bathtub?" I ripped off a piece of dangling tape. "Andy?" Then all at once a cold awareness washed over me. I jumped off the chair, scrambling from the kitchen.

The first thing I saw as I tore into our bedroom was one drawer, then the other, lined up like little soldiers outside the bathroom. *Oh no, please don't let him find them—not after last night.* I turned toward the doorway, my heart jumping into my throat.

"Looking for these?" Andy said from atop of the shell of the linens dresser, my next month's supply of birth control pills between his fingers.

Chapter Nineteen

Double Indemnity

"WELL, ARE YOU?" Andy said evenly.

I stared at the birth control pills in his hand, a blatant display of my own recklessness. "Is that a rhetorical question?" I asked, sarcasm always my first refuge. "Because if it is, you'd know by now they're a little beyond the point."

He tossed them to the sink, coming toward me. "Just tell me the truth. Just tell me you considered the 'starting a family' part of our contract optional."

I couldn't lie to him, not with that hurt in his eyes. "You know it's not that simple. Not with how much that's changed over that last few days. Plus with the fire and everything else I forgot to start the new month, so there's an excellent chance I might already be pregnant. And you know what?" I laid my hand on his arm. "I honest to God hope I am."

He stared at me, that little muscle in his face twitching like it always did when his emotions got the best of him, as he struggled for control. "Really?" he said, moving past me to the window.

I went to his side; he didn't look at me. "Andy, we were strangers. Until I got to know you, could you really expect me to get pregnant? If I did, well . . ." I searched for the words. "I wouldn't be anything more than an incubator for your issue."

"Yet you signed an agreement with this stranger to do just that."

"I did. But even you said I was pretty desperate at the time."

"Which is why I spelled everything out," he said, finally looking at me. "Tossing in every protection so you wouldn't be taken advantage of by me or anyone else. You're forgetting you were as much a stranger to me as I was to you, but I still gave you every advantage. The risk was all mine."

"I'm no threat to you," I said, affronted.

"Except to make me look like a fool. Didn't I start out as one of your silly little stories for TV? Aren't I and our contract still the topic of your book?"

"But I already told you—the book's mainly about me."

"Especially now with those pills guaranteeing you a $50,000 exit."

"I never intended to take a nickel of your money." *God, this hurt.* "Or to fall in love with you."

He looked away. "That's your misfortune."

"You *bastard*," I cried, pushing at him.

He caught my wrists, pressing me back against the wall. "You're right, maybe the biggest bastard there is. I tried to warn you, but you still have no idea what I'm capable of. Julie . . ." His eyes softened. "It's not the pills. Trust me, it's a minor infraction. And that's why loving me *is* a misfortune. Once you learn how much of a bastard I really am, I doubt you'll want me."

I blinked, fighting tears; who was the fool now? I struggled against his hold, wanting to touch him so badly it ached. "You're wrong, I'll always want you. It doesn't even matter what you did, as long as you keep on wanting me."

He leaned in so close I could feel his breathing. "So you do love me after all?"

Love? I was out of my mind with loving him. "Please forgive me for lying to you. Whatever I was thinking at first, I don't feel that way now. I just want to be with you."

He growled something decidedly feral and pulled me to him, crushing his lips to mine, and for the first time since this horrible conversation began my Andy returned to me, the Andy I knew, the Andy I loved. He let go, hanging onto my hand like a lifeline.

"Julie," he said, very quietly, "I have to tell you something."

"Okay. I placed my palm on his cheek.

He turned into it, his eyes closing as he kissed it slowly, almost reluctantly, returning it to his grasp. "I'm not who you think I am."

"I don't care," I said, meaning it. "I know who you are now."

"No. You have no idea." He opened his eyes. "For one thing, I was sick when I was a young man. They told me then it would be difficult, if not impossible, to father a child. The proof being, well . . ." He looked to me, a bit of the rake in his eyes. "I haven't exactly lived the life of a monk. And after twenty-five rather vigorous years, there should've been at least one or two . . . accidents."

Now I was confused. "Then why did you include that clause in your contract?"

"Because if a woman was willing to risk even her fertility, I'd know she'd be taking this seriously."

"So in other words . . ." I slipped my hand from his. "You lied, too."

"Yes. But not about wanting you. I've wanted you more and more every day." He kissed me again, and my mind went blank.

What was this hold he had on me, this ability to make me lose all common sense? Again I was falling down the well, the lies we told each other so tangled, neither of us could claim the moral upper hand. But he needed to keep talking; I knew there was more.

I pulled away from him. "But why go through all the trouble with exit clauses and $50,000 payments if you knew what'd happen in the end? It's almost like you didn't *want* to stay married."

"Because I didn't," he said. "Until I married you."

It was what I wanted to hear, and yet . . . "Then why—"

Outside, Bucky began to bark and we looked toward the living room window; a car pulled into the yard. Before we could make it to the front door there were footsteps on the porch, followed by an insistent banging.

"*Bonjour!* André—*Est-ce que tu là-dedans?!* André! *Bonjour!*"

He instantly paled.

"Who is it?" I said.

He put his hand on my arm. "*Julie.*"

The door swung open.

"Mon frérot! Comment ça va?" In strode a man who could've been Andy fifteen years earlier, tall but even darker, his hair slicked back, a cigarette in his hand. He grasped Andy by the shoulders and kissed him on each cheek. "*Chao!*"

"Marcel," Andy said. He looked to me. "Julie—"

"Ah! *Est-ce la femme? Brava!*" He looked from me to Andy, grinning wide as he dragged on his cigarette. He raked me up and down, eyes hooded. "*Ravi de vous rencontrer, madame,*" he said with every measure of Andy's charm, his head bowed slightly as he threw out his arms. "André, *tu devrais me présente!*"

"Julie," Andy said, "this is Marcel. My brother."

I instantly assumed—*but to hear it!*

"Marcel," he continued, his color high, "this is Julie, my wife."

As Marcel kissed my cheek I caught Andy's eyes. *I'm sorry*, he mouthed, and a dread washed over me. This, I knew, was how it would end.

"*Enchanté*, Julie. Marcel Mercier, à votre service," he said, kissing my other cheek. "*Tu es belle . . .* André *est un homme chanceux*—ah!" He tapped his head. "You have no *français, n'est-ce pas? Je suis désolé.* I said you're very beautiful, which makes my brother a very lucky man.

"And a lazy one!" He opened the door, flicking his cigarette butt into the yard. "Why haven't you answered your phone? I've been calling for three days! How many messages do I have to leave?"

Mercier? "We were away," I said. "On an island."

"Where you can't even get sat phone reception?" He looked to Andy and laughed. "Jesus, this *is* America, isn't it? I mean, I didn't take a wrong turn at Mexico, did I?"

"To what do we owe this pleasure, Marcel?" Andy said tightly. "Where's Lisette?"

"Hm, yes ... Lisette. Well, *mon frérot*, that's why I'm here." He shrugged his shoulders. "You won."

Andy's eyes narrowed. "Marcel—"

"No—really, I'll accept defeat. You said it wouldn't last six weeks, but it didn't last half that. She left with the first boat sailing. Where you ..." He glanced at me. "You do have an exquisite wife. I suppose you can take a few more weeks before you have to pay her off and get back to work. After all ..." He eyed me lasciviously. "You still have six weeks left—"

"Ta gueule, gamin!" Andy cried. *"Elle ne sait pas."* He looked to me. "Not yet anyway."

"What?" Marcel glanced at me. "You never told her about our bet? Why *Andy* ..." he spun the name. "Aren't you *le palourd peu* ..."

"Trou du cul ..." Andy growled. *"Ta gueule."* He looked to me. "Julie, don't listen to him. He's a spoiled little shit and—"

"I'm a shit!" Marcel gaped at him. "Listen, big brother, I—"

"Shut up! Shut up both of you!" I bolted out the door.

It's a good thing I never took my things from the truck; at least I would have something to bring home. *Home.* Where was that? I had no goddamn idea. All I knew was I had to get out of there, and I stomped my foot to the gas, tearing down the trail from the farm. I only had minutes—if not seconds—to do what I had to do, as Andy was sure to follow. I checked the rear view; not yet, so I bore down, mindless of everything else. When I finally hit Main Street I veered into Uncle Jinks' station, startling him so he dropped a ratchet, mid-crank.

"Julie! What the hell!" he cried.

I was already on his porch, next door. "Hurry! Where's your computer?"

"Front room, second floor." He looked to the road, then back to me, stricken. "Oh Christ—I begged him to tell you! Every day! I swear to God!"

But I was already taking the steps two at a time, finding the laptop on a corner desk. As I waited for it to come up I spied a flash of red and black with a long, thick antenna atop a shelf. I picked it up: another satellite phone.

How convenient Jinx's home page was Google. I typed in *Andy Devine.* Nothing but old movie sites. Then I typed in *Andrè Mercier.* Over 35,000 results. *Acting CEO of Mercier Shipping. The second largest privately-owned commercial shipping company in*

France. Headquartered in Marseille. Offices in Belize, *Shanghai. Personal wealth estimated at 1.2 billion dol-* *lars. Forty years old. Single.* I clicked Images. Dozens of Andys flashed across the screen, each one looking more corporate than the next. I pulled down his phone and dialed Denny.

After nearly five rings he answered. "Hello . . .?"

"Denny, it's Julie. Come and get me." A pause. "Had enough?"

Had I? "Yes."

"Where are you?"

"Jinks' gas station."

"Well, ain't it your lucky day? I'm outside of Egg Harbor on the way to A.C. Hang tough, sweetheart. I'll be there in fifteen."

I clicked off, hurling the phone to the floor.

Wasn't it funny, I thought as I stared at the computer screen, how I used to live online, and now, after not being on it in nearly six weeks, it was hardly my salvation? Or was it? A car screeched outside, followed by Jinks yelling and the front door slamming. "Julie—" Andy appearing in the doorway, flushed and heaving.

I jumped back. "Who *are* you?"

"I'm just who I said I was." As he came toward me, his eyes flashed to the computer screen and all his incarnations. "But I'm also someone else."

I slammed the laptop shut. "Right. A fucking liar. Aren't you slumming, *André*?"

"Call me Andy," he said, coming closer.

"S-Stay away from me," I said, my voice quavering.

But he kept coming until I was backed into a corner. "Stay away from me!" I yelled, cowering.

"Andy! For Christ's sake!" Jinks screamed from outside. "Julie!"

Andy was so close I could see the pulse pounding in his neck, his scent so dizzying I couldn't breathe. His hands were frozen an inch from my face, his own a study in anguish. "Please," he said, pleading. "There's a reason for what I did. Please let me explain."

I stared at him. Those eyes. My God—*those eyes*. How often have I looked into them as he was deep inside me, how close have I come to drowning in them?

"Julie!" Jinks called again.

"Please," Andy whispered, backing off.

I squeezed past him, going to the window. "I'm okay, Uncle Jinks. We're just . . ." I glanced back to Andy, his eyes fixed on me.

"We're talking," Andy called down.

"You sure?" Jinks said after a moment.

"I'm fine," I said. "Sorry for upsetting you."

"Well. I'm right here if you need me." He turned, still wary, for the garage.

I went to the bed, slumping atop it. "Okay," I said. "Talk."

I felt the mattress sink as he dropped to the other side, our backs to each other. After a long while he began. "First off you should know I never lied to you."

"Right. Just omitted a few pertinent facts."

"Guilty as charged. But I did have a reason, maybe not a very good one as far as you're concerned, but something

I thought made sense at the time." He sighed. "I've since learned otherwise."

If he was waiting for a snappy comeback, I was all out of snark. So I waited.

"I was born Andrew Devine right here in Iron Bog. I'm an American citizen by birth, and I've never given it up. A copy of my birth certificate's at the local bank in a safe deposit box. But when I was thirteen, my mother took me to France, divorced my father, and married Victor Mercier, a ship owner from Marseille on his way up. Do you remember that photo of my mother you found in the kitchen?"

"Yes."

"That's him in the photo with her. My father commissioned a private investigator, who . . ." He shook his head tightly. "Anyway, Marcel was born shortly after he and my mother married, so she changed my last name to Mercier, partly to spite my father, I think. When she did she also listed my surname as the French derivation of Andrew, but to my close friends, both here and abroad, I've always been Andy."

"So I take it Marcel's never been one of your confidants."

He snorted. "The only good thing Marcel has ever done for me was set up a series of catastrophes that somehow led me to you."

"Well, isn't that ironic?" I said. "Now he's leading you away."

"Don't say that."

"Even if it's true? After all, you did win your bet."

"The bet was in his head, not mine. All I wanted to do was try to make him grow up, so he could take over the family business and I could finally be free of it. His father's not in the best shape, so it's time, and I figured if I took off he'd have no choice." I felt him swiveling around, though I wouldn't face him. "Marcel married a woman he'd only known three days, and that was after fathering a baby with another one. He has a brilliant mind and he could be a great man, but he's ruled by romantic notions instead of logic, especially when it comes to women."

"So you placed a bet with my life and called it *logic*?"

He huffed. "No—look. Marcel married for love and it didn't even last a month. When we married, we already knew what to expect, so—"

"For God's sake Andy—*stop!*" I jumped from the bed, turning on him. "Do you really believe that bullshit you're spouting? There is no *we*—we're over."

He came toward me. "Don't say that. Don't even joke about it."

"Why? I don't even know who you are! I married Andy Devine, not André Mercier—some billionaire ship owner who thinks he can manipulate peoples' lives to make a point."

"I'm still the same person," he said, once again backing me into the wall. "I'm still everything you thought I was and everything that's good for you. Come on Julie . . ." he said softly, "aren't you better off now than before you met me?"

I looked at him squarely. "I was a mess when I met you and I'm a mess now. What's the difference?"

"Yet I see a strong woman. Who knows what she needs to be happy."

"I lost that ability when I met you."

"You're wrong," he said, his arms caging me. "That's when you found it."

Those eyes were on me again, working their mesmerizing magic, and everything in me said to run away. But I couldn't. Either their pull was too strong or I was just a pushover, my anger giving way to the last sparks of desire.

He kissed the hair above my temple. "Julie, you know you need me . . . you know you want me."

"Andy, don't," I whimpered, his breath hot against my ear. I pushed against his chest, a purely superficial effort; I've never felt weaker.

"Don't what?" he said, his tongue tracing down my jawline to my neck, feathering kisses across the swell of my breasts. "You're so beautiful . . . so . . ."

"Ah . . ." I couldn't speak, could barely stand, his hands were on me now, at my hips, pulling them to his. He pressed against me and I ached to touch him, but I wouldn't, I didn't dare. And then he kissed me.

I fell as deep as I could go, lost in his scent, and it was all over. I was overcome by my own craving, but who was I kidding? I was crazy in love and nothing mattered. I threw my arms around him and succumbed.

"Julie, Julie . . ." he groaned, "can't you see how I feel about you? I can't stop wanting you." His hands trailed to my breasts and he dropped his head to them, biting a nipple through the fabric. "I want you all the time, you're like a sickness in me. Oh Julie, *Julie* . . ." He kissed his way up my breasts and back to my mouth, taking it savagely.

I slid down the wall, bent back in his arms, both of us panting as we crumpled to the floor. He tore his mouth away from mine and dragged it down my torso, biting and nipping until finally he shoved my dress up and yanked my panties down, diving into me. I bucked, my head arching back, the sensation so intense I bit my lip to keep from screaming, my fingernails digging into the floorboards as he went at me, relentless. Then all at once I went off, absolutely paralytic.

"Jesus—I love the way you taste . . ." Andy growled as I shook within his grasp. "I love the way you come for me, love the pleasure I can give you . . . love . . ." He kissed my belly, lingering to breathe against it, "love the way you feel when I'm inside you."

He slid up my quavering body, pressing his panting mouth to mine, my hands at his fly, fumbling to free him. "I love you, Andy." I bit his lip, and he groaned. "Andy—did you hear me? *I love you.*" His eyes closed and he raised up ready to enter me, when all at once I had to know. "Andy, please tell me . . . do you love me?"

"Julie . . ." he murmured, "I want you, more than anything in my whole life . . ."

I kissed his cheek, his mouth. "But do you love me, Andy, do you?"

"I—ah . . ." He pressed against me, right at the entrance. "Ah . . . ah . . ." Suddenly he stilled, his eyes wide open, staring at me.

I couldn't breathe.

"Julie . . ." he whispered.

I pushed him off, scrambling to my feet.

"Son of a bitch," I screamed, stepping into my panties. "Bastard."

He grabbed my hand. "No one in the world means anything to me except you. Can't you see—"

"No." I said, snatching my hand back, righting my dress, my hair. "I can't." I ran for the stairs.

"Julie!" He scrambled to his feet, zipping as he followed. "Where're you going! Come back! You're my wife!"

I turned from the doorway. "That's your misfortune."

I was already taking my things out of the truck when he caught up with me. "You can't be leaving."

"That's exactly what I'm doing," I said, slinging my purse over my shoulder. "Whatever I've left, send to Channel 8 News in Philly. They'll know where to find me."

"Julie!" He gaped at me, panicked. "Please don't leave. I have so much more to tell you. But when I'm near you . . ." He palmed his forehead, as if he were in pain. "Julie, please. Let's talk about this. *Please.*"

I hefted my overnight bag. "I heard all I wanted to hear—or didn't." At which he had the grace to blanch.

"Julie!" Jinks ran over. He shot Andy a filthy look. "I'm so sorry, I tried over and over to make him tell you, but he wouldn't listen."

"I don't blame you," I said, hugging him quickly. "Thank you for everything."

Andy shoved between us, turning me around. "Julie— give me a minute to explain and I know you'll understand. Jinks'll help us—won't you, Jinks? You'll see it isn't so easy. It's so much more complicated than that."

I could hear a car pulling up behind me. "It's not complicated, Andy. You either love me or you don't. I have to be more to you than how I make you feel. I have to be everything."

"You are," he whispered, "but I just can't feel it."

"But I can." I touched his cheek, my heart breaking. "Goodbye, Andy."

Denny called from the car, "You need some help there?"

"No," I opened the back door, tossing in my overnight bag. "We're all through."

"Julie!" Andy gasped.

I don't remember getting into the car, but somehow I found myself inside, Denny pulling it into gear, and Andy outside the opened window, his hand thrust through it and clamped onto mine.

"If you think I can give you up this easily," he said, his face ashen, "then you have no idea what I'm capable of."

"Then fight for me, Andy," I said, squeezing his hand before I let it go. "But make sure you know what you're fighting for. Until you do please don't come after me."

I could see him in the side mirror as we pulled out, growing smaller as the road and the forest took us. Was I going in or coming out? I couldn't decide.

Denny took hold of my hand. "I guess it's pretty stupid of me to ask if you're all right."

I could feel his palm pressing down on my wedding rings. "Just as long as you don't say 'I told you so.'"

"Oh Jesus Christ," he said after a moment. "You went and fell in love with him, didn't you?"

The diamonds sparked, catching the sun. I yanked them off, zippering them into my wallet. "In the worst possible way," I said, the tears finally falling.

Chapter Twenty

Back, After a Brief Commercial Interruption

WHERE WAS I? Oh yes, I was walking down the street in Center City, turning the corner into the WPHA building, decked out in a blazer, sweater and tweed A-line, a leather messenger slung across me. (The bag is new, by the way. I bought it from that sweet little advance I got for the book I can't bring myself to continue writing.) It's a gorgeous November day, the kind that got you all excited about winter coming on—blindingly sunny with a frosty nip to the air, but just warm enough to make all that winter-enthusiasm seem token. I walked into the building's marbled lobby, past the security guard who smiled in surprise and said, "Ms. Knott! Welcome back!" my three-inch heels clipping smartly as I nodded and pressed the UP button at the elevator bank. (Damn tricky thing, getting back into those heels.) It was all so old it seemed new again.

"Come on down, Julie, we need to talk." In truth, I sincerely doubted anything Gil, my former station manager, had to say would rock my world, but I managed to spare him an afternoon. For crying out loud, it wasn't as if I didn't have anything to do. Licking your wounds takes more time than you think.

Andy's efficiency in finding me was indeed impressive. With all the global resources of a billionaire, I shouldn't have expected anything less. By the night I left, he'd found not only Denny's cell number, but Brent's; he'd already given up trying to get me to answer mine. I deleted every message without listening, as I instructed both my protectors to do as well. By the next morning, Andy was on Brent and Denny's doorstep, behind whose door I was barricaded.

"I'm sorry, Mr. Devine, she won't see you," Brent had said in a most diplomatic manner. "I'm sure you understand."

"Could you please ask her again?" Andy had pleaded so desperately, Brent said, he nearly relented. "I won't be long. You can stay with us if you like."

"I'm sorry," Brent said, "but it's no good. She said if you persist she'll go where no one could find her, including me or Denny. And in her current state, that's a scenario I simply can't allow." He came off the stoop, placing a hand to Andy's shoulder. "Perhaps if you just gave her some time . . ."

Andy took a deep breath, his gaze shooting up toward my window; I jumped back, hoping the curtain still hid me. He was pale and drawn, wearing the same clothes as the day before. I grunted; my fist flying to my mouth. He looked back to Brent.

"Tell her . . . tell her I have to go back to Marseille. I don't want to, but if I don't . . ." He coughed, handing Brent an envelope. "Give her this for me, would you please? My personal number's inside. I'm available any time of the day or night. Tell her, well . . ." He coughed again, nodding. "Anyway, thank you."

By the time he walked away I was back on the bed. A few moments later a knock came at my door.

"Julie?" Brent said, "May I come in?"

What a goddamned gentleman. "Of course."

"He gave me this," Brent said, placing the envelope on the bedside table. "How are you, darling?"

I laughed; a short burst or irony. "Why, peachy, doll." I swiped my eyes. "Are you blind? Isn't it apparent?"

"Oh absolutely," he said, falling to his haunches before me. "Your exuberance is only matched by your unfailing wit."

I laughed for real. "Oh, Brent!" I said, planting a smooch on his forehead. "Oh Brent . . ." I sobbed, crumpling against him. "He looked awful, didn't he?"

"Nearly as awful as you," he said. "Which is why you're probably perfect for each other." He held me out, thumbing tears from under my swollen eyes. "Why don't you see him, Julie? Anyone can see the man's about to die, he's so in love with you."

"Then why won't he tell me!" I shot back. "I poured my heart out to him, made an absolute ass of myself, but when I asked him point blank, he froze. I'm sorry, but I'm never settling again."

"But you already did when you married him. You know he never promised you love. What made you think you had the right to demand it?"

"Now you're playing the other side of the fence?" I sat back. "Don't you think once you cross that sexual line, you have a right to expect it?"

Brent eyed me wryly. "There's a few people walking the street outside the bus station who'd beg to differ."

"It's hardly the same thing."

"You'd be surprised how much it isn't. My dear, I can't possibly know what's in either of your heads, or how you'll sort this out. The only thing I can do is be here for you if you need me." He nodded to the bedside table. "See what he has to say. Who knows? It might be just what you want to hear." He left.

I plucked Andy's note from where it sat against the lamp, fingering the word **Julie** written in his spare script across the envelope. I stared at it a very long time, my heart in my throat, before I could summon the nerve to open it. When I finally did, it read:

Ma petite Julie –
   The time I spent with you was the happiest of my life. I've never known such joy with another person as my experiences nearly always have been otherwise. As much as I have disappointed you—and I do consider

*that an understatement—I'm working toward the day
we will be together again, when I have proven myself
worthy of your trust and, more importantly, your love.
For the interim, I'll respect your request for privacy,
but have enclosed my business card with my personal
number. Call any time of the day or night; I will be
here for you.*

      Yours always,
      Andy

I fingered the card; *Compagnie du Mercier, André L. Mercier, Président-Directeur-Général.* It listed several numbers and contacts for offices in Marseille, Belize City, and Shanghai, faxes, email addresses, and something called Radio Telex. On the back was a handwritten number, which I suppose was the satellite phone he'd kept at Uncle Jinks. Then maybe it wasn't; who knew? There was so much I didn't know about him.

Why would someone do it? Why would a CEO (or *PDG*?) of an international company advertise for a wife on a utility pole, then settle down in obscurity in the woods? Whatever reason he had probably wasn't worse than my own, but why wouldn't he tell me? Especially knowing I was a journalist and there was the risk I'd eventually find out? But I didn't, did I? Maybe I wasn't much of a journalist after all.

Which still gave me pause as I rode the Slowest Elevator in the World up to Gil's office. After a month of haunting Brent and Denny's, as Brent had the gallery and Denny had since found a job with an independent production company, I received a call from Gil's assistant saying he wanted to see me. As far as Gil knew, I had simply gone out of town for the duration. I had not gotten married after knowing my intended for six days, I had not lived in the woods for six weeks, I had not had my heart summarily broken, I had not spent the first week afterward unable to get out of bed, the subsequent two too numb to do much more than watch TV and drink too much wine. The week after that I felt a bit of the fog lifting after a package arrived from Iron Bog, containing the rest of my things and a note from Uncle Jinks:

Dear Julie –

As you probably know, Andy had to close the house and return to France, but before he left he dropped off your things at my place hoping you might stop in. But unlike Andy I'm a realist, and I figure you're going to need this stuff way before you cool off enough to come get it. In case you're wondering, we did find good homes for the chickens and Betsy, and Bucky is here with me and missing you. (I was, and I did miss Bucky terribly.) But while I've got your attention, I think you should know something about Andy. After you do, it might lighten your load a bit.

I knew both his parents, and neither were what you would call model figures. But it was his mother who was as scheming as she was beautiful. She used her own son against his father more than once, to the point she forced Andy to choose between them. When he couldn't, or wouldn't, she did it for him, and one

*guess will tell you who paid the price. I have a pretty
good feeling all this somehow fits into what's going on
now.*

> *Please don't give up on him, Julie. You might not
> believe it now, but he's worth it.*

> *Take care,*
> *Jinks.*

I was finding it hard to believe anything now; if someone were to tell me we were on planet Earth, I believe I'd
ask for proof. So it was with a bit of numbness and quite
a lot of skepticism that I tapped on the half-opened door
of Gil's office. He looked up from his screen and smiled
broadly, waving me in.

"Miss Julie! How the hell *are* you?" he cried, jumping
up. "Come in and tell me all about it!"

"About what, Gil?" I said, sitting down. "Aren't you
here to tell me?"

"Haw-haw!" he guffawed, his belly jiggling. "Same ol'
Julie, still full of fire!"

Why he was pandering to me, I couldn't figure out.
"Gil," I finally said. "I'm kind of busy, so if you could cut
to the chase . . ."

"Oh right, right," he said, with solemnity. "Denny had
told me a while back you were working on a book. How's
that coming, by the way?"

Proceeding as fast as a full stop, I thought, not that he
needed to know. "Just fine. Almost through." *With maybe
the first paragraph.* "Been a great experience, too. A real
voyage of discovery." *Like sailing over a cliff.*

"That's terrific! Because, my dear . . ." He looked at me, most businesslike. "I'd like to offer you your old job back."

"Really," I said, piqued for the first time in weeks. "And what makes you think I'd be interested?"

His brow arched, expecting that. "Because I'm going to make it too attractive to refuse."

He'd have to do better than that; I was so over pretty packages. "Okay," I said, "wow me."

Seemed he was ready to. "For starters, three years, your old position with a twenty percent raise, three spots per week, a personal assistant, plus you can even bring Mr. Denny back if you like. But . . ." His eyes lit. "That's not the best part."

"Oh?" The raise, the extra spot a week, and the assistant all were nice; I couldn't speak for Denny, but I was sure he'd take a smug satisfaction in being asked. "Then what is?"

"Well, I'll tell you." He shot me a cavalier glance. "Seems MSNBC has caught on to you and is now a fan, and they would like to replay one of your spots every Friday on "Morning Joe." He threw out his hands. "National exposure, Miss Julie. Think of it—right up there with Jeanne Moos."

I gripped the arms of my chair. "You're joking."

"Ah ha!" He pointed to me. "I thought that would get you! Let me hear you say no now!"

How could I? It was all I ever wanted and he knew it. But I also knew if I jumped on too quickly he'd only hogtie me again. My memory wasn't that short, after all.

I rose, glancing at my watch. "Look, I have to be somewhere. Let me think about it, okay?"

"Sure, sure," he said, rising with me. "Just don't let me wait too long. Offers like this can shrivel up in the sun, if you know what I mean."

"Oh, absolutely. Which makes me think . . ." I eyed him squarely. "Why all of a sudden this offer anyway? It didn't have anything to do with the network making it so sweet, did it?"

Gil came around the desk, leaning against it. "Let's not mince words, Miss Julie. I think we can both see our way around a mutually beneficial deal. But without each other, we sort of have nothing, don't we? So I wouldn't drag my feet if I were you . . . savvy?"

Our gazes met; held. Oh hell, what did I have to lose?" Okay. I think I have an old contract lying around in my hard drive. I'll revise it and send it on by."

"It's done," he said, reaching to his desk. "All you need to do is sign. Here." He handed me a sheaf of papers. I took a look, falling back in my chair.

"This is from *Richard*!"

"Well, he's still your agent, isn't he?" he said, matter-of-factly. "Who do you think sold me on the idea?"

"*Richard*? But . . . but . . ." I had no answer for him.

"Look, so he's a shitty fiancé. You're well rid of him. But the man's one hell of a salesman. This *is* a deal too good to turn down. Take it home, look it over, and come back tomorrow. Run with it, sweetheart. What the hell?"

Richard did this? I couldn't figure him out. Why

was he doing this for me? Unless . . . I shoved the papers in my messenger. "Let me take a look. I'll get back to you."

"That's all I'm asking." He reached out and shook my rather-startled hand. "Come back tomorrow anytime. I'll be waiting."

Lately everyone had an open-door policy as far as I was concerned, the fact of which I passed to an equally-skeptical Denny over dinner at Spasso. He turned the last page of the contract, pushing it toward me.

"The bastard fuck wants you back, that's why," Denny said, chopping into his Chicken Fontinella. "I mean, you do realize that?"

"No kidding," I said, "but why?"

He took a slug of wine, looking at me as if it were obvious. "Oh I forgot—you've been under a rock lately. Because Annika Eden dumped him, is why."

"Seriously?" I said, pushing my salad aside. "Again?" I smiled most evilly. "Isn't that just too bad."

"Yeah, isn't it?" Denny said, just as gleeful. "His loss, your gain."

I looked at him, horrified. "You can't think I want that bastard back?"

"Well, yeah—but only in the most selfishly beneficial way. I say let him grovel and lick your heels while you cut his commission and promise him nothing. You were his cash cow when no one would give him the time of day. It's payback time, Jules."

"But he hasn't even tried to call me."

"He doesn't have to." He flicked the contract. "With

this, his bloated little ego is leaving it up to you. He figures you can't resist."

"Oh yeah?" I snatched it from the table, shoving it in my purse. "Watch me."

So I didn't call him, not that night, not the next day. In between Gil called and texted at least five times, but I wouldn't budge, taking some measure of satisfaction in the brown leather journal that still lay unopened beside my laptop, its contents pressing most heavily upon my brain. But even though I was no closer to finishing the book than the day I started, it still gave me a measure of security: that story was all my own. Then that night, Richard finally called. And even more miraculously, I picked up.

"So how's the wife?" I said.

Richard coughed. "So you heard about that."

"Yeah. From everyone but you. So give me a good reason why I should continue this conversation, you rat-bastard piece of shit," I said, surprisingly calm for all his fiery death scenarios I had once enacted in my head.

"Because I *am* a rat-bastard piece of shit, and I want to make it up to you. And I'll do it for free."

"Well, aren't you just like me," I said. "I would've killed you for free, too."

He laughed softly. "I probably would've handed you the gun." He sighed. "How are you, Julie?"

"Fabulous, no thanks to you. So let's get down to it. Why the contract?"

"No matter what you think, no matter what I've done—and I'll be the first to admit what I did to you was unconscionable—I've never stopped being your agent. Fact was that last contract was so minor league I should've never considered it. The station made so many changes it was an insult. Then they saw their numbers tank and started to panic, letting go of the best talent they had. By the way, that was a smart piece of work, your dropping under the radar for a while. Only made you more valuable. Where did you go, if I may ask?"

"Certainly not Seattle," I said. "That would've been way too crowded."

He laughed again. "Too crowded for me these days, too."

"Like Philly," I said, "So I'm thinking maybe I should be going—"

"Well don't," he interjected. "Not now. Not for a while. Julie, I'm serious. This is a good deal. As your agent, as someone . . ." I could hear his throat working. "Who still cares about you very much, I think you should seriously consider it. With the MSNBC clause, it's your ticket to the big show."

Didn't I know it. But why did it have to come through him? "Why are you doing this, Richard? And don't bullshit me. Tell me the truth."

"Because I fucked up, Julie. I know it. I just want to make it up to you, that's all."

"Wouldn't have anything to do with your girl dumping you, now would it?"

Silence, then: "It has everything to do with my girl dumping me. Because if I were you, I would've dumped me, too."

Now I was just plain irritated. "Richard, I'm not in the

mood for your being cute. I know you're not that selfless, so answer my question."

"It's the truth, dammit, and just to prove it, I'm taking no commission on the contract."

"Oh stop it—that was when we were together. I'll cut it to ten, but you take it."

"Look, I'm sending you a revised contract, so just quit arguing with me and accept it. I'm doing right by you whether you want me to or not, and I'm going to keep doing it until I can hold my head up to you again. Until then, call me anything you want, but don't underestimate me. I'm going to absolutely make it up to you, with interest."

And in the following couple of weeks, I quickly found out how much he meant it. For my grand return on December first, he arranged for the station to launch a publicity campaign, online, on air, in print, and on billboards warning, "Get ready for a new Julie!" commissioning a top Hollywood firm to make sure I looked totally A-List in front of the camera, hiring me a personal trainer, and weaseling from the station a wardrobe allowance. He opened a bank account in my name only, restoring all the money he had frozen, including an additional $5,000. He found a great row house in Northern Liberties and even paid the security and the first six months' rent, furnishing it with the nicest pieces from our old penthouse, including that tea table Andy and I had talked about. I promptly put it in the closet. But the best part was how he tweeted everyday what a shit he'd been to me, and how blinded he'd been by that soprano succubus Annika Eden.

"That last part's not necessary," I told him over mulled cider and cheese. "Looks so petty."

"Petty would be tweeting how fat she's gotten." He pulled out his phone, his grin all malevolence. "On second thought . . ."

I couldn't believe I'd actually told Brent I wouldn't mind if he came for Thanksgiving dinner, and the truth was it didn't bother me at all. Fact was, amid the hubbub over my return, I pretty much didn't feel anything anymore, except when something innocuous would punt a memory byte to the fore. Such as the twinge I felt reaching toward the cheese tray, passing over the brie for the stack of crackers beside it.

"Brie should be served with a nice crusty baguette," I said, nipping into a cracker.

"What?" said Richard idly, finishing the tweet. The crowd roared on TV and he looked up. "Son of a bitch!"

"Damn, there goes Penn State down the shitter," said Denny. "I should've went to Louisiana."

"Yes, just imagine our float in the Sugar Bowl parade," Brent drawled, coming in from the kitchen. "Total queens from Gay Bingo." He flipped a towel over his shoulder. "Okay, my quarterbacks—dinner is served. *Ya'll.*"

I dropped the cracker back to the cheese plate; suddenly the idea of cramming myself full of turkey and fixings held as much appeal as a root canal, even though Brent was an excellent cook. I took another sip of wine instead.

Richard inspected the bottle. "Wow, we pretty much killed that, didn't we?"

"Don't worry," Denny said. "We have a couple of bottles of this great pinot for dinner. Got it from a local vintner up in Bucks County."

"Oh yeah?" said Richard. "Anyone I know?"

"Silver Drum Winery," Denny said. "Ever hear of them?"

His eyes widened. "Oh yeah. They're fantastic. Had a bottle of Beaujolais from them last week. Good stuff."

Beaujolais . . . I thought, sipping again. *Serve Beaujolais with a nice, fresh* . . . My head began to spin. Before I knew it the glass slipped from my hand I was staring up at Richard.

"Julie!" he cried, blanching. "Julie!"

It suddenly occurred to me I was crumpled on the floor. I scrubbed my hand across my eyes. "What . . . happened?

He helped me to the sofa. "One minute you were sipping wine, then the next you dropped like a rock." He grabbed a magazine from the table, fanning me. "Have you eaten anything today?"

I caught the clock on the mantel; it was going on three. "Coffee, this morning. I think."

"Damn girl—cried Denny, "get over to this table and eat!" But as I made my way to it I felt my knees weakening. I grabbed the wall, feeling ready to go down again.

"That's it," Denny said, his arm around me, "you're going to the hospital. Brent!"

He already had his jacket on. "I'm getting the car."

"I'll get your coat," Denny said, leading me back to the sofa. "Now stay put."

I felt more horrible than I ever had in my life. I picked up a cracker and nipped it; as benign as it was, I wanted to hurl.

I felt the sofa sink as Richard sat beside me. "I'm coming with you."

"No," I shook my head. "That's not necessary. I'll already have two nursemaids."

He slipped his arm around me, turning my face toward his. "I'm not asking your permission. I'm going." He felt my forehead. "My God, you're warm."

Another memory byte clicked. "Probably an old snakebite come back to haunt me."

Richard looked at me. "What?"

Within a half-hour, I was on the fast track to the ER, the patient load surprisingly light for a holiday. After answering about three dozen pertinent questions, I was zipped to an examining room, ordering all my protectors to stay behind. A nurse came in, poked, prodded, took my temperature and blood pressure, and had me pee in a cup, all while letting a glucose drip snap me surprisingly back into focus. About a half hour later a doctor came in.

"How're you feeling?" she said.

"Much better," I said, sipping water.

"You were pretty dehydrated," she said.

I instantly felt stupid. "I've been pretty busy lately."

She smiled. "I know. I've seen your pictures all over town. So is this the new Julie?"

"Ha!" I laughed. "Are you shocked?" I rolled my eyes. "Please don't tell anyone."

"Your secret's safe with me," she whispered, detaching

the IV. "But you really do have to take care of yourself. Especially now."

"I know, I know," I said, properly chastised. "But my trainer wants me to lose some more weight, and that's probably why I got so dehydrated." I sipped more water. "Don't worry. It won't happen again."

"It better not," said the doctor. Then she stared at me. "Wait a minute. You don't know, do you?"

I was mystified. "Know what?"

She stood, crossing her arms as she came up to me. "Ms. Knott—you're pregnant."

Chapter Twenty-One

Mother Knows Best

THANK GOD PENNSYLVANIA doctors were bound by privacy laws. So far, she was the only one who knew I was pregnant. And that's how I intended to keep it, at least until I could think straight again.

"You didn't know, did you?" the doctor asked.

"No," I said, gulping water now. "But I should've. Oh my God—am I about six weeks?"

"Yes, very early on. Is that about the time of your last ovulation?"

"About the time I forgot to start the next month of pills."

"Hm," she said, sitting down to fill out her report, "that'll do it. I'm assuming you have a gynecologist? Might I suggest seeing her as soon as possible? Your urine came back positive, but you do need other tests to be sure."

"Doctor . . ." I said tentatively, hoping it wouldn't come out wrong, "may I please ask that you don't . . ." I hoped my expression told her the rest.

"Ms. Knott—I wouldn't think of it," she said with all candor. "I did the urine test myself, so believe me, no one knows." She patted my hand. "Don't worry. That's not what we're about here. You just take care of yourself. As far as the official diagnosis goes?" She scribbled onto the report. "I'll put down dehydration and fatigue, which are the real reasons you ended up here anyway. Now, I want you to take a couple days rest. Does that work?"

"Yes, thank you," I said. *Pregnant!* Andy's face flashed into my head, and I nearly burst into tears. As if we weren't complicated enough, this only made it worse.

She scribbled a bit more then handled a folder to me. "Take this to the desk over by the door, and you're ready to go." She held out her hand and I shook it." Take care, my dear. I sincerely hope it works out for you."

So do I, I thought, but instead I just smiled gratefully and took my folder to the discharge desk. Maybe I still had a few things to feel grateful about, like having health insurance. Wasn't any question now how badly I needed this job now. But how long would I be able to keep my condition off-camera? I already knew the answer. As if I could keep it from anyone for very long. Especially the one person who needed to know about it the most.

As I entered the waiting room my three escorts quickly surrounded me. "How are you? What'd they say? Are you all right? Do you need a wheelchair?" they all said at once, bombarding me with questions.

"I'm all right!" I said, fending them off. "I was just pretty dehydrated and I need something to eat."

"Thank God, darling," Brent said, visibly relieved. "Might I suggest we return to Thanksgiving?"

"Right after this punt," said Denny, turning back to the TV.

"Dude, I'm so winning this game," Richard said, his fingers wrapped around a Starbucks. "This kicker sucks."

Brent sighed. "I'll get the car and meet you out front."

Richard turned to me. "You *are* okay, right? I mean, we're due at 30 Rock Monday."

I leveled my gaze. "I'm fine. I just need food and a good night's sleep."

He eyed me a moment. "Stellar." Then turned back to the game. "Ooh! Damn! Look at that!"

"Ha!" Denny yelled, arms raised. "You owe me, dude! You frickin' *owe me!*"

I'd already come to this conclusion a while ago, but its impact was never more apparent: I knew too many men. As Richard adjusted his package, as Denny spit into the trash can, before I became asphyxiated by their testosterone smog, I needed to get in touch with my sisters in the worst way. *In the worst possible way.*

I ARRIVED EARLY at the studio Monday morning after spending the long Thanksgiving weekend angsting and sleeping off a turkey tryptophan overdose. I wanted to catch Terri, my assignments editor, potential confidant, and the mother of four, before Richard and I left for New York and NBC. As expected, she was in her office pouring over leads. I knocked on the jamb and she smiled, waving me in.

"A man just called saying he has a two-headed cat." She squinched her face in distaste. "I'm betting one's vestigial. *Gross.*"

"No kidding." I looked over my shoulder, slipping into a chair. "Terri . . . do you have a minute? I'd like to talk to you about something, if it's okay."

"Absolutely," she said, looking concerned. "Close the door." After I did, she said, "What's going on? Is everything okay, sweetie?"

I had thought about the best way to tell her, but decided to just come out with it. "I'm pregnant."

She slapped the desk. "I *knew* there had to be a reason you hooked up with that snake again!" Then all at once, she reddened. "Oh my God—I'm so sorry! Don't take that the wrong way!"

It took me a moment before it sunk in. "You mean you think . . .?" I made a gagging noise. "Oh Terri! Hell no! It's not Richard! Jesus! *No.*" We both laughed, then all at once I teared up. "Actually, it's much worse than that."

Terri handed me a tissue. "Tell me, sweetie, then who?"

I blew my nose. "Remember the day Richard dumped me? And you sent us to do that story about the flyer you found on a utility pole?"

She thought a moment. "You mean that guy looking for a wife?" Her face went from confusion to clarity. "It's *his*? But Denny came back saying you never got the story!

Holy cow—talk about off the record! What'd you do, meet him on the sly?"

"Better than that," I said. "I married him."

"*What?* When?"

"Six days after we met. I wasn't at my parents like everyone heard. Except for breaking up with Richard, they think nothing in my life has changed. They still don't know I married Andy and moved off the grid into the Pine Barrens. In fact, very few people do."

"And how was it?" Terri asked, wide-eyed.

I swallowed hard, trying to put it into words. "Like nothing I ever imagined, Terri. Like a great big wonderful dream."

Saying it cracked the floodgates, because after that I couldn't stop. I told her about Andy's contract and the book deal, about our wedding and the house in the woods, about Jinks and Bucky and Betsy, about the lake, the garden, the peach trees and the chickens, and about the fire and our honeymoon, at least as much as I could say. The telling made us laugh and at the end, when I told her about Marcel and the real Andy, we were both grabbing tissues.

"You have to let him know, Julie," Terri said. "It's his child, too. That is . . ." Her face grew stern. "If you decide to keep it. If you think he'll take that choice away from you, then maybe you—"

"Terri, I love him. And I miss him so much I don't know how I make it through the day." I blew my nose. "I want to go ahead with this pregnancy, but he needs to want me in spite of it. I don't want him back if he feels obligated. I want him to love me *because* of me and not because of this baby."

"Which sounds like a tall order, from this end." She sat back in her chair, looking as non-committal as I'd ever seen her. "So what do you want to do?"

"I don't know," I said honestly. "Right now he's in France, and since I threatened to disappear if he tried to see me again, I don't think he'll come unless I call him. So I'll just go on with work until I figure it out."

"Or you start showing," Terri said. "With some bulky clothes—and you thank your lucky stars it's going on winter—you could probably stall out anyone knowing through your fifth month. Unless he's got you with twins or you start blowing up like a Macy's balloon. I'd watch the salt if I were you, keep a light exercise schedule, and just try to eat healthy. Does Richard know?"

"No, just you. By the way, once everything's set I'm blowing Richard off."

"Good luck with that. From everything I've seen he looks like he wants back in."

I got up. "Then bet on the two-headed cat. That's got a better chance of happening."

My GRAND RETURN came and went, and I was firmly back in the saddle. I moved into my new digs, and with the aid of my new salary, declined Richard's offer of paying my first six months' rent. My first spot premiered on "Morning Joe" the second week of December, and by the third I had appeared live on the panel as a guest.

My star was rising unabated, and with the station ratings shooting up, Gil was more than happy, even hiring Denny back with a solid, five-year contract. I felt responsible for him losing his job, so I took some solace in the fact that, whatever I decided to do, he was taken care of. While all this was going on, I quietly passed my ten week mark, now starting each morning with my head in the crapper. With my gynecologist's Seal of Approval, I was officially pregnant, and although healthy as a horse, I'd never been more miserable.

Every week my belly grew I missed Andy more and more. Over and over I debated calling him, especially when I was in the studio and I had unlimited access to overseas calls. But I also wondered why he hadn't called me, why he hadn't pushed past Brent when he had the chance, busting down the door if he had to. Then I got to thinking maybe he would've if he truly loved me, which only got me more depressed. Christmas came and so did New Year's, which I spent with my parents in Florida, wanting family around me even if it was the detached facsimile that was my own. But my parents were warmer to me than they'd been in years, and I thought maybe they could somehow sense their line continuing inside me. I truly wanted to tell them, but it almost seemed traitorous to Andy, and truth be told, way too sticky. Odd, wasn't it? That for me, telling strangers was easy, but telling those closest to me was impossible. I pondered that on long walks in the Florida sun, thinking maybe that's why I'd always been drawn to the peculiar, feeling out of place with anything cutting too close to home. Maybe it was the distance that attracted me, polar opposite to someone knowing me too well. Maybe I, like my parents, found a measure of emotional security in that detachment. Maybe only now we were discovering it didn't work.

The holidays over, I was back on the street, the winter rewarding me with a wealth of outdoor crazies, allowing me to bundle up in a thick coat and hide my growing girth. Thank God for Denny, as he always knew how to shoot me at perfect angles, my scarves and jackets leaving no one the wiser. Yet I was well aware it was only a matter of time as by mid-February I was closing in on fourteen weeks, my thickening waistline and bulging breasts were getting more and more difficult to camouflage.

"This is going to be one big baby," the doctor said, prodding me. "Get up. You're going to the ultrasound room."

I instantly panicked; I've been trying to get out of it for weeks. Although I had long become accustomed to being pregnant, I still hadn't fully accepted the fact there was a real baby inside me. And I knew a sonogram would put an end to that right quick.

She poked me up. "Go. *Now*."

A half hour later, with my bladder ready to burst, my doctor stood behind the technician as she moved the wand over my jelly-slathered belly. My head was turned to the wall, my mouth so dry I couldn't swallow.

"Ah now—see that?" my doctor said. "Everything looks terrific. And not a twin in sight, just one big baby. Come on, Julie, take a look."

My heart pounded out of my chest, which only kicked up the fetal heartbeat. "I don't know if I—can." The words clumped in my throat like chunks of bile.

The doctor took my hand. "Julie, it's okay, she's beautiful. That's if she *is* a she, it's too early to tell." She tilted the monitor toward me. "Come on. Look."

I couldn't hold out any longer; if anything, curiosity took over and then something even stronger: the need to make whatever inside me real. I turned my head.

"There now," the doctor said, "see?"

I couldn't breathe, my hand flying to my mouth. Up on the screen an arm moved, floating in the amniotic air, and suddenly I wasn't alone in this anymore. There were two of us in it now, me and this child Andy and I had put together. And both of us wanted him now more than ever.

"He's—perfect," I said, my eyes clouding.

The doctor squeezed my hand. "He sure is. Now, no more worries. You're doing great inside there, okay?"

Perhaps, but as I got dressed, I knew that wasn't the *inside* I was worried about. My heart wanted to call Andy, but my head still cautioned me to wait. I was never more confused. Then my phone *dinged*! for a text. It was Terri.

A woman staying at the Ritz-Carlton left a message; says her story'll beat anything you've ever done; wants to see you ASAP; leaving tonight. I called to verify; you're expected; Presidential Suite Viviane Mercier. Good luck.

"Jesus Christ." I grabbed my purse.

I ran from the medical building to the street, throwing up my arm. In less than a minute, a cab pulled to the curb, just as a blue Bentley passed us on the other side of the street. I slunk back. *Oh God, please don't let that be Richard.*

"Ritz-Carlton," I said to the driver, "and hurry."

I SOON FOUND out that the marble-columned façade of the Ritz-Carlton Hotel, as well as the drop-dead gorgeous Presidential Suite, perfectly suited the penchant for drama that was Viviane Mercier. I was let in by a distinguished-looking man in a jacket and tie, who I took as the butler.

"Ms. Knott?" he said in his very British accent.

"Yes," I said and he opened the door wide. "I believe I'm expected."

"You are. Please come in." He led me to one of two sofas in the living room, a coffee table set with high tea between them. "Mrs. Mercier will be right with you," he said, then promptly disappeared through the dining room. And true enough, less than a minute later, a door to the next room opened and out walked, in the most basic of terms, my mother-in-law.

A similar scene flashed through my head from over a year ago, when Richard had taken me to meet his parents in blue-collar Bristol, PA. We had met at an Olive Garden because they thought the unlimited salad and bread such a good deal. This from a man who had made millions on Comcast stock, which he had started buying years earlier when he was cable box installer.

But where Richard's working-class roots had only

made me snicker at his champagne affectations, I instantly knew I was in another league altogether when Mother Mercier entered the room. Medium height, dark hair gathered into a chignon, attired in a tastefully fitted white blouse and fluted black skirt, a string of pearls at her neck, she was elegance enshrined. At least sixty years old, she was stunningly beautiful with a quietly voluptuous figure, porcelain skin, and startling blue eyes, every inch her son's mother, yet singularly her own woman. Instinctively I stood up, my heart kicking up considerably as she glided toward me, hand extended, a most cordial smile on her face.

"*Bon après-midi*, Ms. Knott," she said. "So good of you to come."

"Thank you, ma'am," I said, her handshake surprisingly firm for all her airs of gentility. "*Ravie de faire votre connaissance.*"

She tilted her head, clearly surprised. "*Parlez-vous français?*"

"Well, I can greet you, bid you goodnight, offer you some gourmet dishes and utter a few words not suitable for children, that's about the extent of it. But I'm hoping to learn more in the future."

"Really," she said pleasantly, her gaze washing over me. "I expect lately there hasn't been time." She swept her hand to the sofa. "Won't you please have a seat? I've ordered us tea."

I tried not to take her former aside as a dis. "It looks lovely. Thank you ma'am." She sat on the sofa opposite, and poured from the china teapot.

"I'm leaving for Bermuda in just a little while," she said, handing me a cup, "and I always find it hard to eat the first night. So I try to have at least a little bit before I go."

"First night, ma'am?"

"I'm sailing on the *Madeleine*. A freighter, but the accommodations are quite luxurious, a little-known secret of which many world travelers take advantage." She swept her hand again. "Please, help yourself."

"Thank you." I took a plate, placing a single strawberry atop it. I had absolutely no appetite, my stomach so jumpy, mostly from wondering when she'd cut the chitchat and get to it.

My answer came when she leveled her gaze into mine. "My son *will* divorce you, Ms. Knott. You should expect it."

It was as abrupt a shift of gears as flicking off the light switch. I set the plate to the table with a *clank*. "Oh? Did Andy tell you that? Did he send you to find me?"

She settled her own cup noiselessly. "I haven't seen nor spoken to André in over six months, and then only briefly when he received the news his father died. I found *you* by simply turning on the television. The observation about my son comes from knowing him very well. And although, you, Ms. Knott . . ." she observed me, her eyes hooded, ". . . appear to satisfy his physical preferences, it can never be more than that."

Boy if she didn't come out swinging. "How could you possibly know what we were like together?"

"Because I know my son. I know you've served your

purpose as an able playmate while he bided his time. But now that he's finished, I'm afraid, so are you."

I sprang to my feet. "What are you talking about? How can you—"

"Please sit, Ms. Knott," she said calmly. "Honestly, it's not my intention to be cruel. I'm just trying to give you a bit of enlightenment to save us all any more pain." But I couldn't move; I could only stand there, staring, my fists clenched. "Please, Ms. Knott," she said, inclining her head, "I do have more to tell you."

I don't know why I did, but I sat, fool that I was.

"Thank you." She placed a tiny quiche on her plate, brushing her hands over the table. "Mercier Shipping has been a family business for over two hundred years, but five years ago another shipper threatened a buyout when market changes left us most vulnerable. André was then quite content working as a ship's engineer, even though everyone knew he was capable of bigger things. So when his stepfather fell ill he agreed to step in temporarily, even though it soon became apparent he'd never work again. But he proved such an excellent manager, he turned the company around. Even so, he remained adamant he'd only stay until Marcel was able to take over."

"Andy did mention Marcel has a *brilliant* mind."

"Which he stores in his *penis*," she said wryly, either ignoring my sarcasm or adding to it. "He falls in love like other people brush their teeth. In any event, I believe the purpose of André's sabbatical was to force Marcel to face up to his responsibilities, and in the two months while he was in America, he not only ran the company, he proved he was born to do it, which, in fact, he was. Because of this, André has been turning over operations to his brother and very soon now—if not already, he will leave." She glanced over the rim of her teacup, her eyes like ice chips. "And when he does, he'll go back to the sea."

"I wouldn't be so sure of that," I said.

"Hm, that's very interesting." She took a sip of her tea. "Why is that, do you think?"

Pure speculation, I knew, but ... "Because I believe he loves me."

"Really," she said, leaning forward. "Has he told you this?"

"No, but—"

"And he never will." Which she said with such certainty I was nearly inclined to believe her. But I couldn't.

"I think you're wrong." I looked to my clenched hands; my knuckles were nearly white. "He's told me he wants to make a life with me. He married me, after all."

"Yes, he has. But tell me, Ms. Knott—where is he now?"

Any other woman with an ounce of self-respect would've refused to answer and stormed out. So why didn't I? Maybe the need to defend what we had made the possibility of a future a little more tangible, and that spurred me on. "We argued, those months back and I asked him to stay away. He's respecting my wishes, that's all."

She waved dismissively. "Too simplistic, don't you think? We French are a passionate people. If he loved you, if he truly wanted you, he would break down walls to get to you." She demurely crossed her hands atop her lap. "So again, where is he now?"

Why she was taunting me, I had no idea, but I'd had enough. "You know damn well where he is, so why this cat-and-mouse? Tell me what you really got me here for."

She cocked her brow in an unspoken *touché*, reaching to a silver box on the table to pull out a cigarette. "I don't really smoke anymore, maybe once or twice a month. But at times like this it seems appropriate. Do you mind?"

"Of course not," I said, as all former smokers usually did. "Go ahead."

"Thank you." She flicked a lighter then drew in delicately, her eyes never leaving mine. "Did you ever wonder how a man could reach forty years of age and never marry? Gay, was the old exception, but that's not even true anymore." She inhaled, exhaled. "Didn't you ever think it odd in Andy?"

"No." I affected my best imitation Gallic shrug. "He'd been waiting for me."

That irritated her and her cheek twitched; another affectation cutting too close to the bone. "He'd been waiting for no one. His heart is too cold to let anyone in. And proof of that is you, *ma chère*. As far as he's concerned, you were just a prop.

"What was it I heard from Marcel, who I understand you've had the pleasure of meeting? Seems he mentioned something about a bet between he and André which, most unfortunately, involved you."

"Yes," I said, the anger rising again. "About who could stay married the longest."

She uttered a derisive sigh, distinctly French and so like Andy I winced. "Well, I can assure you, if André did make such a bet, it wasn't to win or lose it, but to simply get Marcel to play." She inhaled once more then crushed the cigarette into her plate.

"But, the game's over, Ms. Knott, and both my sons have come out winners. Marcel takes control of the company, and André goes back to the life he lived before— a pretty man flitting about with no commitments. *Ma chère*," she said, her voice softening, "I am telling you this as one woman to the other, and not to make things more difficult for you. But I know my son—he can't commit to anyone. Believe me . . ." Her face stiffened with a faraway anger. "He first proved it to me. I only want to prepare you for the eventuality and save you the heartbreak." Her eyes narrowed. "Especially if you're intending to enlighten him with your bit of news anytime soon."

I don't know how she did, but she knew. "What news?"

"Ms. Knott—please. I'm a mother twice over. You get to know the signs." She dropped her gaze to my belly, my hands idly over it. "Mostly it's the hands. They're always protecting it. Did you know the doctors told him the likelihood of his ever having a child was slim?"

"I assure you most definitely it's his."

"Well then." Her mouth curved into a brittle smile. "You've proved them wrong, haven't you?"

The butler stepped into the doorway. "Madam, it's time."

"Yes, *merci*." She stood. "I'm truly sorry, Ms. Knott, but I must go. The ship leaves in an hour." She smiled again. "Well, then. Do pay attention to what I told you, and although you may not believe me, I do only have your best intentions in mind." She held her hand out. "*Au revoir*, Ms. Knott."

I stood, staring at her hand thrust in the spirit of fidelity. Except right then, with Andy so close and so far away, I wasn't feeling especially felicitous. I looked up, squaring my gaze into hers.

"First off, *ma chère belle mère*, the name's Mrs. Devine, and if Andy's out to break my heart, I'd rather have him do it in person and not by proxy. Although I do thank you for your selfless concern." I grabbed my purse.

Her eyes flared like two bolts of blue lightning. "You have no idea what you're setting yourself up for—he *will* disappoint you!"

"I'll take my chances," I said, walking out.

I rode back to the station in a fog of anger and indecision. There was no story to file, so I recycled an old one, and in a burst of panic I called Andy's number, letting it ring once before I quickly hung up. I fled the studio and walked home in a daze.

I went to bed, only to wake up near midnight. I needed to think, and I knew there was really only one place I could go, rummaging through a wooden box on my dresser until I found the key. I shoved it in my pocket and jumped into my clothes. The only thing I needed now was a car. I ran outside and, hailing a cab, went straight to the airport. Forty minutes later, I was on my way.

Funny how I didn't know how to get there, then suddenly I did. I crossed one bridge, traversed the Pines, then crossed another, going east until I couldn't go any further. I made a right then traveled nearly the length of the island, ending up where we really began. I sunk the key into the cottage's lock and stepping inside, found a blanket then went straight to the back porch.

The moon, nearly full, was high, lighting a path from the rumpled sand to the horizon, the stars pocking the sky with pinpoints of light. It was cold but the salt air tempered it, and wrapping the blanket around me, I tucked myself into the porch's wicker loveseat. With my hand on my belly, I cast my hope across the water, and drifted off to sleep.

I OPENED MY EYES. It was light, but it was the footsteps that woke me. I shivered awake, turning toward them.

"Julie? *Julie!*"

Chapter Twenty-Two

Ship to Shore

"RICHARD!" I CRIED, bolting upright. "What in hell are you doing here!"

He flapped the collar of his jacket, tightening it around his throat. "A better question would be why you're sleeping outside in February. It's cold as *balls* out here!"

What the *fuck* was he doing here? "How did you find me?"

"Well, it's simple," he said wryly. "Your Twitter feed."

"*What?* I don't *have* a Twitter feed!"

"Oh yes you do. I feed it for you. And I got this from one of your contacts who works there." He whipped out his phone, showing me the tweet. *Why is JK at the airport Rent-a-Wreck at one AM?* "So me being curious, I went there." He lifted a brow. "Who would think those bombs have a GPS in them?"

I grabbed his phone. "What the hell! Now you're spying on me?"

"Well, someone has to." He grabbed back his phone. "Since you're lying to me."

"What?" I cried, flabbergasted.

"I'm doing everything I can to launch your career into the stratosphere, where it should've been a long time ago, and you're still fighting me every step. You don't tweet, you don't Facebook," he ticked off on his fingers. "You're ignoring your blog, you didn't show up for the drive time interview you had at WMMR yesterday—"

"Oh shit." When I was at the Ritz-Carlton. "I totally forgot about that."

"And it wasn't because you were out on a shoot, either, because for some goddamned reason you recycled a story that was just on last month. Now, how the hell can we run that on 'Joe' on Friday?"

"I'm shooting this afternoon. I'll send them that."

"You know damn well they need a two-day lead. You'd never make it." He waved his hand dismissively. "But that's not what's got to me. What's *really* killing me is right *there*." He threw open my blanket, jabbing his finger toward my belly. "You're pregnant, aren't you?"

My mouth dropped. I tried to answer, but nothing came out.

"Yeah, I thought so. Why the fuck didn't you tell me?"

I gaped at him, wrapping the blanket back around me. "How—how—?"

"It's why you ran away from me last summer. It's why you passed out on Thanksgiving. And it's why I saw you coming out of that gynecologist's office yesterday, isn't it?"

I think I'm going to be sick. "I would've told you sooner or later."

"You should've told me right from the jump." He paced the porch, looking so bruised I nearly felt chastised, until he leaned against the railing to face me. "All right, look—it might even be to your advantage. Baby bumps are hot right now. We'll get you working that whole smokin' mama thing, and I'm sure we could shoot some killer spots around it. And after we're married—"

"Married!" Again he floored me. "You want to *marry* me?"

"I've always wanted to marry you," he said, as if obvious. "Just because I had a bout of temporary insanity doesn't mean I never would. You knew I'd come back."

"I did? You threw me out on the street!"

"Oh, that was just Annika having a hissy fit. She told me just the other day how sorry she is about it."

That got me standing. "You're still *talking* to her?"

"Purely as a client. Don't worry, we're so over even the crack of dawn can't get past us. I already told her, next week's opening is the last one I'm going to."

I couldn't help but laugh. "Oh Richard, you truly are predictable. Go to the opening. I really don't care."

"Julie, listen to me." He grasped me by this shoulder. "You're thinking I'm the same Richard who screwed you over last year, but believe me, I'm not. If it takes the rest of my life, I'm going to make it up to you. I've changed, really I have, but one thing hasn't: I love you. I've always loved you. And I do want to marry you." He reached in his pocket, bringing out the engagement ring I had thrown at him six months earlier. "Julie, will you marry me?"

I looked at him, same handsome face, same slick delivery, and I thought: *if this were six months ago, I would've fallen at his feet.* He said he loved me. But how could I really be sure? Did the proof lie in what he said? Or was the real test in what he did? Or was it more in how he made me feel? Did I *feel* loved? And would I feel it even without him telling me? The answer came to me, almost instinctively.

"Richard, I can't marry you. And even if I could, it wouldn't work out. You're not the only one who's changed, you know."

"I know you've changed and I'm willing to accept that. I'm also willing to take it one day at a time. What have we got to lose? If we find out it's not working, we can always split up later, but for now, we let's give it a try. Marry me."

Oh my, didn't this sound familiar? So why now did I hear it so differently? "I'm sorry, but I still can't marry you."

"And *I'm* sorry," he huffed, looking affronted, "but I won't have my kid born a bastard. Call me old school, but there it is."

"*Your* kid?" I laughed out loud. "Oh, sweetie, do I have a surprise for you."

A car door slammed; a dog barked. Richard stiffened, incensed. "I don't care what your surprise is, because I got a bigger one for you. You *are* going to marry me, so stop acting like a two-year-old and—"

The back door opened and Bucky barreled out, nearly knocking Richard down as he ran toward me. I fell to my knees and he leaped into my arms. "Bucky!" I cried, hugging his ruff. I looked past him; my heart clenched. *Andy!*

"What the—?" Richard turned, eyeing him. "Who the fuck are you?"

"Andy Devine," he said, looking straight at me, "and what I want is my wife."

Richard sucked in a breath. "Your *wife!*" He whirled around and I stood up, gathering the blanket around me. "You're already *married*? Then is he the—"

"Richard don't!" I cried. "I haven't—"

"*Richard . . .?*" Andy growled, as lethally as I'd ever heard him. He looked tired but magnificent, in a business suit and overcoat, his tie loosened yet very much the corporate intimidator. "So you're *Richard*," he said, smiling most malevolently.

"Yeah," he said, thrusting his chin. "What the fuck is it to you?"

Andy's eyes narrowed. "Less than you think, but just to keep things peaceful, you'd better leave."

"I don't think so," he said. "We're talking business here."

"Talk it later," Andy said. "I need to speak with my wife."

Richard laughed. "Oh yeah? Well, you had plenty of chances to speak to her in the last few months, but I haven't seen you around, have I? Seems to me you've lost your place in line, buddy."

"Richard," I said. "Don't do this. Just go."

He whirled around to me. "Hey! I'm not done with you yet! Just sit there and be quiet!"

I looked past him to Andy, that little muscle in his cheek thumping wildly. "Oh, *Je vais te casser la geule*. Come on, *putain*." He tapped Richard's shoulder. "Time to go."

Richard spun around, shoving Andy back against the railing. "And I said beat it cheese eater! Get the fuck out of my face!"

Andy's eyes flared and in a flash he was on him, grasping Richard under the chin until he was red and sputtering. "And yet, that's exactly where am, aren't I, *espèce de salaud*? Now, fly away like the little chicken you are before I wring your fucking neck."

He flung him loose and Richard stumbled back, clutching his throat and gasping. "Yeah okay, hard case— big fucking man! See how big you are when you hear from my lawyers! We'll see who's fucking big then!"

Andy threw up his hands. "What is it with these guys? Always the lawyers! Come on, *femmelette*," he taunted Richard. "You want to take me on? You want to finish this?" He slid his coat off. "Come on and finish it like a man you little shit—I'm ready."

Richard blanched, lunging for the door. "Go fuck yourself," he squeaked, bolting through it like a jackrabbit, Bucky snarling and hot on his heels.

"Ha!" Andy laughed. "Look at that! Shit stains right through to the front door!"

I nearly choked. "I-I guess he's skipping the colonic today!" We laughed until we were nearly breathless, then it was just me and Andy and the great divide that gaped between us. His gaze, vividly liquid, settled on me.

"Julie . . ." he said.

I straightened my back against the arm of the love-seat, the blanket still firmly around me. "What brings you here, Andy? It's certainly a surprise."

"Why should it be?" he said. "After all, you called me."

"I did?" I remembered dialing him from the studio, but . . . "You got that? But it only rang once and I hung up."

"It was enough."

"But how did you know I'd be here?"

"I took a chance," he said. "I saw the number and traced it back to your television station. Call me presumptuous, but I hopped the next plane. You see, I just happened to be in Paris, so I caught a direct flight to Philadelphia, as luck would have it."

"Yes . . ." I said idly. "As luck would."

His hand slid to the seat, his fingers just an inch or two from mine. "I had this vague notion you needed me. At least I hoped."

A million thoughts swirled around my head, my heart pounding so heavily it was hard to think. As cold as it was on that porch I could still feel the heat from his body, or it could've been the sun, now up and blinding me as it rose over the water.

"Andy . . ." I said, not capable of much else. "I did try to call you, but . . ."

He looked toward the beach. "Everything I did while we were apart went toward working my way back to you. I also hoped it would give you time to think about forgiving me, and when you tried calling, I thought maybe you had. But I wasn't about to guess, sitting on the other side of the Atlantic. I knew I had to come here and find out for myself."

"Did you also find out your mother summoned me?"

Shock spread over his face. "*What?*"

"Yesterday afternoon, but only with the purest of intentions. He wanted to warn me of your imminent desire to divorce me."

His fists clenched and he stood up, falling back against the railing. "*Ma mère* wouldn't know a good intention if it bit her on the *derrière*. He reached into his coat, pulling out a cell phone. "I'll straighten this out right now—"

"Ah! Look at that! So you do believe in them after all."

He reddened slightly. "In this context, yes." He showed me the face of the phone. "Look—four bars."

"Put it away," I said. "We fought our own battle, and I think I won." *My God, it was good to see him.* "I don't believe you're half as callous as she thinks you are."

His mouth crooked. "Only half?"

I pulled the blanket tighter around me and looked at him in all seriousness. "I think you know what she would've said, Andy. Is there anything you'd like to clarify?"

He seemed relieved I asked. "God yes." He looked to the loveseat. "May I?" I nodded and he sat, though keeping a respectable distance between us. "I think I know what she's referring to, and if I'm right, it's only because she made it impossible for me."

He shifted, stretching his long legs out on the porch.

"When my mother refused to go back to America that summer when I was thirteen, what she didn't know was my father had already set a private investigator after her."

"Those photos I found were from him."

"Yes. And two days later, my father was in Le Havre." He shook his head. "God, how they fought that night. The neighbors thought they'd kill each other, but no one dared come in, not even the police. I'd been at a friend's house, but when I came in my father went mad, pouncing on me."

He leaned forward on his knees, his hands in his hair. "'Who do you love, Andy?' he asked me. 'Who means more to you—your mother or me?' He warned me to choose right because if I didn't . . ." He swallowed hard. "He pulled a knife from his boot—he said only one of them was getting out of there alive."

Andy turned to me, the muscle in his cheek thumping violently. "How could I choose? I was thirteen years old! How many times did I have to come between them? Which one did I have to love more?" He looked out to the ocean, his face calming. "So I didn't, and that's when my father said I was dead to him. And as far as my mother was concerned? By the end of the month I was in Swiss boarding school and that . . ." He sat back. "Was the end of that."

I reached for his hand. "Oh Andy. How our parents do fuck us up."

He squeezed it. "But not now. Not anymore."

I looked at him. "So tell me. What's changed?"

"Many things," he said, "but mostly this." He turned

to me, placing my hand over his heart. "I love you. I have for a long time, but now I'm finally able to say it. *Je t'aime*."

As he brought my hand to his lips a tiny sound escaped me, neither good nor bad but more like astonishment.

"I know I've put you through a lot," he said, "and I can't blame you if you don't trust me. And I don't think you're just going to jump in my arms and expect everything to go back as it was. But I want you to know I'll keep trying until it either is or you tell me it's over. But until that happens, I intend to make good on my promises to you so you aren't beholden to bastards like that," indicating Richard, I'm sure, "ever again." He reached into his jacket pocket and pulled out an envelope. "This is for you."

"What is it?" I said, reluctant to take it.

"Go ahead." He pressed it into my hands. "Take a look."

I opened it to a fold of papers and another envelope. The first was the deed to the cottage in my name, the second, a check for $100,000.

"Andy!" I said with a gasp, "you must be joking."

"Oh, right," he said with all seriousness, "it's not enough, is it? Well, consider it a down payment anyway. I'll be sending you more. I'll send you anything you want. Just tell me what you think it should be."

I put everything in the envelope and handed it back. "Andy, you don't owe me a thing."

"Oh yes I do," he said adamantly. "I probably owe you much more. I've been a bastard, and I want to make it up to you."

First off, I was having a hard time with the fact both Richard and Andy shared the same disparaging opinion of themselves. Second off, I knew only one of them actually believed it. Third off, could there really be men out there capable of such selflessness, without expecting anything in return? I mean, really, weren't we all out for something? I knew I was. And a few minutes ago I actually I got it.

"Andy, I'm not perfect. And if I recall correctly, I think you had a bit of a problem with me, too."

"What, with the birth control pills?" He waved me off. "Who needed them anyway? As I told you, they were probably overkill."

I started to laugh. I mean *hard*. Until there were tears streaming down my face.

"What?" he said. "What's so funny?"

"Andy," I said, swiping my eyes, "that's an understatement if I ever heard one." I dropped the blanket from my shoulders and taking his hand, placed it over my belly.

He seemed confused at first, then suddenly his hand jolted away. "Christ," he breathed, his eyes widening, "are you . . .?"

I took his hand again, placing it back on me. "Yes. And don't be ridiculous—it's most definitely yours. Conceived right here, I'm thinking."

He pressed his hand against me, a warmth radiating from it, a smile slowly spreading across his face. "Wow," he said, grinning. "I never thought I could do it."

"I never thought I could do it either," I said, "yet here we are."

He took both my hands, kissing them. "But why didn't you tell me sooner?" Then he waved his hand. "No, don't bother—I know the answer to that. I'd love you whether this happened or not. But I have to tell you . . ." His grin broke wide. "I'm really happy it did."

"So does this mean . . .?" I let him finish that.

He cupped my chin and kissed me, so deeply and so full of romance I shivered, right down to my swollen ankles. "Let's go inside," he said, helping me up.

But before we did I went to the railing, looking out to the ocean and the rumple of clouds laying low on the horizon. "You know, it wasn't my attempted phone call that brought you to me," I said.

Andy stood behind me, his hands falling atop my belly. "No? Then what?"

I looked across the water, imagining the wide ocean, the ships that sailed on it, the long lonely space that separated this island from the other side. "Andy, you don't, by any chance, believe in telepathy?"

"I didn't," he said, kissing my neck, "but I do now."

SIX MONTHS LATER . . .

One advantage to marrying a billionaire was you could buy any kind of car you wanted. Our considerable fortune bought me a used Jeep Patriot, fuel-efficient enough to get me back and forth from Philadelphia, big enough for Andy and the infant seat, and rugged enough to ride me up and down the sugar-sand trail to town. I was on my way back from one such excursion to the big city that morning, snagging a quick meeting with my editor, Mina Riley, as she made her way from D.C. to New York.

"So?" I said as we sat at the food court in 30th Street Station. "What did you think?"

Mina eyed me over the rim of her coffee. "Quite frankly, Julie, I have to tell you, I never thought I'd see the finished manuscript. I honestly figured I had gifted you with five grand."

"For what it's worth," I said, chagrined, "I'm truly sorry about that."

"Well, don't be," she said adamantly. "You've redeemed yourself. I just finished it on the train and Julie, I love it. But I do have to ask—what took you so long?"

I thought back to the day Andy and I met at the firehouse, our wedding and those crazy first weeks of our marriage, our long separation and finally getting back together, and then after, how the writing eluded me for so long. "You know how I kept a journal when we first got married?"

"Right." She laughed. "Which you kept it under the dresser in the bathroom with your birth control pills."

I nodded. "While we were separated I couldn't bring myself to look at it, and then when we got back together and I finally started writing, I didn't know how to end it. I'm still not sure I ended it right."

Mina placed a well-manicured hand over mine. "Let me ask you. Are you happy?"

Oh man, I had to think about that because, truth be told, I was so many things these days. I was a wife, a mother, a TV journalist, and an author, but mostly I was just busy as hell, spending a good amount of time exhausted, muddy, bug-bitten, wet, shit-smeared (from various different species, human and otherwise), achy, itchy, rushed, on-deadline, milkified, entranced, awed and very much in love.

"You know, it's crazy," I said, "but I really haven't had the time to consider it. But if doing what you love is what makes you happy, then I guess I am."

"Well that's good," she said, patting my hand. "Because crazy love makes for great copy. So I want you to keep going with this."

"Keep going!" Writing that book had been like giving birth, and she wanted me to keep going? "And write about what?"

"Life on the farm. Andy, the baby. The animals. That jar you found in the yard with the Indian-head pennies in it. The neighbor with the shotgun and the still. The tree frogs. All of it. Julie." She eyed me squarely. "You think it's those odd folks out there making your stories, but that's not it at all. It's the angle at which you see them that makes them so unique. Your knack for looking below the surface and saying 'hmm ... maybe things aren't quite what they seem.' That's what makes you divine, Miss Julie, and that's what I want to buy."

"Really?" I said, basking a bit in the ego boost.

"Really." They called her train. "Damn, I have to go." She leaned in to press her cheek to mine. "Keep writing, and I mean it. See you soon."

"*Au revoir*," I had said, waving as she disappeared down the stairway.

The Jeep bumped into a rut and I winced, my full breasts bouncing. I had expressed them before I left, but already they were leaking into my bra. Probably because the baby drained me dry at every feeding, in full possession of all of Andy's vigorous appetites. *Supply and demand*, my doctor had said at the size of my enormous boobs. If they were this big now, and the baby only six weeks old, I could expect a centerfold offer for *Penthouse* by the end of six months.

I steered the Jeep around another turn, passing the ruins of the old stagecoach stop. The Iron Bog Historical Society had been out the week before, and they were pretty sure they could get the people up in Trenton to give it historical status, which would make it eligible for restoration funding. But Andy had pretty mixed feelings about that. For one, he wouldn't accept it; if he wanted it fixed he could certainly afford it on his own. Marcel had continued to prove he had a head for running the business; Andy's quarterly share was almost an embarrassment of riches. But rather than restore a shine to the darker side of his family, he donated a sweet sum to the local school system, for repairs, technology, and Wi-Fi, bringing Iron Bog fully into the twenty-first century.

But he couldn't fool me. There was another, more selfish reason why he demurred. Restoration to the old ruins would bring tourists a little too close to the insular paradise he'd carved out of these woods, populated by a cow, chickens, mud, and mushrooms, and a house on a lake surrounded by Pines and clean air and a whole lot of nothing else. Except for me and the baby and oh yeah—Bucky, running full-bore up to me as I pulled into the yard.

The baby squealed from Andy's arms as he walked out of the barn. "Hey, Luc, see? The lunchwagon's arrived. Now we can both eat."

"Sorry," I said, taking the baby, "but Mina's train was late. But the good news is Gil's approved the new format. Now I only have to be in the city once a week. Denny and the assistants will take care of the rest."

"Terrific," he said, leaning in to kiss me, tweaking a nipple that instantly soaked my blouse.

"Andy!" I cried, laughing as I slapped his arm. "Isn't it bad enough I'm ready to explode!" I shifted the baby to the other shoulder.

His mouth crooked. "Just testing the teat, *ma belle*. Got to get back into practice, you know. Betsy'll be calving again by next month."

"Oh man, it'll be so nice being the milker instead of the milkee." I went to the porch and, sitting down, lifted my blouse and unhooked my bra. Almost instantly Luc latched on, slurping happily as his little hands kneaded the air. I kissed his silky head, feeling the milk drain from me. Andy propped a foot on a step, watching us.

My boys, I thought.

There was a time in the not too distant past when I thought I knew too many men. Now I knew these two were all I needed. And maybe one more, if we were lucky enough. And a *mademoiselle* or two, to make it even.

"Mina wants me to write another book."

"About what?" Andy said.

"About the farm, the animals. The people around here. The Pines."

"About our life."

"I suppose."

Andy leaned forward, his gaze washing over us. "*Tu es ma vie. Je t'aime.*"

I smiled, understanding perfectly.

About the Author

Gwen Jones, after spending years writing several un-publishable novels, decided to learn what she was doing wrong or give it all up. So after earning an MFA in Creative Writing from Western Connecticut State University, she's now *so* good they even allow her to teach there. An unabashed born-and-bred native of Southern New Jersey and the Jersey Shore, she lives with her husband, Frank, and the absolute cutest cat in the world, Gracie. To see more, visit her website at gwenjoneswrites.com.

Visit www.AuthorTracker.com for exclusive information on your favorite HarperCollins authors.

Give in to your impulses . . .
Read on for a sneak peek at four brand-new
e-book original tales of romance
from Avon Books.
Available now wherever e-books are sold.

THE CUPCAKE DIARIES:
SWEET ON YOU
By Darlene Panzera

THE CUPCAKE DIARIES:
RECIPE FOR LOVE
By Darlene Panzera

THE CUPCAKE DIARIES:
TASTE OF ROMANCE
By Darlene Panzera

ONE TRUE LOVE
A CUPID, TEXAS NOVELLA
By Lori Wilde

An Excerpt from

THE CUPCAKE DIARIES: SWEET ON YOU

by Darlene Panzera

Darlene Panzera, author of *Bet You'll Marry Me*, launches a delicious new series that proves business and pleasure don't mix . . . or do they?

Andi cast a glance over the rowdy karaoke crowd to the man sitting at the front table with the clear plastic bakery box in his possession.

"What am I supposed to say?" she whispered, looking back at her dark-haired sister Kim and their redheaded friend Rachel as the three of them huddled together. " 'Can I have your cupcake?' He'll think I'm a lunatic."

"Say 'please,' and tell him about our tradition," Kim suggested.

"Offer him money." Rachel dug through her dilapidated Gucci knockoff purse and withdrew a ten-dollar bill. "And let him know we're celebrating your sister's birthday."

"You did promise me a cupcake for my birthday," Kim said with an impish grin. "Besides, the guy doesn't look like he plans to eat it. He hasn't even glanced at the cupcake since the old woman came in and delivered the box."

Andi tucked a loose strand of her dark blonde hair behind her ear and drew in a deep breath. She wasn't used to taking food from anyone. Usually she was on the other end—giving it away. Her fault. She didn't plan ahead.

Why couldn't any of the businesses here be open twenty-four hours a day, like in Portland? Out of the two dozen eclectic cafes and restaurants along the Astoria waterfront promising to satisfy customers' palates, shouldn't at least one cater to late-night customers like herself? No, they all shut down at 10:30 P.M., some earlier, as if they knew she was coming. That was what she got for living in a small town. Anticipation, but no cake.

However, she was determined not to let her younger sister down. She'd promised Kim a cupcake for her twenty-sixth birthday, and she'd try her best to procure one, even if it meant making a fool of herself.

Andi shot her ever-popular friend Rachel a wry look. "You know you're better at this than I am."

Rachel grinned. "You're going to have to start interacting with the opposite sex again sometime."

Maybe. But not on the personal level Rachel's tone suggested. Andi's divorce the previous year had left behind a bitter aftertaste that no amount of sweet talk could dissolve.

Pushing back her chair, Andi stood up. "Tonight, all I want is the cupcake."

Andi had taken only five steps when the man with the bakery box turned his head and smiled.

He probably thought she was coming over hoping to find

a date. Why shouldn't he? The Captain's Port was filled with people looking for a connection. If not for a lifetime, then at least for the few hours they shared within the friendly confines of the restaurant's casual, communal atmosphere.

She hesitated mid-step before continuing forward. Heat rushed into her cheeks. Dressed in jeans and a navy blue tie and sportcoat jacket, he was even better looking than she'd first thought. Thirtyish. Light brown hair, fair skin, sparkling chocolate brown eyes. *Oh, my.* He could have his pick of any girl in the place. Any girl in Astoria, Oregon.

"Hi," he greeted.

Andi swallowed the nervous tension gathering at the back of her throat and managed a smile in return. "Hi. I'm sorry to bother you, but it's my sister's birthday, and I promised her a cupcake." She nodded toward the see-through box and waved the ten-dollar bill. "Is there any chance I can persuade you to sell the one you have here?"

The guy's brows shot up. "You want my cupcake?"

An Excerpt from

THE CUPCAKE DIARIES: RECIPE FOR LOVE

by Darlene Panzera

In the second installment of Darlene Panzera's
new series, another Creative Cupcakes
founder discovers that a little magic may be
the secret ingredient in the recipe for love.

Rachel pushed through the double doors of the kitchen, took one look at the masked man at the counter, and dropped the tray of fresh-baked cupcakes on the floor.

Did he plan to rob Creative Cupcakes? Demand she hand over the money from the cash register? Her eyes darted around the frilly pink-and-white cupcake shop. The loud clang of the metal bakery pan hitting the tile had caused several customers sitting at tables to glance in her direction. Would the masked man threaten the other people as well? How could she protect them?

She stepped over the white-frosted chocolate mess by her feet, tried to judge the distance to the telephone on the wall, and turned her attention back to the masked man before her. Maybe he wasn't a robber, but someone dressed for a costume party or play. The man with the black masquerade mask covering the upper half of his face also wore a black cape.

"If this is a holdup, you picked the wrong place, Zorro." She tossed her fiery red curls over her shoulder with false bravado and laid a protective hand across the old bell-ringing register. "We don't have any money."

His hazel eyes sparkled through the holes in the mask, and he flashed her a disarming smile. "Maybe I can help with that."

He turned his hand to show an empty palm, and relief flooded over her. No gun. Then he closed his fingers and swung his fist around in the air three times. When he opened his palm again, he held a quarter, which he tossed her way.

Rachel caught the coin and laughed. "You're a magician."

"Mike the Magnificent," he said, extending his cape wide with one arm and taking a bow. "I'm here for the Lockwell party?"

Rachel pointed at the door leading to the back party room. The space had originally been a tattoo shop, but the tattoo artist had relocated to the rental next door. "The Lockwells aren't here yet. The party doesn't start until three."

"I came early to set up before the kids arrive," Mike told her. "Can't have them discovering my secrets."

"No, I guess not," Rachel agreed. "If they did, Mike the magician might not be so magnificent."

"Magnificence is hard to maintain." His lips twitched as if he were suppressing a grin. "Are you Andi?"

She shook her head. "Rachel, Creative Cupcakes' stupendous co-owner, baker, and promoter."

This time a grin *did* escape his mouth, which led her to notice his strong, masculine jawline.

"Tell me, Rachel, what is it that makes you so stupendous?"

She gave him her most flirtatious smile. "Sorry, I can't reveal my secrets, either."

"Afraid if I found out the truth I might not think you were so impressively great?"

Rachel froze, fearing Mike the magician might be a mind reader as well. Careful to keep her smile intact, she forced herself to laugh off his comment.

"I just don't think it's nice to brag," she responded playfully.

"Chicken," he taunted in an equally playful tone, making his way toward the party room door.

Despite the uneasy feeling he'd discovered more about her in three minutes than most men did in three years, she wished he'd stayed to chat a few minutes more.

Andi Burke, wearing one of the new, hot pink Creative Cupcakes bibbed aprons, came in from the kitchen and stared at the cupcake mess on the floor. "What happened here?"

"Zorro came in, gave me a panic attack, and the tray slipped out of my hands." Rachel grabbed a couple paper towels and squatted down to scoop up the crumpled cake and splattered frosting before her OCD-about-kitchen-safety friend could comment further. "Don't worry, I'll take care of the mess."

"I should have told you Officer Lockwell hired a magician for his daughter's birthday party." Andi bent to help her, and, when they stood back up, asked, "Did you speak to Mike?"

Rachel nodded, her gaze on the door to the party room as it opened and Mike reappeared.

Tipping his head toward them as he walked across the shop, he said, "Good afternoon, ladies."

An Excerpt from

THE CUPCAKE DIARIES: TASTE OF ROMANCE

by Darlene Panzera

In the final installment of Darlene Panzera's
charming series, one lonely cupcake decorator
will learn that love is worth the risk . . .
once she gets a little taste of romance.

Focus, Kim reprimanded herself. *Keep to the task at hand and stop eavesdropping on other people's conversations.*

But she didn't need to hear the crack of the teenage boy's heart to feel his pain. Or to remember the last time she'd heard the wretched words, *"I'm leaving"* spoken to her.

She tried to ignore the couple as she picked up the pastry bag filled with pink icing and continued to decorate the tops of the strawberry preserve cupcakes. However, the discussion between the high school boy and the young woman she assumed to be his girlfriend kept her ears attentive.

"When will I see you again?" the boy asked.

Kim glanced toward them, leaned closer, and held her breath.

"I don't know," the girl replied.

The soft lilt in her accent thrust the familiarity of the conversation even deeper into Kim's soul.

"I'm going to the university for two years," the girl continued. "Maybe we'll meet again after."

Not likely. Kim shook her head, and the bottom of her stomach locked down tight. From past experience, she knew that once the school year was over in June, most foreign students went home, never to return.

And left many broken hearts in their wake.

"Two years is a long time," the boy said.

Forever is even longer. Kim drew in a deep breath as the unmistakable catch in the poor boy's voice replayed again and again in her mind. And her heart.

How long were they going to stand there and torment her by reminding her of her parting four years earlier with Gavin, the Irish student she'd dated in college? Dropping the bag of icing on the Creative Cupcakes counter, she moved toward them.

"Can I help you?" Kim asked, pulling on a new pair of food handler's gloves.

"I'll have the white chocolate macadamia," the girl said, pointing to the cupcake she wanted in the glass display case.

The boy dug his hands into his pockets, counted the meager change he'd managed to withdraw, and turned five shades of red.

"None for me." His Adam's apple bobbed as he swallowed. "How much for hers?"

"You have to have one, too," the girl protested. "It's your birthday."

Kim took one look at his lost-for-words expression and took pity on him. "If today is your birthday, the cupcakes are free," she said. "For both you and your guest."

The teenage boy's face brightened. "Really?"

Kim nodded and removed the cupcakes the two lovebirds wanted from the display case. She even put a birthday candle on one of them. A heart on the other. Maybe the girl would come back for him. Or he would fly to Ireland for her. *Maybe*.

Her eyes stung, and she squeezed them shut for a brief second. When she opened them again, she set her jaw. Enough was enough. Now that they had their cupcakes, she could escape back into her work and forget about romance and relationships and every regrettable moment she'd ever wasted on love.

She didn't need it. Not like her older sister, Andi, who'd recently lost her heart to Jake Hartman, their Creative Cupcakes financer and a news writer for the *Astoria Sun*. Or like her other co-owner friend, Rachel, who'd just gotten engaged to Mike Palmer, a miniature model maker for movies who also doubled as the driver of their Cupcake Mobile.

All she needed was to dive deep into her desire to put paint on canvas. She glanced at the walls of the cupcake shop, adorned with her scenic oil, acrylic, and watercolor paintings. Maybe if she worked hard enough, she'd have the money to open her own art gallery and she wouldn't need to decorate cupcakes anymore.

But for now, she needed to serve the next customer.

An Excerpt from

ONE TRUE LOVE
A CUPID, TEXAS NOVELLA
by Lori Wilde

Find out how the magic behind *New York Times*
bestselling author Lori Wilde's Cupid, Texas
series began with this heartwarming
story of a love that inspired a legend.

Whistle Stop, Texas
May 25th, 1924

I met John Fant on the worst day of my life.

There he was, the most handsome man I'd ever seen, standing at the bottom of my daddy's porch clutching a straw Panama hat in his hand, the mournful expression on his face belying the jauntiness of his double-breasted lightweight jacket and Oxford bags with sharp, smart creases running smoothly down the fronts of the legs. An intense, magnetic energy radiated from him, rolled toward me like heat waves off the Chihuahuan Desert. I felt an inexplicable tug square in the center of my belly.

His gaze settled heavily on my face. There were shadows under his eyes, as if he'd been up all night, and there was a tightness to his lips that troubled me. A snazzy red Nash

Roadster sat on a patch of dirt just off the one-lane wagon road that ran in front of the house. It looked just as out of place as the magnificent man in my front yard.

My knees turned as watery as the mustang grape jelly I'd canned the summer before that hadn't set up right, and suddenly I couldn't catch my breath. I hung onto the screen door that I was half hiding behind.

"Is this Corliss Greenwood's residence?" he asked.

"Yessir." I raised my chin and stepped out onto the porch. The screen door wavered behind me, the snap stretched out of the spring from too many years of too many kids slamming it closed. Without looking around, I kicked the door shut with my bare heel.

He came up on the porch, the termite-weakened steps sagging and creaking underneath his weight.

Shame burned my cheeks. *Please, God, don't let him put one of those two-tone wingtips right through a rotten board.*

He was tall, with broad shoulders, and even though he was whip-lean, he looked as strong as a prizewinning Longhorn bull. A spot of freshly dried blood stained his right cheek where he must have cut himself shaving. He'd shaved in the middle of the day, in the middle of the week? His hair was the color of coal, and he wore it slicked back off his forehead. His teeth were straight and white as piano keys, and I imagined that when he smiled, it went all the way up to his chocolate brown eyes. But he wasn't smiling now.

Mr. Fant had caught me indisposed. I must have looked frightful in the frayed gray dress I wore when cleaning. The material was way too tight around my chest because my breasts had blossomed along with the spring flowers. Strands of unruly hair were popping out of my sloppy braid and falling around my face. I pushed them back.

Another step closer and he was only an arm's length away.

My heart started thudding. His masculine fragrance wafted over to me in the heat of the noonday sun, notes of leather, oranges, rosemary, cedar, clove, and moss. Perfume! He was wearing perfume. I'd never met a man who wore perfume before, but it smelled mighty good, fresh and clean and rich.

My daddy always said I would have made a keen bloodhound with the nose I had on me. A well-developed sense of smell can be good for some things, like telling when a loaf of warm yeast bread is ready to come out of the oven, and inhaling a snout full of sunshine while unpinning clothes from the line, but other times having a good sniffer can be downright unpleasant—for instance, when visiting the outhouse in August.

"Is Corliss your father?"

My throat had squeezed up, so I just nodded.

"I'm John Fant."

I knew who he was, of course. The Fants were the wealthiest family in Jeff Davis County. Truth be told, they were the wealthiest family between the Pecos River and the New Mexico border. The Fants had founded the town of Cupid, which lay twenty-five miles due north in the Foothills of the Fort Davis Mountains, and they owned the Fant Silver Mine, where my father worked. Three years before, when John had returned home with a degree from Maryland State College, his father, Silas Fant, had turned the family business over to his only son.

The screen door drifted open against my calf, and I bumped it closed again.

He arched a dark eyebrow. "And you are . . . ?"

"Millie Greenwood." I barely managed to push my name over my lips.